Praise for *Inheri*

A PICK-THE-PATH EXPERIENCE

T0280011

JESSIE AWARD
Outstanding Innovative and Immersive Storytelling

JESSIE NOMINATIONS
Outstanding Lead Actor (Darrell Dennis)
Outstanding Production of the Year (Large Theatre)

"*Inheritance* is what theatre should be. It breaks boundaries, embraces new technology ... It is excellent. It should be required viewing. See it, ask questions, and enjoy the beauty of these incredible artists along the way."

—Vancouver Presents

"[*Inheritance*'s] creative team is definitely onto something ... [The play] digs into land claims and entitlement in engaging new ways, using a lively mix of humour and interactive technology to work through heavy concepts. Viewers go out into the night with the knowledge that land issues will never be solved with an easy click of the button. And more importantly, with plenty to think about their own role in the matter."

—*Georgia Straight*

BY THE SAME AUTHORS

Daniel Arnold & Medina Hahn

Tuesdays & Sundays

Any Night

Darrell Dennis

Peace Pipe Dreams: The Truth about Lies about Indians

Darrell Dennis: Two Plays (Tales of An Urban Indian / The Trickster of Third Avenue East)

Inheritance

A PICK-THE-PATH EXPERIENCE

BY

Daniel Arnold, Darrell Dennis, and Medina Hahn

FOREWORDS BY

Miles Richardson and David Suzuki

INTERVIEW WITH THE CREATORS BY

Annie Smith

STUDY GUIDE BY

Danielle Kraichy

TALONBOOKS

© 2022 Daniel Arnold, Darrell Dennis, and Medina Hahn
Foreword, "Two Solitudes" © 2022 Kilslaay Ḵaaji Sding Miles Richardson, O.C.
Foreword, "The Play" © 2022 David Suzuki
"A Short History of the Secwépemc People and Their Territory" © 2022 Adams Lake and the
Neskonlith Secwépemc, Peter Douglas Elias / Perisor Research Services
Interview with the creators © 2022 Annie Smith and Theatre Research in Canada
Study guide © 2022 Danielle Kraichy

All rights reserved. No part of this book may be reproduced, stored in a retrieval system, or
transmitted, in any form or by any means, without the prior written consent of the publisher or
a licence from Access Copyright (The Canadian Copyright Licensing Agency). For a copyright
licence, visit accesscopyright.ca or call toll-free 1-800-893-5777.

Talonbooks
9259 Shaughnessy Street, Vancouver, British Columbia, Canada V6P 6R4
talonbooks.com

Talonbooks is located on xʷməθkʷə̓y̓əm, Sḵwx̱wú7mesh, and səlilwətaʔɬ Lands.

First printing: 2022

Typeset in Minion
Printed and bound in Canada on 100% post-consumer recycled paper

Cover design by andrea bennett. Interior design by Typesmith
Cover illustration by Presley Mills
Inside front cover: VinceTraveller, *Cabin in the Woods*, via Flickr (CC BY 2.0)
Inside back cover: Carol Highsmith, *Olympic National Park*, via Flickr / Raw Pixel (CC BY 2.0)

Talonbooks acknowledges the financial support of the Canada Council for the Arts, the
Government of Canada through the Canada Book Fund, and the Province of British Columbia
through the British Columbia Arts Council and the Book Publishing Tax Credit.

Rights to *Inheritance: a pick-the-path experience*, in whole or in part, in any medium and
by any group, amateur or professional, are retained by the author. Interested persons are
requested to contact Antje Oegel at the AO International Agency, 540 President Street, Unit 2E,
Brooklyn, NY 11215, USA; telephone: 917-521-6640; email: aoegel@aoiagency.com; website:
www.aoiagency.com.

LIBRARY AND ARCHIVES CANADA CATALOGUING IN PUBLICATION

Title: Inheritance : a pick-the-path experience / by Daniel Arnold, Darrell Dennis, and Medina
Hahn ; forewords by Miles Richardson and David Suzuki ; interview with the creators by Annie
Smith ; study guide by Danielle Kraichy.
Names: Arnold, Daniel (Playwright), author. | Dennis, Darrell, author. | Hahn, Medina, author.
| Suzuki, David, 1936– writer of foreword. | Richardson, Miles (Miles G.), writer of foreword.
| Kraichy, Danielle, writer of supplementary textual content.
Description: A play. | Includes bibliographical references.
Identifiers: Canadiana 20210200529 | ISBN 9781772013627 (softcover)
Classification: LCC PS8601.R6465 I54 2021 | DDC C812/.6—dc23

CONTENTS

Two Solitudes

FOREWORD BY

Kilslaay K̲aaji Sding Miles Richardson, O.C.

Inheritance: a pick-the-path experience immerses the audience in a situation reflective of Canada's current reality of two solitudes, namely: (1) the continuing fact of ancient Nations who have been in this place since beyond human memory and who intend to continue our Nationhood in our Homelands, and (2) the relatively new nation-state of Canada, defined by its British legal and cultural traditions.

The play begins with a young settler woman, Abbey, and her partner, Noah, riding up by boat to the property she is set to inherit from her father, describing the property line encasing a vast mountainous landscape and its high real-estate value. When they arrive, they come across an Indigenous man, Frank, who invites them in and argues that Abbey's father told him he could stay at the house. Frank notes that his own house and most of the other houses on his reserve are covered in mould, so he doesn't have anywhere else to go. After Abbey asks Frank to leave, he reminds her that her father invited him to stay there and adds that maybe *she* should be the one to leave and stop squatting on *his* land – a contention Abbey begins to contest as the audience is invited to choose which direction to take the story next.

The play's dialogue mirrors the disputes about territory and power that settler Canadians and Indigenous Peoples must face today. What makes this dialogue emotional, difficult, seemingly complex, and gut-wrenching is that Canada's story is built on a big lie: the lie that Indigenous Peoples are not human and therefore not competent to have fundamental human rights. This big lie is exemplified by the colonialist and racist principle of terra nullius (a Latin legal phrase meaning "land belonging to no one") that underlies the Doctrine of Discovery that colonizers used to justify taking Indigenous lands.*

---

* See this book's glossary, page 256.

"We Are All Here to Stay"

How can we even begin a dialogue when the story on one side is presented as truth but rests on denying the humanity of the other side? This inequitable situation becomes even more pernicious in the "post-truth" world we now seem to be inhabiting.

As I have learned from the respected Anishinaabe spiritual leader Nii Gaani Aki Innini Elder Dr. Dave Courchene, as we enter this dialogue with an argument, it is important to begin in proper ceremony, reminding ourselves that we are all in this together.

Reconciliation requires that we come to terms with these two solitudes. Reconciliation requires a meeting of the minds amongst Peoples about what is true. The reality is that on this planet everything is connected. That's the truth. It's natural law. We can't do away with it, negotiate with it, or try to overrule it without consequences. We can only seek to understand and act in accordance with it. In Indigenous worldviews, everything is connected, and sustainability requires that we accept that lives throughout all of Creation are of equal importance to our own. Another common understanding amongst Indigenous Peoples is acknowledging your responsibility if you choose to take from the rest of Creation – a common value that can be described as reciprocity, a responsibility to help maintain the balance of life in all of Creation. In what we call Canada today, Indigenous Peoples have thrived in their territories for hundreds of generations. Is this a coincidence? I think not. Applied to our relations with each other, recognition of this interconnectedness and responsibility means that we, as settler Canadians and Indigenous Peoples, must live with each other in a way that enables our respectful coexistence into the future.

In the landmark Aboriginal Title case *Delgamuukw v. British Columbia*, Supreme Court of Canada Chief Justice Antonio Lamer wrote, "Let us face it, we are all here to stay,"* in effect asserting that, going forward, we – both settler Canadians and Indigenous Peoples – have to find a good way to live with each other in the future. We must share.

Being here to stay means coexisting, in the manner envisioned in the Gä·sweñta' / Two-Row Wampum,** in which Indigenous Peoples and the

---

* *Delgamuukw v. British Columbia*, [1997] 3 S.C.R. 1110, at para. 186, scc-csc.lexum .com/scc-csc/scc-csc/en/item/1569/index.do (last modified August 5, 2021).

** A treaty between the Haudenosaunee and the Dutch made in the seventeenth century, which the English soon after became party to when they displaced the Dutch as the predominant colonial force in North America.

TWO SOLITUDES

nation of Canada exist alongside each other as equals, with neither party seeking to dominate, assimilate, or control the other.

Be Who We Say We Are

Until now, we have been two solitudes. We *must* choose to change this. That is the purpose of the dialogue in *Inheritance*. And we must choose that we are all here to stay. We must choose to be all in this together. Let's celebrate our differences, strive to understand the truth, and base our actions on this understanding.

Canada is a work-in-progress. It must become the story of "we," rather than the story of "us and them." We must define and empower this "we" and stand up for what we know to be true.

Embrace this dialogue at every level. Engage in these issues. They will determine your and your descendants' future. Seek the truth, listen, and learn. And choose wisely for our future together.

Kilslaay Kaajii Sding Miles Richardson, O.C., is a citizen of the Haida Nation and an Officer of the Order of Canada. He served as President of Xaadée 'Wáadluuwaan Née / XaaydaGa 'Waadluxan Naay (the Council of the Haida Nation). He was a member of the BC Claims Task Force that recommended the process for conducting negotiations to build a new relationship between First Nations and the Governments of Canada and British Columbia, and served as Commissioner and Chief Commissioner of the BC Treaty Commission.

The Play

FOREWORD BY

David Suzuki

With no hope of escaping their extreme poverty in Japan, my grandparents left their homeland for a one-way trip to Canada early in the twentieth century. They knew little if anything about the flora, fauna, or First Peoples of the continent. Like all settlers arriving in North America after contact, they had heard of vast forests, abundant marine life, and precious minerals, "resources" to be exploited by ingenuity and hard work.

My grandparents knew of British Columbia's anti-Asian bigotry encountered in legal and social restrictions on employment, housing, education, and civic participation. They couldn't vote whether as citizens or Canadian-born until 1949. But they didn't know that racism was embedded in the very fabric of the country, through the infamous Indian Act that reduced Indigenous people to a state of wards of the government.

My parents were born in Vancouver, Dad in 1909, Mom in 1911, as was I, in 1936. None of my grandparents spoke more than rudimentary English, but while Mom and Dad were fluently bilingual, my second language was French. I never had a conversation with any of my grandparents, never asked them about the "old country," what they expected in Canada, how they were treated, and whether they were glad they came. In other words, I was deprived of my roots. Instead, I became a Canadian, steeped in the history of England (of which we were told Canada was a part).

Way back in the fourteenth and fifteenth centuries, as technology developed to allow sailing over vast distances and navigating back home, explorers "discovered" new continents – Africa, North and South America, Australia ... – that were already fully occupied by human beings who had thrived there for millennia. The newcomers were driven by "resourcism," a perspective through which trees, fish, minerals, soil, water, all become opportunities for exploitation. But this way of seeing the world has no reciprocity; it takes without limit or responsibility.

Obviously, this perspective clashes with cultures in which Nature is seen as the source of all that matters for spiritual, physical, and social sustenance. The ecocentrism of Indigenous Peoples is grounded in a web of relationships with all other species of animals and plants (often referred to as "relatives") and air, water, soil, and sunlight. These sacred elements of life sustain people who acknowledge responsibility to act properly so that Nature can continue to be abundant and generous.

But the attachment to and responsibility for place of the Indigenous Peoples are impediments to those who seek opportunity above and below ground and water. Without respect and care, how can one tear at Mother Earth without harming her? But resourcism is the foundation of our legal, economic, and political systems.

We have laws to define borders around property and states and human rights, but what about the right of a songbird to live out its life as it evolved to, the right of a river to flow as it has for millennia, or the right of a forest to exist as a community of organisms?

As Indian British economist Sir Partha Dasgupta's recent analysis demonstrates, economics is fundamentally flawed by ignoring Nature and ecosystem services as an "externality," their loss being simply the price of doing business.* Just as egregious is the construction of an economy whose progress is measured by constant growth – the creed of cancer and an impossibility in a finite world.

We are told that democracy, whereby all eligible voters have a say in government priorities and actions, is the best political system; but those most affected by government action or inaction do not vote, namely children, future generations, the atmosphere, oceans, forests, fish, and so on. So they aren't on the political agenda. The ministers of Fisheries and Oceans, of Natural Resources, and of Environment and Climate Change are not primarily charged to protect fish, oceans, natural resources, the environment, or the atmosphere; their constituency is people who vote and use them.

Our world view, in which we see ourselves outside of and atop Nature (anthropocentrism), is embedded in our laws, economy, and politics, and is thus inevitably unable to protect the web of relationships that sustains us. Ever since Rachel Carson's 1962 science book *Silent Spring* galvanized

---

* See Partha Dasgupta, "The Economics of Biodiversity: The Dasgupta Review – Full Report" (London, UK: HM Treasury, February 2, 2021; updated April 23, 2021), assets.publishing.service.gov.uk/government/uploads/system/uploads /attachment_data/file/962785/The_Economics_of_Biodiversity_The_Dasgupta_ Review_Full_Report.pdf.

an environmental movement,* the thrust of activists has been within this anthropocentrism and thus focussed on laws to channel human behaviour, green economics, and Green parties, not the transformation of the systems themselves.

We need transformative change. The history of our inability to act to avoid climate change reveals that, so long as we elevate human constructs like the economy and elections above Nature and her laws, we will fail. What is desperately needed is an understanding of why Indigenous Peoples have resisted the genocidal policies of the settler nation ever since contact. They are the ones who can provide leadership to inculcate the values and perspective from their cultures and languages. But first, Canadians have to work to overcome the legacy of racism and genocidal policies of the country and work towards a genuine reconciliation.

That's what makes this play so important.

David Suzuki is a renowned geneticist, science broadcaster, and environmental activist. Host of the long-running CBC television show *The Nature of Things*, he is also the author of more than fifty books. For his support of Canada's Indigenous Peoples, he has been honoured with eight names and formal adoption by two First Nations.

---

* See Rachel Carson, *Silent Spring*, Fortieth Anniversary Edition, introduction by Linda Lear, afterword by Edward O. Wilson (Boston: Houghton Mifflin Harcourt, 2002), as well as Joni Seager's *Carson's Silent Spring: A Reader's Guide*, Reader's Guides series (London, UK: Bloomsbury Publishing, 2014).

Production History

Inheritance: a pick-the-path experience was first produced by Alley Theatre and Touchstone Theatre, in association with Vancouver Moving Theatre and the Vancouver Aboriginal Friendship Centre, at the Annex Theatre in Vancouver, British Columbia, on the unceded, Traditional, and Ancestral Lands of the xʷməθkʷəy̓əm, Sḵwx̱wú7mesh, səlilwətaʔɫ, and Stó:lō First Nations, from March 3 to 15, 2020, with the following cast and crew:

FRANK: Darrell Dennis

ABBEY: Medina Hahn

NOAH: Daniel Arnold

THE HOST and **RAIN**: Michelle Bardach

Director:	Herbie Barnes
Associate Projection Designer and New Media Operator:	Yvonne Wallace
Projection Design Team:	Chimerik 似不像
Sound Designer and Composer:	Mary Jane Paquette
Set Designer:	Lauchlin Johnston
Props Designer:	Bill Beauregarde
Lighting Designer:	Jill White
Costume Designer:	Carmen Thompson
Production Manager and Technical Director:	Mimi Abrahams
Associate Production Manager:	Andrew Pye
Stage Manager:	Yvonne Yip
Apprentice Stage Manager:	Diana Bartosh
Post-Show Facilitator:	Renae Morriseau
Secwépemc Creative Advisors:	Mayuk Manuel and Percy Casper
Outreach and Engagement Coordinator:	Eugene Crain
Outreach and Engagement Assistant:	Krys Yuan
Research and Evaluation Leader:	Jennica Nichols
Emotional Support Worker:	Ray Thunderchild

Advocacy and Advisory Council:

Maxine Matilpi (Project Lead for Revitalizing Indigenous Law for Land, Air and Water [RELAW], West Coast Environmental Law), Kathleen Cunningham and Krista James (British Columbia Law Institute), Stephen Mussell (lawyer with Mandell Pinder), Justin B Neal (Testify, a project from the Indigenous Laws and the Arts Collective), Fawn Adolph (Vancouver Aboriginal Friendship Centre Society)

Local Territories Advisors:

Te'ta-in Shane Pointe (xʷməθkʷəy̓əm Nation); Agi Mathias Paul (Sḵwx̱wú-7mesh Nation); and Charlene Aleck (səlilwətaʔɬ Nation)

Inheritance was developed with assistance from the following:

Alley Theatre, Touchstone Theatre, National Arts Centre / Centre national des Arts, The Cultch, Arts Club, Firehall Arts Centre, Citadel Theatre, Anvil Centre, Theatre Replacement's PushOFF, Banff Centre for the Arts' Playwrights Lab, David Diamond at Theatre for Living, ArtStarts in Schools, Shadbolt Centre for the Arts, Magnetic North Theatre Festival, Jim Sibley at UBC, Western Canada Theatre, Vancity Community Foundation, Vancouver Foundation, BC Arts Council, and Canada Council for the Arts / Conseil des arts du Canada. The playwrights especially thank Larry Grant and Shane Pointe (xʷməθkʷəy̓əm), Agi Mathias Paul (Sḵwx̱wú7mesh), Carleen Thomas and Charlene Aleck (səlilwətaʔɬ), and Percy Casper and Mayuk Manuel (Secwépemc) for their consultations and endorsement of this play's development.

Cast

FRANK, in his forties, Secwépemc

ABBEY, in her thirties, of settler/immigrant descent

NOAH, in his thirties, of settler descent

In audiovisual recording:
THE HOST and RAIN, Frank's daughter
(written to be played by the same performer)

Time and Place

This play takes place now, on Secwepemcúl'ecw, the Territory of the Secwépemc Nation, in what is currently called the Canadian provinces of British Columbia and Alberta. For a brief history of the Secwépemc people and their Territory, see page 261.

A Note on How to Read This Play

Inheritance was written to be an interactive theatre experience in which the audience chooses what happens in the story. You are reading a revised and updated version of the premiere production, in which audience members were given handheld devices to vote on what would happen next in the play.

This script can still be interactive for you, if you read it how a theatre audience would experience it:

If you are reading this play in print form, when the script comes to a **Choice-Point**, decide what you want to happen next, then flip to the appropriate page.

If you are reading this play in digital form, when the script comes to a **Choice-Point**, decide what you want to happen next, then click or tap on your choice to be taken to the appropriate scene.

And so on. This will take you, ultimately, to your chosen ending.

Once you've completed a reading of the script in this manner, you can then go back and read all the other choices and scenes. That way, the various versions will make more sense.

If you just read this script page by page like you would a standard play, you will quickly become confused.

Pre-Show

You've entered a space that hosts a number of locations: a forest, mountains, a river.

In the middle of it all is the porch and living room of a grandiose, but aging, log cabin. Leaning against the porch is a dirty shovel.

In the living room, by the fireplace, is a hunting rifle.

There is also a projection screen or screens.

Amped-up hard-rock music plays.

At Curtain

The lights dim and a video plays on the screen not unlike an airplane safety tutorial, with a voice-over.

THE HOST (in voice-over) addresses the audience.

THE HOST: Hello and welcome to *Inheritance: a pick-the-path experience.*

Speaking of inheritance …

THE HOST acknowledges the Ancestral and Traditional Indigenous Territories that the play is being presented on and the appropriate supporters. For the premiere production, this Land Acknowledgment was as follows:

We respectfully acknowledge that we are all currently on the unceded, Ancestral, and Traditional Territories of the xʷməθkʷəy̓əm (Musqueam), S̱k̲w̱x̱wú7mesh (Squamish), and səl̓ilwətaɁɬ (Tsleil-Waututh) First Nations.

What do we do with this reality, you may ask? Well, welcome to this play.

Before we begin, we wish to acknowledge that we have an emotional support worker here today. Should you ever need the support.

The support worker stands to make their presence known.

We also wish to thank those who have supported this project:

*Logos are projected. **THE HOST** acknowledges the support. For the premiere production, this was as follows:*

The Canada Council for the Arts, the British Columbia Arts Council, BC Gaming Corporation, the City of Vancouver, the Vancouver Foundation, Vancouver Civic Theatres, Vancity Credit Union's Community Partnership Program, MacMillan Learning, the National Arts Centre of Canada, Electric Company Theatre, and the many others found in your program.

Now. Fasten your seat belt and make sure your chair is in the upright position, because in this play YOU determine what happens next. Oooooooh!

Every so often the story will come to a **Choice-Point**. You'll be presented options for how things should proceed, and you'll have *fifteen seconds* to cast your vote. After that the performance will resume according to which choice received the most votes.

So everything in the past is already set; but you … determine the future. Kinda like life.

Each of you should have a clicker. Take a moment to press the power button. The glowing green light means the device is on and ready to receive your vote. After you've voted, your clicker will automatically turn off after a few minutes. So before voting again, I'll remind you to turn it on.

Voting is entirely anonymous. You chose your seat, so we have no idea who has which device.

And just so you know, there are no right or wrong choices. Every path leads somewhere. Vote how you wish. Drama? Humour? An ethical choice? There are no rules.

All good? Let me hear you say it: All good?

If the audience isn't that vocal:

Hello? Are we all good?

If the audience clearly says, "All good":

Good.

So. Let's try a few questions to practise.

Questions are also projected.

How old are you?

    A.   Under 30

    B.   Between 30 and 55

    C.   56 or older

    After fifteen seconds, the results are projected.

Good. Here's another:

Do you identify as Indigenous to the land now called North America?

    A.   Yes

    B.   No

    C.   Prefer not to say

    After fifteen seconds, the results are projected.

Great. Now let's try affecting the action onstage.

    FRANK enters the living room – with a butcher knife and two dead rabbits. He goes to the stereo to put on some music –

CHOICE-POINT PRE-SHOW

THE HOST: Choice-Point. Frank wants to listen to some music. What does he choose?

    A.   The Clash

    B.   The Halluci Nation

    C.   Enya

You have fifteen seconds.

    The fifteen-second clock ticks down. When all the votes are tabulated:

You chose:

    *The results of the **Choice-Point** are projected and **THE HOST** announces the choice.*

Now you know how to play. I hope you enjoy. And I'll be back ...

Act One

SCENE 1

FRANK finds the track he's looking for and presses "play" on the stereo.

Music blasts (whatever the audience chose – The Clash, The Halluci Nation, or Enya).

He rocks out OR headbangs OR dances along to the music.

Then he steps onto the porch, places the rabbits on a board on the railing, and starts to butcher them – he's obviously experienced at this – all while grooving and lip-syncing along to the music, enjoying himself.

He suddenly stops – looks up and around, his mood changed, now serious.

He goes inside, shuts the music off, and stands there, listening.

He steps back onto the porch and listens again. Far in the distance: the sound of a motor. He stands there, wondering.

Lights fade on him as the sound of the motor gets closer and closer, and louder and louder.

SCENE 1.1

The motor suddenly cuts out as the lights snap up on
ABBEY and NOAH, in a boat, drifting on the water.
ABBEY is on her cellphone, fighting for signal. She
intersperses English with Arabic.

ABBEY: Can you get there for me? They only speak Arabe, and they won't have any money ... Someone needs to be there. Shu? Shu fi? Āime, you're breaking up. (*half-laughing*) Maman. I'm not on "vacation." I'm going to get Bayey to sign those papers ...

NOAH is lazily playing with the water out the side of the
boat and drinking a Hey Y'all (vodka iced tea).

ABBEY: What guy? ... No, he won't help because I don't work for him anymore ... I don't work with Immigration anymore. And the family doesn't even know him. They only ever dealt with me. They trust me ... Shu halHaké, ya Āime!? I had to file, had no choice ... He was inappropriate, he took advantage. Someone had to stand up to him ... I know, I know, Mom ... Listen, this family needs help and if no one's there, they'll end up on the street ... Can you meet them tomorrow for me? ... Hello? Āime? Āime? Dammit!

ABBEY's signal is obviously gone. She hangs up.

Sorry babe. I'm going to have to call back when we get there.

NOAH: Yeah, yeah, do what you gotta do. It's important.

NOAH offers her a beer. She takes it, gladly.

NOAH: I'm just excited. Finally coming out here. I'm on a boat! (*beat*) Oh hey, can we see your property yet?

ABBEY: Yeah. (*pointing*) Starts about there, and goes all the way to the other side of the lake ...

NOAH: Whoa.

ABBEY: And see the highest mountain way out there? Property line basically follows the river to the other side of that.

NOAH: Holy, seeing it on maps just doesn't do it justice. No wonder it's worth so much. Man ... what a place to grow up. Thanks for finally bringing me here, babe. And still a couple days before your dad gets back, so lots of time to ... "get back to nature," if you know what I mean.

ABBEY smirks. They get lovey-dovey ...

ABBEY: Okay, before it gets dark.

She pulls the engine – and the lights cut out as the sound of the revving engine fills the theatre again.

SCENE 1.2

When the lights rise, FRANK is sitting on the porch, eating his dinner. A hunting rifle is perched nearby.

We hear the sound of the motor boat arriving. As it gets closer, FRANK doesn't seem to change. As if he's waiting, patiently, for a storm.

Offstage, the motor cuts out. A few moments later, ABBEY and NOAH walk on, slowly, backpacks over their shoulders. They've seen FRANK, and ABBEY is checking him out, confused. They stop in front of the porch. A beat as they all suss each other out. FRANK nods.

FRANK: 'Lo there.

ABBEY: ... Hey.

FRANK: Nice evenin'.

> *NOAH's confused. What's going on?*

ABBEY: Sorry, can I help you?

FRANK: I'm doing okay. Can I help *you*?

ABBEY: Sorry, who are you?

FRANK: Name's Frank. You?

> *ABBEY's not saying anything.*

NOAH: ... Uh, Noah, hi.

ABBEY: Is Danny around?

FRANK: (*considering how to answer*) ... No ...

NOAH: Man of few words, okay.

ABBEY: Do you know him, or ...?

FRANK: Depends who's asking.

ABBEY: His daughter.

FRANK: Ohhhh! Oh, okay. Ha. Sorry about that. Just never can tell who's gonna wander up off the river. (*standing*) Hey, I'm Frank.

He goes to shake ABBEY's hand, but she is skeptical. And eyeing the rifle.

FRANK: Uh, yeah, your dad was going away but said that I could uh, stay, while he was gone. He didn't tell you? Well, yeah, said he had to go check out a claim up north, but that I should stay. Did he know *you* were coming?

ABBEY: Yeah.

NOAH: Yeah, we were gonna – spend a few nights on our own here first, then he gets back on, like, Sunday, and I officially "meet the focker."

ABBEY: Okay ...

NOAH: Actually supposed to be here a couple days ago but decided to stay in a hotel first. So now's the kind of ... "*rustic* romance" –

ABBEY: Okay ...

FRANK: Well hell, guys. Romantic getaway, and here I am instead.

> *Beat.*

Well, no worries, I'm a heavy sleeper, I can wear earplugs, and there's plenty of room. Don't let *me* stop you. Come on in. There's more if you're hungry. You make it from town all in one day?

NOAH: ... Yeah, yeah.

FRANK: Man, that's a long trip, eh? Though probably nicer by boat. I had to drive my truck in. That is one bumpy ride, even in a four-by, you could charge admission for a ride like that.

> *FRANK bounces around. NOAH and FRANK kind of chuckle, but not really. FRANK sees NOAH eyeing the rifle.*

FRANK: Oh, I've seen a bear out there.

> *NOAH instantly looks around, afraid.*

FRANK: Anyway ... Bring in your stuff. I fixed the pump, so the water's running now. Cleared all the crap outta the fireplace so you can actually have a fire if you want. (*indicating his dish*) And like I say, there's more where this came from.

> *ABBEY's still trying to take this in. NOAH's unsure, caught in the middle.*

NOAH: … I'm kinda hungry.

FRANK: C'mon in.

FRANK goes into the house – taking the rifle with him.

ABBEY: Something's wrong.

ABBEY is looking around the yard, inspecting her turf.

ABBEY: There's no way my dad's just letting this guy stay here.

NOAH: Why, why not?

ABBEY: First off, why didn't he *tell* me some guy was gonna be here. And second, my dad's a recluse, doesn't talk to anyone. Doesn't trust – anything. The guy's a squatter, it's obvious.

NOAH: … "Obvious"?

ABBEY: Yes. My dad's got … bad history with the Native people around here, Noah. People trespassing, he gets into fights; they even gave him a concussion once – put him in a coma. But now he's just *letting* this … guy stay in his place? No way.

NOAH: Holy. You never told me that.

ABBEY: It was, like, five years ago. You were on a "break" with me, remember?

NOAH: So, what, there's a feud or something? Is this gonna be a problem …?

ABBEY: No, no. But my dad *hiring* this guy … is weird.

Beat.

NOAH: Well, can you call him, make sure? (*beat*) Hon. Can you call him?

ABBEY: Yeah, I guess.

Beat. NOAH and ABBEY look up to the house.

NOAH: Or … well, do you want to just … go back?

ABBEY: No. God, no. This is my place.

ABBEY suddenly walks up the porch and into the house. NOAH reluctantly follows.

Inside: FRANK is not in the living room. But ABBEY spots the rifle perched against the fireplace. She goes immediately to a side table – but something's wrong. She looks around.

NOAH: What?

ABBEY: The phone.

She looks around the room; it's nowhere.

(*calling to FRANK*) Hey! Hey, uh – (*to NOAH*) what's his name again?

NOAH: Uhhh, Frank?

ABBEY: Hey! Frank!

NOAH: I *think* it's Frank.

ABBEY: Can you come out here a sec?

After a moment, FRANK steps in, wearing an oven mitt.

FRANK: M'lady?

ABBEY: Um, do you happen to know where the phone is?

FRANK: Oh uh … (*beat*) No don't know.

ABBEY: What do you mean, you don't know?

FRANK: I mean, I don't know. There was no phone when I got here.

ABBEY: We've always had a landline, right here.

FRANK shrugs. Then ABBEY continues to look around – for the phone, but also for clues as to what's going on. NOAH tries in vain for service on his cell.

NOAH: Last place we got signal was in the middle of the lake, right? So that's, what, like an hour?

ABBEY goes off to check out the rest of the house. NOAH and FRANK stand there awkwardly.

NOAH: Sorry, man. She's usually really nice.

FRANK: I'll take your word for it.

FRANK sets the table for some dinner, while NOAH kind of pokes around for the phone.

FRANK: (*privately to NOAH*) Hey, is she … a bit Native?

NOAH: What? Abbey? No! Ha ha. No. Not that – … No, her mom's a bit Lebanese.

FRANK: Ah. Yeah, cuz her dad is ALL White.

NOAH: … So you, uh, you know him, eh?

FRANK: Yeah, was working some odd jobs for him round here. Clean the place up.

NOAH: Right, cuz – Cool.

> *Another beat.*

Hey, sweet ride out there, man, what year is it?

FRANK: Seventy-six.

NOAH: Sweet. Vintage. (*beat*) Yeah, I know nothing about trucks, I don't know why I asked. (*beat*) I know a lot about *vans*. (*beat*) I'm a drummer. In a band. Also manage a few bands. (*beat*) So I have toured in a lot of *vans*.

> *Another beat.*

FRANK: What kind of music?

NOAH: We're not really into labels. "Indie rock," I guess some people say.

FRANK: Cool. Rock star.

> *ABBEY re-enters slowly. She has a cellphone in her hand.*

ABBEY: My dad's cellphone is here.

NOAH: What? You're *sure* it's his?

ABBEY: Yes, I bought it for him.

NOAH: Why would he leave it here?

> *ABBEY looks to FRANK.*

ABBEY: Has this been here the entire time?

FRANK: Where was it?

ABBEY: On his dresser.

FRANK: (*shrugging*) I just work for the guy. I don't go into his bedroom.

> *Beat.* ***ABBEY*** *looks at where the home phone should be. So does* ***NOAH***.

NOAH: ... Huh. Well, shoot.

> ***ABBEY*** *looks at* ***FRANK***, *then around the house. She decides:*

ABBEY: (*to FRANK, very nicely*) Okay, listen, uh ... I don't mean to ... be rude or ... obviously I'm a little freaked out ... and seeing as how *we're* here now, could we maybe ask that maybe you ...?

> *She waits for* ***FRANK*** *to offer to leave, but he doesn't, so:*

Well, that maybe *we* could stay here now?

FRANK: Of course, yeah, like I said, more the merrier.

> *Upbeat,* ***FRANK*** *leaves for the kitchen.*

(*from offstage*) Oh, but I've been staying in the orange room upstairs. That's not your room, is it? Cuz I can move into another room if you need.

> ***ABBEY*** *looks to* ***NOAH*** *for help. But* ***NOAH*** *shrugs, "It's not really my place, is it?"* ***ABBEY*** *looks at the rifle by the fireplace. She then calls to* ***FRANK***:

ABBEY: No, I was thinking, like ... it would be good if we could be here ... alone? (*beat*) Like, do you have anywhere else you could go?

> *After a beat,* ***FRANK*** *slowly re-enters, no longer in a good mood.*

FRANK: Seriously?

ABBEY: I'm sorry, /* I just –

FRANK: I'm here cuz the walls of my house are covered in mould. Actually most of the houses on my reserve are covered in mould, so ... kinda between places.

ABBEY: ... We could – give you some money for a hotel or something?

---

*   Slashes within the text indicate overlapping lines of dialogue.

FRANK: Listen, I understand it freaks you out to have an Indian around –

NOAH: Hey, / whoa, whoa –

ABBEY: That has nothing to do with ... / what I'm –

FRANK: But last I checked this wasn't *your* house. It's your dad's. And he said I should stay here, so that's what I'm gonna do. So you can either take your money and go back to a hotel yourself, and stop squatting on my land. Or you can, you know, stay here and we can, like, all be friends maybe.

> *Beat.*

ABBEY: *Your* land.

FRANK: If you wanna talk about who should leave, I'd like to talk about that.

NOAH: (*having noticed something on the floor*) Ummmmmmmmm –

CHOICE-POINT 1.2

THE HOST: Choice-Point. Noah is looking at a bloodstain on the floor ...

    A.   Should Noah confront Frank about it, privately?
        ▶ **Go to Scene 2B, page 26**

    B.   Should Abbey see the bloodstain, too?
        ▶ **Go to Scene 2C, page 30**

    C.   Should Frank take their money?
        ▶ **Go to Scene 2A, page 20**

Again, make sure your device is on. And you have fifteen seconds.

    The timer starts ...

    Votes are in.

You've chosen ...

    The results are projected and **THE HOST** *says the choice.*

SCENE 2A

Frank takes their money ...

Replay the last few moments ...

FRANK: So you can either take your money and go back to a hotel yourself, and stop squatting on my land. Or you can, you know, stay here and we can, like, all be friends maybe.

Beat.

ABBEY: *Your* land.

FRANK: If you wanna talk about who should leave, I'd like to talk about that.

NOAH: (*having noticed something on the floor*) Ummmmmmmm – maybe we *should* go, babe.

ABBEY: This is my house.

NOAH: Yeah. But – no one wants, like, blood – bad – blood. Anywhere. On the – anywhere.

ABBEY: What?

*All **NOAH** can do is bite his lip.*

NOAH: Okay, man. She's pretty stubborn. She did grow up in this house. And we really did plan on having some – alone time here. So seriously we don't want to put you out, we'll give you some money for a hotel. Seriously. (*to ABBEY*) Babe, you got any cash?

ABBEY: Uh ...

NOAH: Here, here's twenty, forty, sixty, eighty ...

ABBEY: I've got forty ...

NOAH: There, one twenty. How much was our room again?

ABBEY: Here.

ABBEY gives FRANK the rest of NOAH's money.

NOAH: Yeah, uh, yeah ... take it, man. We don't want to put you out.

Beat.

FRANK: Sure. Sure, whatever.

He takes their money.

FRANK: Well, help yourself to the meal in there. Just made a fresh rabbit stew. Oh but, bit of a mess in the kitchen, you want me to clean up before I go?

ABBEY: Oh no, no worries. (*thinking she's being nice*) Feel free to take your stew if you want.

FRANK receives this as another shutdown.

FRANK: Right. I'll get outta your hair then.

He goes upstairs to pack.

ABBEY: (*calling after him*) I didn't mean … it doesn't matter, either way.

ABBEY and NOAH stand there awkwardly.

NOAH: I think we just gave him over two hundred bucks.

ABBEY: Whatever, as long as he goes.

NOAH: I think I had a fifty in there …

ABBEY: I don't know what's going on here … Stay here, I'm going to go look around. Can you check my dad's cell history, see if there's anything weird?

ABBEY heads off down the hallway to inspect the place. NOAH looks again at the floor, at the stain, not sure if he should say something about it.

FRANK comes back on, pack over his shoulder. A large hunting knife on his belt.

FRANK: You know … (*deciding not to say it*) Whatever. I left the stew for ya. (*waving their money*) Thanks for the money. Nighty night!

FRANK leaves out the front door and disappears into the woods.

NOAH watches him go. He scrolls through the cellphone … becoming intrigued by something.

After a moment, ABBEY comes back in, holding a map.

ABBEY: This was on his desk, just sitting there.

Confused, she lays the map down on the table. It also appears projected on the screen. NOAH comes over and looks too.

ABBEY: It's a map of our property. Looks like ... he hid the Deed to our land? somewhere on the property. But drew a *map* of how to find it ...?

NOAH: ... Huh? (*looking over ABBEY's shoulder*) ... Why the hell would he do that?

ABBEY: (*reading*) "The physical bearer of the Land Deed need only bring the Deed to my lawyer (details below) and is thereby entitled to this entire property"?? ... "all the riches thereon ... and all the rights therein"??

NOAH: What the hell ...?! So, wait, so ... whoever finds the Deed ... owns the land?

ABBEY: (*reeling*) No ... / That can't be –

NOAH: That's insane.

ABBEY: "However if the Deed is not brought to my lawyer by Friday, April 17 ..."

NOAH: Wait, that's ... tomorrow?

ABBEY: "... at 3 p.m., then I hereby bequeath all of the aforesaid rights unto the sole chosen beneficiary of my entire estate, namely the Right Honourable *Queen of England*" –?!? – "for her to use as she deems fit ..."

NOAH: The Queen!

ABBEY: "... as it is she from whom my grandfather obtained our first 160-acre parcel of land, for a whopping Ten Dollars."

NOAH: Whoa, only ten / bucks?

ABBEY: "Again, if the Deed is not brought to my lawyer by Friday, 3 p.m., then I hereby return the land unto you, O Queen. It's your problem, you can bloody well deal with it."

ABBEY is stunned and can't continue. NOAH reads on:

NOAH: "Written in sound mind ... Danny Mitchell."
Stamped, dated, like, two weeks ago. Jesus ... This can't be ...
(*flipping through the papers*) ... is this a joke?

ABBEY: I don't know.

NOAH: This has to be a joke. Or maybe … You did say his mind might be starting to go, right?

ABBEY: Sure, forgetting a few things. But this?

She thinks, looking out the window, then paces.

NOAH: Is this really his signature? Do you know?

ABBEY looks at the paper.

NOAH: Hon …?

ABBEY: One sec, just let me think.

NOAH: … Hon, is this his signature?

ABBEY takes the paper.

ABBEY: Oh my god. That guy could have it. He could have the Deed.

NOAH: Wait. What?

ABBEY: That's why he's living out here – that's why he said it's *his* land. He already has the Deed.

She goes to grab the rifle.

NOAH: Whoa, whoa, babe –

But she's already got the rifle and is going to the door.

NOAH: Abbey, whoa, wait!

ABBEY: What.

NOAH: Jesus, *think* – okay? Who knows what happened out here, the guy has a frickin' HUGE knife – so the safest thing to do is go call this in. Call your lawyer. The cops. Cuz what if this "map" thing isn't even legally sound? I mean, you can't just give away a multimillion-dollar property with a handwritten note! And this may not even be your dad's signature. Frank could have written this.

ABBEY: You want to take that chance?? If it is legally binding, and he shows up with the Deed – we're screwed. Out of everything.

She turns to go.

NOAH: Oh my God. Our *lives* are more important than –

NOAH and ABBEY start wrestling for the control of the gun.

NOAH: Abbey! Let the authorities handle / this!

ABBEY: We let him go and it could all be gone. / All of it.

NOAH: I don't – care. Let the police – Abbey!!

THE HOST interrupts:

CHOICE-POINT 2A

THE HOST: Choice-Point:

A. Should Abbey break free with the gun, and run after Frank?
    ▶ **Go to Scene 3B, page 49**

B. Should Noah get the gun, and he and Abbey go back to catch Frank in a lie?
    ▶ **Go to Scene 3A, page 42**

C. Does it not matter, and let's follow Frank instead?
    ▶ **Go to Scene 3C, page 56**

Again, make sure your device is on. And you have fifteen seconds.

The timer starts ...

Votes are in.

You've chosen ...

*The results are projected and **THE HOST** says the choice.*

SCENE 2B

Noah confronts Frank about it, privately.

Replay the last few moments ...

FRANK: So you can either take your money and go back to a hotel yourself, and stop squatting on my land. Or you can, you know, stay here and we can, like, all be friends maybe.

Beat.

ABBEY: *Your* land.

FRANK: If you wanna talk about who should leave, I'd like to talk about that.

NOAH: (*having noticed something on the floor*) Ummmmmmmmm – maybe we *should* go, babe.

ABBEY: This is my house.

NOAH: Yeah. But – no one wants, like, blood – bad – blood. Anywhere. On the – anywhere.

ABBEY: What?

*All **NOAH** can do is bite his lip.*

NOAH: Hey Frank, could we maybe, uh, talk this blood – out – man to man?

FRANK: Excuse me?

NOAH: Maybe, Abbey, you can leave, so me and Frank can deal with this – man to man.

ABBEY: Now *you're* asking me to leave?

NOAH: Abbey! Just go ... blow off some steam, okay? Go look at your dad's phone, check his call history and stuff. Look around outside, see what you can see.

ABBEY: See what I can –??

NOAH: You're always asking me to "man up," so – let me handle this! Man to man.

FRANK: Is Drummer Boy saying he wants to fight me? I really don't get what he's saying.

ABBEY: That makes two of us.

NOAH: Just –! Give us a second alone, Abbey! How hard can that be?

ABBEY: … You're acting very weird.

> *She leaves. NOAH watches her leave … a distance from the house.*

> *A beat.*

> *NOAH slowly ambles over, closer to the rifle.*

NOAH: So tell me, Frank … You've been staying here a while, no phone, her dad's cell just sitting there. And uh … what's that?

> *NOAH points to the blood on the floor. FRANK goes over and looks.*

FRANK: That … is a stain of blood.

> *NOAH immediately grabs the rifle, points it!*

NOAH: Hands up! Hands up! Hands where I can see 'em! Don't move. Don't move!

> *FRANK is totally casual.*

FRANK: Do you even know how to use that thing?

NOAH: … Yes!

FRANK: You have to take the safety off.

NOAH: I know.

FRANK: Then you have to cock it.

NOAH: I know that, shut up.

FRANK: You also need bullets.

NOAH: Whatever man! Tell me why there's blood on the floor and her dad's cell is just – But mostly tell me why there's blood on the floor!

FRANK: All right, you wanna know?

NOAH: Yeah.

FRANK: You *really* wanna know? You think you can handle it? City Boy. Rock Star.

NOAH: ... Whatever man, yes.

FRANK: All right ...

FRANK rips the gun from NOAH's hands.

FRANK: But once I tell ya: I'll have to kill ya. (*laughing at his own joke*) Hahaaahaaaa! No, seriously. First. Never, EVER, believe someone when they say a gun isn't loaded.

NOAH: Wait, what?

FRANK: Second, don't ever EVER grab a firearm unless you're ready to use it. And third. This is what happened: I came in earlier today. Knife in hand. Fresh from a kill. I put on a good song: (*naming the artist the audience chose at the beginning*). And I started dancing around – with my kill. A couple'a dead rabbits. Just ... (*dancing with pretend dead rabbits*) ... Uh ... Uh ... Oww.

Beat.

NOAH: Sorry. Rabbits?

FRANK: That's right. They must not've bled out all the way.

NOAH: That's the blood of rabbits?

FRANK: Rabbit stew. Try some.

FRANK points to a bowl on the table. NOAH goes over, tries it.

NOAH: Oh yeah. Tastes good.

FRANK: But glad to know you thought I was a murderer. That's great. That I give off that vibe? Cuz that's totally the vibe I'm going for. "Father Murderer." Or at least: "White Guy Killer."

NOAH: ... Okay ... I'm sorry, dude. She said her dad doesn't have good history with ... you know. So. We're obviously pretty freaked out here.

FRANK: I hear ya. I hear ya. I'm just razzin' ya. Yeah, it's her dad's blood, I frickin' hate that guy. Ha haaa! I'm joking! I'm joking! Lighten up!

Beat.

Listen, why don't you call your lady back in, let's just sit down, and talk about all this. Over some dinner. You guys gotta be hungry, right? Rabbit stew.

> *FRANK starts dancing again.*

> *Blackout.*

▶ Go to Scene 2C.1, page 33

SCENE 2C

Abbey sees the bloodstain, too ...

Replay the last few moments ...

FRANK: So you can either take your money and go back to a hotel yourself, and stop squatting on my land. Or you can, you know, stay here and we can, like, all be friends maybe.

Beat.

ABBEY: *Your* land.

FRANK: If you wanna talk about who should leave, I'd like to talk about that.

NOAH: (*having noticed something on the floor*) Ummmmmmmm – maybe we *should* go, babe.

ABBEY: This is my house.

NOAH: Yeah. But – no one wants, like, blood – bad – blood. Anywhere. On the – anywhere.

ABBEY: What?

All NOAH can do is bite his lip.

NOAH: Hey Frank ... Could you ... step off ... for a bit ... and let ... me and uhhh .... Uhhh –

ABBEY: Abbey.

NOAH: Yeah, can you ... let us chit- ... chat?

FRANK: Is he having a stroke?

ABBEY: I don't know.

NOAH: Just –! Can you give us a second ... to discuss this, please?

FRANK: So now *you're* asking me to leave too?

ABBEY sees NOAH trying not to look at the bloodstain – but doing a bad job of it.

ABBEY: What is that?

A beat.

ABBEY: Hey. Frank. What the hell is that?

NOAH: I think we can remain calm. Everybody! We can remain calm!! It looks like – blood, but maybe it's not. Maybe it's not?

FRANK walks over, bends down, looks.

FRANK: Oh yeah. That's blood.

ABBEY suddenly rushes to the fireplace, where the rifle rests, and grabs it!

NOAH: Hey, whoa – Jesus! Abbey!

FRANK: Ha ha, it's not your dad's!

ABBEY has the rifle trained on him. FRANK is just laughing.

NOAH: Abbey!

FRANK: Hey, lady, you wanna do damage with that thing, you're gonna need to load it.

ABBEY blanches. She slightly lowers the weapon.

FRANK: All right, you wanna know what happened? You think you can handle it? Think you city slickers can handle it?

He's walking toward ABBEY.

NOAH: Oh God ...

FRANK snaps the gun out of ABBEY's hands.

FRANK: But once I tell ya: I'll have to kill ya. (*laughing at his own joke*) Ha haaa! No, seriously. First, never, EVER, believe someone when they say a gun isn't loaded.

NOAH: ... Wait, what?

FRANK: Second, don't ever, EVER, grab a firearm unless you're ready to use it. And third. This is what happened: I came in earlier today. Knife in hand. Fresh from a kill. I put on a good song: (*naming the artist the audience chose at the beginning*). And I started dancing around – with my kill. A couple'a dead rabbits. Just ... (*dancing with pretend dead rabbits*) Uh ... Uh ... Oww.

Beat.

NOAH: Sorry. Rabbits?

FRANK: That's right. They must not've bled out all the way.

NOAH: That's the blood of rabbits??

FRANK: Rabbit stew. Try some.

> *FRANK points to a bowl on the table. NOAH goes over, tries it.*

NOAH: Oh yeah. Tastes good.

FRANK: But glad to know you thought I was a murderer. That's great. That I give off that vibe? Cuz that's totally the vibe I'm going for. "Father Murderer." Or at least: "White Guy Killer."

ABBEY: Okay … I'm sorry, Frank. My dad doesn't have good history with … you know. So. Obviously I'm a little …

FRANK: … I hear ya. I hear ya.

> *Beat. FRANK puts the gun down.*

Listen, we really got off on the wrong foot here. Why don't we all just sit down and talk this out. Over some dinner. You guys gotta be hungry, right? Rabbit stew.

> *FRANK starts dancing again.*

> *Blackout.*

SCENE 2C.1

Lights rise on ABBEY and NOAH eating dinner at the table. FRANK sits with them. ABBEY is scrolling through her dad's cellphone history.

NOAH: This is SO good! Isn't this good?

ABBEY: Mm-hm.

NOAH: I've never had rabbit before. Maybe cuz they're so cute. (*to his bowl*) I'm sorry, little guys. But you're so good!

FRANK: Veggies and spices from the garden, too.

NOAH: Wow. Yeah. Love that. (*sing-songish*) Organic! Thanks, man.

FRANK: Thank the Creator.

NOAH: … Cool. Yeah. Hey, our drinks are probably cold now, anyone want?

> *FRANK and ABBEY indicate no.*

NOAH: Okay then, drinkin' alone.

> *NOAH goes off.*

FRANK: So yeah – as I was saying – last year I was scoping around for work, got to talking with your dad. First he brought me on just to fix a fence, but then trying to smooth out that damn road, haul off some old equipment –

ABBEY: That was you? He mentioned he had some guy cleaning up the property, but …

FRANK: "Some guy." Y'know, he never said much about *you*, either. *Anyway* – after a while we started … talking about the land. What could be done with it. What *should* be done with it.

> *ABBEY looks up. NOAH re-enters, sipping another Hey Y'all.*

ABBEY: What do you mean?

FRANK: How it could be … put to use. He was wondering what to do with it.

ABBEY: Wait, my dad told you about the plans, right?

NOAH: Uhhhh, sure no one wants a drink? Hey Y'all. Vodka with Southern iced tea, real good. You wanna try?

ABBEY: We're cleaning up the property to sell half of it and turn the rest into an eco-resort. The master plan was submitted, like, last year.

FRANK: Right, a plan that would disrupt our salmon run just so rich folks can clamber all over the land with their latest kill. While the people who actually live out here need access to those same hunting and fishing grounds for our livelihoods.

NOAH: Okay, it's not gonna – disrupt – it's gonna be a real back-to-the-land experience, Frank, eco-friendly. A retreat, not some macho sport-shooting thing. We plan to hire locals, people from the reserve. An employment program for new refugees. As low a footprint as possible –

FRANK: I know the plans.

ABBEY: Okay. So then what kind of conversations were you having?

FRANK: Just, what else could be done with the land. And who should have the right to do that. You know.

ABBEY: Sorry. You're being very vague.

NOAH: Ab ... (*to FRANK*) You mean, like, you're referring to, like, the fact that this land was originally your people's, kind of thing?

FRANK: Sure, that "kind of thing," yeah.

ABBEY: Oh my God –

FRANK: Your old man's pretty conflicted –

ABBEY: – sure, sure, we're *all* conflicted, but we have to be practical. I'm sorry, is that why you're here, to try and stop us developing our land? Are you from the reserve?

FRANK: Yeah.

ABBEY: Right. Okay, well, I've spent the last three years getting all the permits – we need to do this, my dad's broke, his mind is going, and this is all we have. So you may think you're, like, "spiritually converting some rich old mining tycoon here," but you're not. Anyway, sorry, just – I need to know where I stand here. I feel a bit – you know.

FRANK: I can see that. All right. I'm sure you know that *all* the land around here is recognized, even by your government, as the Traditional Territory of my people –

ABBEY: Wait – This is *private* land, you want everyone to give all their land back? Where do you want us to go?

FRANK: If I may?

ABBEY: If you want to reclaim territory there is so much Crown land. So much. Don't try and take it from some frail old man just cuz –

NOAH: Maybe we could just listen?

   Beat.

FRANK: My – Our issue is not with your dad. Or you, even.

ABBEY: Good, cuz my family worked hard for this, it wasn't easy. And they actually worked with and *helped* the Native – or First Nations people around them, so – It's not just –

FRANK: Trust me, no one is trying to boot anyone off the land.

ABBEY: Then what?

FRANK: My problem, our problem, as the original Peoples of this land, is with your government, yes, not with individual landowners. *However*, you do vote. But okay, I'll be very specific. Do you know what the word "unceded" means?

ABBEY: Yes. It means a right or property not formally given up. I deal with contracts all the time.

FRANK: Bingo! Give the lady a cigar. A large portion of land that Canada and private "landowners" are sitting on is unceded land. Meaning never formally surrendered. No treaties, nothing. Almost all of BC, large parts of Québec, a lot of the North, your capital city of Ottawa, all unceded. Including this property we're sitting on right now.

ABBEY: Okay but –

FRANK: Which means technically you are squatting on this land. And once I explained that to your dad and he really understood it, he started to see things in a different light.

   Beat.

ABBEY: Okay, what are you saying here? You've had some conversations about what he should do with his land, and what? That's it, that's where we stand?

FRANK: That is where we stood. Before he left. Now there's something else.

FRANK exits into the hallway. ABBEY is stunned.

NOAH: Babe. It's okay.

ABBEY: No – it's not okay, it's definitely not okay.

NOAH: Okay, okay.

ABBEY: Their whole Nation has filed an official land claim for all the properties around here. Not just Crown land, but all the private land – the town, the farms, our entire property – everything.

NOAH: Whoa.

ABBEY: And now this guy's "talking" to my dad about a change of plans?! This is all we have. I'm already eighty *grand* in debt over this.

NOAH: ... Holy.

ABBEY: How do I take care of everyone?

NOAH: Wait, eighty? I thought it was fifty.

ABBEY: Lawyer fees.

NOAH: ... Frickin' lawyers.

A beat. Then FRANK enters with some papers. Beat. He smiles at them, then lays a piece of paper down on the table. It also appears projected. It's a map of the property.

FRANK: According to this, your dad hid the Title Deed to this land, somewhere on the property. But drew a *map* of how to find it.

NOAH: ... Huh? (*looking over ABBEY's shoulder*) ... Why would he do that?

ABBEY: (*reading*) "The physical bearer of the Land Deed need only bring the Deed to my lawyer (details below) and is thereby entitled to this entire property" – ?? – "all the riches thereon ... and all the rights therein." What / the hell?

NOAH: Holy ... so, wait, so ... whoever finds the Deed ... owns the land?

FRANK: And can decide what to do with it.

ABBEY: (*reeling*) No ... this can't be ...

NOAH: That's insane.

ABBEY: "However if the Deed is not brought to my lawyer by Friday, April 17 ..."

NOAH: Wait, that's –

FRANK: Tomorrow.

ABBEY: "... at 3 p.m., I hereby bequeath all of the aforesaid rights unto the sole chosen beneficiary of my entire estate, namely the Right Honourable *Queen of England*" –?!? – "for her to use as she deems fit ..."

NOAH: The Queen!

ABBEY: "... as it is she from whom my grandfather obtained our first 160-acre parcel of land, for a whopping Ten Dollars."

NOAH: Whoa, only ten bucks?

FRANK: They were givin' away what wasn't even / theirs –

ABBEY: "Again, if the Deed is not brought to my lawyer by Friday, 3 p.m., then I hereby return the land unto you, O Queen. It's your problem, you can bloody well deal with it."

ABBEY is stunned and can't continue. NOAH reads on:

NOAH: "Written in sound mind ... Danny Mitchell."
Stamped, dated, like, two weeks ago. Jesus ... This can't be ...
(*flipping through the papers*) ... is this a joke?

ABBEY: I don't know.

NOAH: This has to be a joke. Or you did say his mind was starting to go, right?

ABBEY: Sure, forgetting a few things. But this?

Beat.

NOAH: Is this really his signature, do you know?

She looks.

NOAH: Hon?

ABBEY: One sec, just let me think.

ABBEY takes the papers and turns to FRANK.

ABBEY: So what are you saying here? What are you saying: my dad gave you this or ...?

FRANK: Just saw it on the table here, after he was gone. Was just sitting there, in plain sight.

ABBEY: And why didn't you show it to me right away? Why all the ... preamble?

FRANK is silent.

ABBEY: Hey. I asked you a question – Why didn't you show this to me *right away*?

FRANK: I wanted you to have some ... context.

ABBEY: ... Context? For what? (*beat*) Oh my God. You already have it. You have the Deed. That's why you're living out here, that's why you said it's your land. You already have the Deed.

FRANK smiles.

FRANK: You *really* hate the thought of that, don't ya?

ABBEY: Oh my god ... Noah, do something ...!

NOAH: Me? What am I ...? Do ...?

FRANK: Hey, hey, okay, calm down. Calm your White Fears, okay? I looked for it, sure. Even though it's a Deed to *stolen property*. Of course I did. Stupid not to. But I couldn't find it. I followed his directions, found the coordinates, even dug all around in case he buried it. But either that map is wrong, or he didn't actually put it there. Or there's something I'm not seeing. I don't know.

Beat.

NOAH: Wait, so ... wait, so ... I don't get it. The map, isn't even ...?

FRANK: Hard to say.

ABBEY looks at the map again, confused.

FRANK: So here's what I'm thinking. I think you should see if this map makes sense to *you*, see if it lines up. Then maybe we all head out and search. Maybe I missed something.

ABBEY: Maybe we *all* search, did I hear that right?

> *FRANK shrugs, "Yeah." ABBEY doesn't like the sounds of this. Her leg is bouncing.*

NOAH: Okay, may I speak? ... um. I think we're, uh ... Basically I just think we need to go back to town. At least back into cell range, and like – you know – get in touch with your lawyer, see if this map is even – *legal*? And try to track down your dad somehow, alert the authorities.

> *FRANK tenses up, shakes his head.*

NOAH: Cuz I mean ... his cell is here? Some weird map? ... And naming a beneficiary for a will is kind of –

ABBEY: It doesn't have to mean he's planning on dying, Noah, people write their wills all the time, I have a will.

NOAH: You do?

ABBEY: Sure.

NOAH: Oh. Am I in it? Ha ha. (*off ABBEY's look*) I'm joking, I'm joking!

> *NOAH now talks privately with ABBEY:*

NOAH: Still. Who knows what happened out here? The guy has a frickin' HUGE knife – so the *smartest* thing to do is go call this in. Call your lawyer. The cops. Cuz what if this "map" thing isn't even legally sound? I mean, you can't just give away a multimillion-dollar property with a handwritten note! And this may not even be your dad's signature; Frank could have written this.

> *ABBEY paces, then returns to within earshot of FRANK, confronting him.*

ABBEY: (*to NOAH*) I still think he could be lying. He could have the Deed and is just lying to our faces right now.

NOAH: Oh, Abbey ... Come on ...

ABBEY: Admit it: it's possible.

NOAH: Well, sure it – … Sorry, dude, talking about you like –
(*to ABBEY*) Maybe we should go …?

FRANK: Say it to my face. Whatever you have to say, say it to my face.

ABBEY: Fine. I think I just did.

A tense beat.

NOAH: Hon. Please. Please be –

ABBEY: If we leave or "look at the map again" or even turn our backs for a second, he could drive off, waltz in with the Deed tomorrow, and I am screwed.

FRANK: You are quite the piece of work, aren't ya. Chip off the ol' block.

NOAH: So what, Abbey, what are you suggesting, you want to search his stuff??

A beat.

CHOICE-POINT 2C.1

THE HOST: Choice-Point:

    A. Should Noah and Abbey try to leave and catch Frank in a lie?
       ▶ **Go to Scene 3D, page 58**

    B. Should Frank get his way, and they look at the map again?
       ▶ **Go to Scene 3F, page 70**

    C. Should Abbey search Frank's belongings?
       ▶ **Go to Scene 3E, page 63**

Again, make sure your device is on. And you have fifteen seconds.

    The timer starts ...

    Votes are in.

You've chosen ...

    *The results are projected and **THE HOST** says the choice.*

SCENE 3A

They go back to catch Frank in a lie.

Replay the last few moments ...

ABBEY turns to go –

NOAH: Oh my God. Our *lives* are more important than –

NOAH and ABBEY start wrestling for the control of the gun.

NOAH: Abbey! Let the authorities handle / this!

ABBEY: We let him go and it could all be gone. / All of it.

NOAH: I don't – care. Let the police – Abbey!!

NOAH finally uses all of his strength and shoves ABBEY away, taking the gun from her.

NOAH: That's ENOUGH. I don't care if you were raised to fight first, ask questions later, that's not how I was raised and that's not how we're gonna do this. We're gonna go back – we're gonna get on the boat, we're gonna go back to where we can make some calls, and we're gonna make those calls. IF this is even legally sound, THEN we decide what to do. And if at that point you STILL think he has the Deed for some reason – then we get your lawyer, or cops. We're not – vigilantes, Christ.

Beat. He lets that settle. Then:

NOAH: (*grabbing his stuff*) Grab your stuff, let's go. We are calling this in.

He leaves, taking the rifle with him. A moment passes. ABBEY looks around, then grabs her stuff too.

Lights fade.

SCENE 3A.1

Moonlight. The forest. The riverbank.

A flashlight beam flickers around the area, the riverbank, the trees, the boat swaying gently in the current, all unoccupied.

Then NOAH enters, carrying the rifle. ABBEY is right behind him, with the flashlight. They're both carrying their backpacks.

NOAH stops, scoping out the area. ABBEY's flashlight scans the area again. They can't see anything out of the ordinary.

ABBEY: C'mon. If we're going, let's go.

NOAH: I thought I ... heard something.

ABBEY gets on the boat.

NOAH: This is creepy.

ABBEY: This was your idea.

NOAH: It's so *dark* out here. There's, like, NO streetlights?

NOAH gets onto the boat too.

FRANK: (*from the shadows*) Abbey Mitchell?

NOAH: Jesus!

ABBEY's flashlight beam catches FRANK – standing on the bank. She suddenly grabs the rifle from NOAH – dropping the flashlight. Darkness, shadows. NOAH scrambles to retrieve the flashlight. ABBEY raises the rifle to FRANK! NOAH quickly shines the light again, finding FRANK ... standing there in the exact same position.

NOAH: Man ... what the hell?

FRANK: Anything actually in that cartridge, little lady?

ABBEY: ... Of course.

FRANK: Really, eh? I took out the shells when you guys arrived.

ABBEY fires into the sky.

NOAH: Abbey!

ABBEY: Yeah, I saw that.

NOAH: Guys! What are you doing man? What's going on?

Beat of standoff.

FRANK: Okay, hold on. Hold on. Calm down. There was something I should have told you before I left. Your dad made this weird "map" thing. Did you find that?

ABBEY and NOAH again aren't sure how to respond ... so FRANK chuckles.

FRANK: Guess so. What do you make of it?

ABBEY finally chooses to speak.

ABBEY: You tell us.

FRANK: All right. Last year I was scoping around for work, got to talking with your dad. First he brought me on just to fix a fence, but then trying to smooth out that damn road, haul off some old equipment –

ABBEY: That was you? He mentioned he had some guy cleaning up the property, but ...

FRANK: "Some guy." Y'know, he never said much about *you*, either. *Anyway* – after a while we started ... talking about the land. What could be done with it. What *should* be done with it.

ABBEY: What do you mean?

FRANK: How it could be ... put to use. He was wondering what to do with it.

ABBEY: Wait, my dad told you about the plans, right?

NOAH: Uhhh, who wants to have this convo inside by the fire over a drink?

ABBEY: We're cleaning up the property to sell half of it and turn the rest into an eco-resort. The master plan was submitted, like, last year.

FRANK: Right, a plan that would disrupt our salmon run just so rich folks can clamber all over the land with their latest kill. While the people who actually live out here need access to those same hunting and fishing grounds for our livelihoods.

NOAH: Okay, it's not gonna – disrupt – it's gonna be a real back-to-the-land experience, Frank, eco-friendly. A retreat, not some macho sport-shooting thing. We plan to hire locals, people from the reserve. An employment program for new refugees. As low a footprint as possible –

FRANK: I know the plans.

ABBEY: Okay. So then what kind of conversations were you having?

FRANK: Just, what else could be done with the land. And who should have the right to do that. You know.

ABBEY: Sorry. You're being very vague.

NOAH: Ab ... (*to FRANK*) You mean, like, you're referring to, like, the fact that this land was originally your people's, kind of thing?

FRANK: Sure, that "kind of thing," yeah.

ABBEY: Oh my God –

FRANK: Your old man's pretty conflicted –

ABBEY: – sure, sure, we're *all* conflicted but we have to be practical. I'm sorry, is that why you're here, to try and stop us developing our land? Are you from the reserve?

FRANK: Yeah.

ABBEY: Right. Okay, well, I've spent the last three years getting all the permits – we need to do this, my dad's broke, his mind is going, and this is all we have. So you may think you're like "spiritually converting some rich old mining tycoon here," but you're not. Anyway, sorry, just – I need to know where I stand here. I feel a bit – you know.

FRANK: I can see that. All right. I'm sure you know that *all* the land around here is recognized, even by your government, as the Traditional Territory of my people –

ABBEY: Wait – This is *private* land, you want everyone to give all their land back? Where do you want us to go?

FRANK: If I may?

ABBEY: If you want to reclaim territory there is so much Crown land. So much. Don't try and take it from some frail old man just cuz –

NOAH: Maybe we could just listen?

Beat.

FRANK: My – Our issue is not with your dad. Or you, even.

ABBEY: Good, cuz my family worked hard for this, it wasn't easy. And they actually worked with and *helped* the Native – or First Nations people around them, so – It's not just –

FRANK: Trust me, no one is trying to boot anyone off the land.

ABBEY: Then what?

FRANK: My problem, our problem, as the original Peoples of this land, is with your government, yes, not with individual landowners. *However,* you do vote. But okay, I'll be very specific. Do you know what the word "unceded" means?

ABBEY: Yes. It means a right or property not formally given up. I deal with contracts all the time.

FRANK: Bingo! Give the lady a cigar. A large portion of land that Canada and private "landowners" are sitting on is unceded land. Meaning never formally surrendered. No treaties, nothing. Almost all of BC, large parts of Québec, a lot of the North, your capital city of Ottawa, all unceded. Including this property we're sitting on right now.

ABBEY: Okay but –

FRANK: Which means technically you are squatting on this land. And once I explained that to your dad and he really understood it, he started to see things in a different light.

Beat.

ABBEY: (*realizing*) … Oh my God … You already have it. You have the Deed.

FRANK smiles.

FRANK: You *really* hate the thought of that, don't ya?

ABBEY: Oh my god. Noah, do something …!

NOAH: Me? What am I …? Do …?

FRANK: Hey, hey, okay, calm down. Calm your White Fears, okay? I looked for it, sure. Even though it's a Deed to *stolen property*. Of course

I did. Stupid not to. But I couldn't find it. I followed his directions, found the coordinates, even dug all around in case he buried it. But either that map is wrong, or he didn't actually put it there. Or there's something I'm not seeing. I don't know.

Beat.

NOAH: Wait, so ... wait, so ... I don't get it. The map, isn't even ...?

FRANK: Hard to say.

ABBEY looks back at the house ... confused.

FRANK: But now I see what kind of girl he raised, I got a hunch. All right, what's your middle name?

ABBEY: Why?

FRANK rolls his eyes.

FRANK: What am I gonna do, beat you to death with your middle name? Okay ... does it start with an *R*?

NOAH: ... How did you know?

FRANK snickers, shakes his head, then:

FRANK: That son of a bitch. That map. Bottom right-hand corner.

The map is projected again. On the bottom right-hand corner is written: "FORARM." ABBEY looks at the map and reads.

ABBEY: Yeah, I saw that, I have no idea ...

NOAH: "FOREARM" but without the *E*? (*sounding it out*) "Fo-rarm"? "Fo-rar-mm"?

FRANK: I didn't know either. But now that you're in the picture, *Abbey* ... Your last name still Mitchell, like your Dad? (*to NOAH*) Hey Drummer Boy, you guys married or her last name still Mitchell?

NOAH: Yeah. No. No. Yeah. No, not married. Yes, still Mitchell. Why?

FRANK: (*pointing at the map*) So ...

ABBEY: My initials ...

NOAH: "*For* Abbey R. Mitchell."

FRANK: That's why I couldn't find anything. I think that map is coded. For you.

A long pause, as they take that in, and what it means.

NOAH: Wait, so ... wait, so ... the only person who can find the Deed ... is you?

Another beat. FRANK and ABBEY size each other up.

NOAH: I need a friggin' drink.

FRANK: Nice night.

▶ Go to Scene 4, page 77

SCENE 3B

Abbey breaks free with the gun and runs after Frank.

Replay the last few moments ...

ABBEY turns to go –

NOAH: Oh my God. Our *lives* are more important than –

NOAH and ABBEY start wrestling for the control of the gun.

NOAH: Abbey! Let the authorities handle / this –!

ABBEY: We let him go and it could all be gone. / All of it.

NOAH: I don't – care. Let the police – Abbey!!

She kicks NOAH's shin.

NOAH: Ah –!

He releases. She takes the gun and runs outside.

NOAH: Abbey!

She's gone. NOAH takes a moment, rubs his shin – Is there anything he can do but run after her? He grabs the map, rolls it into his back pocket as he reluctantly runs after her.

He stops to close the door behind him – not really thinking.

NOAH: (*running off*) Oh my God ... oh my God ...

The set changes. The house disappears.

SCENE 3B.1

Forest. It's getting dark.

We're now on the road.

NOAH: (*off*) Abbey!!

ABBEY enters. She sees Frank's backpack and starts going through it, eventually taking all the stuff out of it, while also looking around, scared Frank might come out of the woods at any moment ... She still has the rifle.

ABBEY: Come on ... c'mon, c'mon, c'mon ...

She hears something – points the rifle. It's only NOAH who enters.

NOAH: Whoa, whoa, it's just me! ... Jesus ... what are you doing?

ABBEY: He could have it somewhere.

NOAH: Oh man, let's just get outta here, hon ... this is really stupid.

She goes back to emptying Frank's backpack.

NOAH: Ab, leave that, let's just go!

FRANK: (*behind them*) Lookin' for something?

Startled, ABBEY grabs for the rifle, but –

FRANK: Ah, ah!

It's FRANK. He has a rifle trained on her. They are pinned.

NOAH: Holy ... piss. Okay, okay man ... whoa, whoa, whoa – let's all just calm down, okay? Can we all just – please stay calm??

FRANK: You tell me, Rock Star. She's the one reaching for that bolt-action rifle.

NOAH: Abbey??

FRANK: (*definitely not nice*) DROP IT.

NOAH: Abbey, do it!

ABBEY drops the rifle. FRANK kicks it away from them. ABBEY looks determined, a brave face. NOAH looks as if

*he has never, ever, ever imagined he'd EVER be in a
position like this. Ever.*

*FRANK relaxes on the weapon now. He's not here to
hurt anyone.*

FRANK: Relax, Drummer Boy, no need to piss your pants. All right.
So first you kick me out, now you're going through my stuff. Mind if I ask
what for?

NOAH brings the map out.

NOAH: Yeah, we uh … found this, like, "map" thing. Did you … see this?

*Beat. FRANK considers his options, looks at ABBEY, then
nods and smiles.*

FRANK: Sure. And so you figure I have the Deed?

NOAH: Well, she figured, maybe yeah. Why else… I mean, why else,
wouldn't you like – tell us about it?

Beat.

ABBEY: Hey, you were asked a question: Why didn't you tell us
about this?

FRANK: No time. Too busy gettin' kicked out. (*to NOAH*) Geez, she's
a fighter, ain't she. Got that from your old man, I see. All right. Let me
give you some context here.

FRANK lowers the weapon. He's in control, casual.

FRANK: Last year I was scoping around for work, got to talking with
your dad. First he brought me on just to fix a fence, but then trying to
smooth out that damn road, haul off some old equipment –

ABBEY: That was you? He mentioned he had some guy cleaning up the
property, but …

FRANK: "Some guy." Y'know, he never said much about *you*, either.
Anyway – after a while we started … talking about the land. What could
be done with it. What *should* be done with it.

ABBEY: What do you mean?

FRANK: How it could be … put to use. He was wondering what to do
with it.

ABBEY: Wait, my dad told you about the plans, right?

NOAH: Uhhh, who wants to have this convo inside by the fire over a drink?

ABBEY: We're cleaning up the property to sell half of it and turn the rest into an eco-resort. The master plan was submitted, like, last year.

FRANK: Right, a plan that would disrupt our salmon run just so rich folks can clamber all over the land with their latest kill. While the people who actually live out here need access to those same hunting and fishing grounds for our livelihoods.

NOAH: Okay, it's not gonna – disrupt – it's gonna be a real back-to-the-land experience, Frank, eco-friendly. A retreat, not some macho sport-shooting thing. We plan to hire locals, people from the reserve. An employment program for new refugees. As low a footprint as possible –

FRANK: I know the plans.

ABBEY: Okay. So then what kind of conversations were you having?

FRANK: Just, what else could be done with the land. And who should have the right to do that. You know.

ABBEY: Sorry. You're being very vague.

NOAH: Ab … (*to FRANK*) You mean, like, you're referring to, like, the fact that this land was originally your people's, kind of thing?

FRANK: Sure, that "kind of thing," yeah.

ABBEY: Oh my God –

FRANK: Your old man's pretty conflicted –

ABBEY: – sure, sure, we're *all* conflicted but we have to be practical. I'm sorry, is that why you're here, to try and stop us developing our land? Are you from the reserve?

FRANK: Yeah.

ABBEY: Right. Okay, well, I've spent the last three years getting all the permits – we need to do this, my dad's broke, his mind is going, and this is all we have. So you may think you're like "spiritually converting some rich old mining tycoon here," but you're not. Anyway sorry, just – I need to know where I stand here. I feel a bit – you know.

FRANK: I can see that. All right. I'm sure you know that *all* the land around here is recognized, even by your government, as the Traditional Territory of my people –

ABBEY: Wait – This is *private* land, you want everyone to give all their land back? Where do you want us to go?

FRANK: If I may?

ABBEY: If you want to reclaim territory there is so much Crown land. So much. Don't try and take it from some frail old man just cuz –

NOAH: Maybe we could just listen?

Beat.

FRANK: My – Our issue is not with your dad. Or you, even.

ABBEY: Good, cuz my family worked hard for this, it wasn't easy. And they actually worked with and *helped* the Native – or First Nations people around them, so – It's not just –

FRANK: Trust me, no one is trying to boot anyone off the land.

ABBEY: Then what?

FRANK: My problem, our problem, as the original Peoples of this land, is with your government, yes, not with individual landowners. *However,* you do vote. But okay, I'll be very specific. Do you know what the word "unceded" means?

ABBEY: Yes. It means a right or property not formally given up. I deal with contracts all the time.

FRANK: Bingo! Give the lady a cigar. A large portion of land that Canada and private "landowners" are sitting on is unceded land. Meaning never formally surrendered. No treaties, nothing. Almost all of BC, large parts of Québec, a lot of the North, your capital city of Ottawa, all unceded. Including this property we're sitting on right now.

ABBEY: Okay but –

FRANK: Which means technically you are squatting on this land. And once I explained that to your dad and he really understood it, he started to see things in a different light.

Beat.

ABBEY: (*realizing*) ... Oh my God ... You already have it. You have the Deed.

FRANK smiles.

FRANK: You *really* hate the thought of that, don't ya?

ABBEY: Oh my God ... Noah, do something ...!

NOAH: Me? What am I ...? Do ...?

FRANK: Hey, hey, okay, calm down. Calm your White Fears, okay? I looked for it, sure. Even though it's a Deed to *stolen property*. Of course I did. Stupid not to. But I couldn't find it. I followed his directions, found the coordinates, even dug all around in case he buried it or something. But either that map is wrong, or he didn't actually put it there. Or there's something I'm not seeing. I don't know.

Beat.

NOAH: Wait, so ... wait, so ... I don't get it. The map, isn't even ...?

FRANK: Hard to say.

ABBEY looks back at the house ... confused.

FRANK: But now I see what kind of girl he raised, I got a hunch. All right, what's your middle name?

ABBEY: Why?

FRANK rolls his eyes.

FRANK: What am I gonna do, beat you to death with your middle name? Okay ... does it start with an *R*?

NOAH: ... How did you know?

FRANK snickers, shakes his head, then:

FRANK: That son of a bitch. That map. Bottom right-hand corner.

The map is projected again. On the bottom right-hand corner is written: "FORARM." ABBEY looks at the map and reads.

ABBEY: Yeah, I saw that, I have no idea ...

NOAH: "FOREARM" but missing the *E*? (*sounding it out*) "Fo-rarm"? "Fo-rar-mm"?

FRANK: I didn't frickin' know either. But now that you're in the picture, *Abbey* ... Your last name's still Mitchell, like your dad? (*to NOAH*) Hey Drummer Boy, you guys married or her last name still Mitchell?

NOAH: Yeah. No. No. Yeah. No, not married. Yes, still Mitchell. Why?

FRANK: (*pointing at the map*) So ...

ABBEY: My initials ...

NOAH: "*For* Abbey R. Mitchell."

FRANK: That's why I couldn't find anything. I think that map is coded. For you.

> *A long pause, as they take that in, and what it means.*

NOAH: Wait, so ... wait, so ... the only person who can find the Deed ... is you?

> *Another beat. FRANK and ABBEY size each other up, fully aware of the gun in FRANK's hand.*

NOAH: I need a friggin' drink.

> *FRANK suddenly shifts – with the gun in hand – and NOAH and ABBEY jump with fear!*

> *But FRANK is just stretching – looking up at the sky.*

FRANK: Nice night.

▶ **Go to Scene 4, page 77**

SCENE 3C

Let's follow Frank

Replay the last few moments ...

ABBEY turns to go.

NOAH: Oh my God. Our *lives* are more important than –

NOAH and ABBEY are wrestling for control of the gun.

NOAH: Abbey! Let the authorities handle / this!

ABBEY: We let him go and it could all be gone. / All of it.

NOAH: I don't – care. Let the police – Abbey!!

Blackout.

SCENE 3C.1

Outside by the road, FRANK looks out at the land.

FRANK: C'mon, Danny Mitchell, what are you playin' at out here?

Suddenly a thought comes to him:

Wait. Mitchell ... Abbey ...? (*realizing something*) Son of a bitch.

NOAH: (*off*) Abbey!!

A flashlight beam flickers briefly across the forest. Frightened, FRANK starts retreating into the woods, leaving his bag on the road.

A beat.

▶ Go back to Scene 3B.1, page 50

SCENE 3D

Noah and Abbey try to leave and catch Frank in a lie

Replay the last few moments ...

FRANK: You are quite the piece of work, aren't ya. Chip off the ol' block.

NOAH: So what, Abbey, what are you suggesting, you want to search his stuff?

Another tense silence.

NOAH: Sorry, man. Obviously no one's gonna ... Babe, we should just go. Take this stuff and head back. If we leave now, we could start making some calls before it's too late tonight –

ABBEY: I've got a squatter with a virtual free ticket to my / entire inheritance, and you want to put your tail between your legs and go home?

FRANK: Squatter? Squatter?!

NOAH: (*standing up for himself*) No. No. Not go home, go to a place where we can use a phone and call this in! What do you want to do? Root through all his personal belongings just to see if for some reason he's lying – for some reason, he found the Deed, but is not telling us that?? Think about it. If – (*aside to FRANK*) Sorry, dude, talking about you like –

FRANK: No, go.

NOAH: Hon, think about it: if this is legally sound AND he has the Deed, why would he show you that? (*pointing to the map*) He'd just say, "Hey! Want some dinner? I'll get out of your hair, see ya!" Think about it. Why would he even show us this if he already has it? Or if he knew how to find it. Clearly he's just as baffled as we are.

FRANK: Clearly.

NOAH: Except he happened to need a place to stay – don't we all – so now he's caught up in all this.

A beat.

FRANK: Rock Star's making sense to me.

NOAH: So: We're gonna go back. We're gonna get on the boat, go back to where we can make some calls, and we're gonna make those calls. Grab your stuff, let's go. (*grabbing his stuff*) Abbey, let's go. We're calling this in.

ABBEY looks at FRANK, unsure what to do with him.

FRANK: Hey, dude, what do you mean, "call this in"?

NOAH, kind of caught, looks at ABBEY.

ABBEY: You know what he means.

Beat. FRANK decides to play tough despite realizing they're going to call the cops.

ABBEY gets her stuff – her dad's cellphone and the map.

— + —

▶ **If Abbey has previously seen the bloodstain on the floor, add:**

ABBEY takes another look at the stain on the floor.

— — —

Then ABBEY and NOAH leave.

FRANK: Good luck out there.

FRANK stands in the house, thinking about what to do now. He's different now that they're gone. Anxious. He looks out the window and considers. He looks at the stain on the floor, then shakes his head. He takes a couple frustrated stress breaths.

FRANK: Come on, Danny Mitchell. What are you playin' at here? (*a thought hitting him*) Wait. Mitchell ... Abbey ...? (*realizing something*) Son of a bitch.

Blackout.

SCENE 3D.1

By the river ...

Moonlight. The forest and riverbank.

A flashlight beam flickers around the area, the riverbank, the trees. An unoccupied boat sways gently in the current.

Then ABBEY enters, carrying the rifle. NOAH is right behind her, with the flashlight. They're both carrying their backpacks.

NOAH stops; his flashlight scans the area again. So ABBEY stops too. They can't see anything out of the ordinary.

ABBEY: C'mon. If we're going, let's go.

NOAH: ... I thought I heard something. This is creepy.

ABBEY gets onto the boat.

ABBEY: This was your idea.

NOAH: It's so *dark* out here. There's, like, NO streetlights?

NOAH gets onto the boat too. ABBEY puts down the rifle and goes to pull the starter cord.

VOICE: (*from off*) Abbey Mitchell?

NOAH: Holy – ...

NOAH panics, whips around with the flashlight – but drops it. Meanwhile ABBEY scrambles to pick up the rifle but –

FRANK: Ah ah!

It's FRANK. He has a rifle trained on her. They are pinned.

NOAH: Holy ... piss. Okay, okay, man ... whoa, whoa, whoa – let's all just calm down, okay? Can we all just – please stay calm??

FRANK: You tell me, Rock Star. She's the one reaching for that bolt-action rifle.

NOAH: Abbey??

FRANK: (*definitely not nice*) DROP IT.

NOAH: Abbey, do it!

ABBEY drops the rifle. She looks determined, a brave face. NOAH looks as if he has never, ever, ever imagined he'd EVER be in a position like this. Ever.

FRANK relaxes on the weapon now. He's not here to hurt anyone.

FRANK: Relax, Drummer Boy, no need to piss your pants. Feel free to have a seat, you two. I'm not out to hurt you here. Trust me. (*beat*) Or stand, whatever.

NOAH sits.

FRANK: Now let's just *relax*. And think about this. (*beat*) No. Let's *not* use our brains. Let's use our hearts. My daughter would like that.

Beat. He perches too, on the dock, rifle still in hand.

FRANK: She and I were walking in a protest couple years ago. Peaceful walk, some signs, songs, but then a bunch of white guys come out of this bar – and one of 'em punches her right in the side of the head. From behind, you know. I still can't get that image outta my head. I try to defend her, but guess who goes to jail? None of those guys, for spitting on us, calling us names, punching my girl. Nope. I spend the night in jail. So I don't know. I'm starting to think – no, feel – that your dad's bullying me here too, messing with me.

ABBEY: Why would he mess with you?

FRANK: Now that I see what kind of girl he raised. I got a hunch. All right, what's your middle name?

ABBEY: Why?

FRANK rolls his eyes.

FRANK: What am I gonna do, beat you to death with your middle name? Okay ... does it start with an *R*?

NOAH: ... How did you know?

FRANK snickers again, shakes his head; then:

FRANK: That son of a bitch. That map. Bottom right-hand corner.

ABBEY and NOAH look at each other. NOAH opens the map, flashlight:

The map is projected again. On the bottom right-hand corner is written: "FORARM." ABBEY looks at the map and reads.

ABBEY: Yeah I saw that, I have no idea ...

NOAH: "FOREARM" but missing the *E*? (*sounding it out*) "Fo-rarm"? "Fo-rar-mm"?

FRANK: I didn't frickin' know either. But now that you're in the picture, *Abbey* ... Your last name's still Mitchell, like your dad? (*to NOAH*) Hey Drummer Boy, you guys married or her last name still Mitchell?

NOAH: Yeah. No. No. Yeah. No, not married. Yes, still Mitchell. Why?

FRANK: (*pointing at the map*) So ...

ABBEY: My initials ...

NOAH: "*For* Abbey R. Mitchell."

FRANK: That's why I couldn't find anything. I think that map is coded. For you.

A long beat as they take that in, and what it means.

NOAH: Wait so ... wait so ... the only person who can find the Deed ... is you?

Another beat. FRANK and ABBEY size each other up, fully aware of the gun in FRANK's hand.

NOAH: I need a friggin' drink.

FRANK suddenly shifts – with the gun in hand – and NOAH and ABBEY jump with fear!

But FRANK is just stretching – looking up at the sky.

FRANK: Nice night.

▶ Go to Scene 4, page 77

SCENE 3E

Abbey chooses to search Frank's belongings

Replay the last few moments ...

FRANK: You are quite the piece of work, aren't ya. Chip off the ol' block.

NOAH: So what, Abbey, what are you suggesting, you want to search his stuff??

Another tense silence.

NOAH: Sorry, man. Obviously no one's gonna ...

ABBEY: Yeah. I do.

NOAH: Abbey ...

Beat.

FRANK: All right, have at 'er. After all, the place is *yours*, isn't it?

ABBEY: Sure is. You trespass on my property, I'll trespass on yours.

FRANK: Trespass? Ha. FYI, I don't even *need* your dad's permission to be out here. You can't actually convict me of "trespassing" because your own Supreme Court recognizes that my people hold the underlying Title. So *you're* the trespassers here.

This does NOT sit well with ABBEY. But she quashes any response. Instead, she goes off to search Frank's stuff – taking the rifle with her.

FRANK calls after her:

FRANK: In case you forgot, my stuff's in the orange room!

FRANK and NOAH are together again, awkwardly. NOAH glances out the window.

NOAH: So. A '76, eh? (*beat*) Is that really true, the trespassing?

FRANK: Of course it is. Ever heard of the Gustafsen Lake standoff, 1995? Biggest deployment of the RCMP in Canadian history for some Indians doing a Sundance on supposedly "private" land. And the reason they didn't just arrest everyone? They didn't have the legal right. They don't put that in your history books. (*beat*) Yeah so when the cops come in – which they always do – they charge us with "mischief" or "disturbing the peace" or whatever else. Trespassing is too dicey.

NOAH: Wow. Huh. But hey look, I'm sorry man. For her. She's not usually … Usually she's really nice. You just caught her at a … you know …

FRANK: It's fine, Rock Star. I've dealt with a lot worse.

NOAH: But she's not … she's not like … I hope you don't think she's like … "racist."

> *FRANK laughs.*

NOAH: What, it's just when it comes to personal stuff, and her family … she gets protective. "Emotional." She can only see it from her perspective. Isn't everyone like that? Aren't you?

FRANK: Emotional?

NOAH: No, you know … see things from your own "side."

FRANK: Mn, pretty used to seeing things from your side, actually. Pretty used to them being shoved down my throat. Look, Drummer Boy, me and my people live in an upside-down world. Everything we think to be right and true, in the real world is actually the other way round.

NOAH: (*feeling as if he understands*) Yeah … we're trying, though. Aren't we? I mean, we've come a long way since – you know. There's obviously a big movement to rectify all that.

FRANK: A big movement?

NOAH: Sure. Reconciliation. It's a national, you know, movement.

> *FRANK snickers.*

NOAH: You don't think so? You don't feel it? I'm honestly asking.

FRANK: (*making fun of the word "reconciliation"*) "Wrecked-'n-silly-nation"? (*beat*) You own property?

NOAH: Hm?

FRANK: In the city, where you two obviously live, you own property? A condo or something?

NOAH: Sure, barely.

FRANK: (*making fun of the word*) A "condominium"?

NOAH: Sure.

FRANK: Two-bedroom?

NOAH: No man, one-bedroom, no square footage, you don't even wanna know how much I paid and it still doesn't get more than a tiny one-bedroom.

FRANK: (*sarcastic*) Yeah man, that must suck. (*beat*) But you own it.

NOAH: Sure, well the bank does. And I was lucky, I got in before the market blew up.

FRANK: Great, so since there's this big movement going on, this really big "wrecked-'n-silly-nation" movement – does that mean my daughter could come live with you in your condominium?

NOAH: Ha ...

FRANK: No, I'm serious. She's real bright, she got into uni in the fall but we can't find her an affordable place to live. I assume you have a couch. Could she come live with you?

NOAH: Uh ... well ... uh ... Are you sure you'd want her to live with *me*? Ha ha ... I mean I guess we could talk about it ...

FRANK: Oh, you'll consider it! Really?

NOAH: I don't know, man – okay, I get it, it's not that easy to rectify things. We all gotta live together.

FRANK: No, no, that's not what I'm saying. What I'm saying is if this movement you're talking about was really BIG – then people would be willingly *offering* up their places – like they do to refugees. There would be news stories *every day* about conditions on reserves, how many people have to share single rooms, how we're not allowed to own the land our house is on, how I can't even afford to fix my mould-infested walls. When graves of Native kids are found there wouldn't just be some boohoos and flags at half-mast, there would be some real change, as if they actually thought of us as human beings. But you people have the attention span of a fruit fly, so after spending a few days shaking your heads and saying, "How awful," and feeling something for a second, you quickly forget and move on, until it happens the next time and the next time ... Wash, rinse, repeat. Sure, the word "reconciliation" is floating around, but it's not a "movement," it's at best "an idea" that people bandy about when it suits them. Or because it makes them feel better at a party or an art gallery.

NOAH: Hey man, that's not fair, okay? At least we're talking ... that's a start. Even my parents are, like, reading books by residential school survivors.

FRANK: Buddy, I got a guy giving this land to the Queen, and your girlfriend rootin' through my stuff. "At least we're talking"? "That's a start"? There's only so many *years* we can hear that before –

A beat while FRANK tries to calm his emotions.

NOAH: ... Before what? Say it, dude, before what?

FRANK: Nope. Too tired to get into this, kid. I'm going for a walk.

Surprisingly, ABBEY enters from outside the house. She has her dad's rifle hanging over one shoulder and in her hands ... another rifle, which she holds up while she addresses FRANK:

ABBEY: Hey, so I assume this is legal? You've got this registered. Only use it during hunting season?

FRANK snickers, shakes his head.

ABBEY: Just asking: if we call this in, would you go up for possession of an illegal firearm?

FRANK: (*to NOAH*) She went into my truck, ya believe that; she went into my frickin' *truck*.

ABBEY: You said I could search your stuff.

NOAH: Abbey ...

ABBEY: What?

FRANK: (*to NOAH*) Hey does *she* know about this big "movement" of yours?

NOAH: Ab, calm down, okay? I don't think they need a licence for things like that. I think they just ... you know.

FRANK: What, you think we can just carry any weapon we want wherever, whenever? "Roam free on the land like we used ta"?

NOAH: I would assume you get some sort of – don't you?

FRANK: Of course you'd *assume*, you're worse than *her*. Listen, before we can legally carry any sort of firearm, we still need a Chief Firearms

Officer to approve it, like everyone else. And I don't mean Indian Chief. It's a white bureaucrat sittin' in some office who doesn't know diddly-squat about hunting or fishing.

ABBEY: So basically what you're saying is: it's not registered.

FRANK looks at her, anger at the surface.

FRANK: I'm through talking to you, lady. You can fend for yourselves out here ...

NOAH: Frank ...

FRANK goes off upstairs.

NOAH: Hon ... let's keep this civilized.

ABBEY: Civilized? Look at this thing.

NOAH: I guess you didn't find a Deed.

ABBEY: No, but ... he could have it on him.

NOAH: Hon, think about it: if this is even legally sound AND he has the Deed, why would he show you that? (*pointing to the map*) So can you just drop it, and keep this civilized? Please.

FRANK re-enters, bag over his shoulder. He goes to retrieve his rifle – but ABBEY steps in his way.

FRANK: Okay ... You clearly don't want me here so I'll just take my stuff – *all* of the stuff that belongs to *me* – and get outta your hair. No harm, no foul.

He goes to retrieve his rifle again and reaches for the map – so ABBEY raises her rifle.

ABBEY: Don't move.

A beat.

FRANK continues toward his stuff. ABBEY lifts the rifle and fires! Ceiling dust falls to the floor ... and in that moment, FRANK grabs his own rifle: a standoff.

NOAH: Oh God, oh God ... Abbey. Dude. Please, just ... holy Christ ... can we just talk? No one wants – let's just talk, okay?!

FRANK: I took out the shells. When did you load that thing?

ABBEY: Outside.

NOAH: Guys, can we just agree to put the frickin' weapons down? I mean – obviously, right? – obviously we can sort this out without ... right?

FRANK: Okay, Abbey? Wanna do what your boyfriend says? Put 'em down? (*realizing something*) Wait. Abbey ...? Abbey ... Mitchell? Son of a bitch ... All right, what's your middle name?

ABBEY: Why?

    FRANK rolls his eyes.

FRANK: What am I gonna do, beat you to death with your middle name? Okay ... does it start with an *R*?

NOAH: ... How did you know?

    FRANK snickers, shakes his head, then:

FRANK: That son of a bitch. That map. Bottom right-hand corner.

    ABBEY and NOAH look at each other. NOAH opens the map.

    The map is projected again. On the bottom right-hand corner is written: "FORARM." ABBEY looks at the map and reads.

ABBEY: Yeah I saw that, I have no idea ...

NOAH: "FOREARM" but it's missing the *E*. (*sounding it out*) "Fo-rarm"? "Fo-rar-mm"?

FRANK: I didn't frickin' know either. But now that you're in the picture, *Abbey* ... Your last name's still Mitchell, like your dad? (*to NOAH*) Hey Drummer Boy, you guys married or her last name still Mitchell?

NOAH: Yeah. No. No. Yeah. No, not married. Yes, still Mitchell. Why?

FRANK: (*pointing at the map*) So ...

ABBEY: My initials ...

NOAH: "*For* Abbey R. Mitchell."

FRANK: That's why I couldn't find anything. I think that map is coded. For you.

A long beat as they take that in, and what that means.

NOAH: Wait so ... wait so ... the only person who can find the Deed ... is you?

Another beat. FRANK and ABBEY size each other up.

NOAH: I need a friggin' drink.

FRANK: (*looking up at the sky*) Nice night.

▶ **Go to Scene 4, page 77**

SCENE 3F

Frank gets his wish and they look at the map again.

Replay the last few moments ...

FRANK: You are quite the piece of work, aren't ya. Chip off the ol' block.

NOAH: So what, Abbey, what are you suggesting, you want to search his stuff??

A tense silence.

NOAH: Sorry, man. Obviously no one's gonna ... Babe, we should just go. Take this stuff and head back. If we leave now, we could start making some calls before it's too late tonight –

ABBEY: I've got a squatter with a virtual free ticket to my / entire inheritance, and you want to put your tail between your legs and go home?

FRANK: Squatter? Squatter?!

NOAH: (*standing up for himself*) No. No. Not go home, go to a place where we can use a phone and call this in! What do you want to do? Root through all his personal belongings just to see if for some reason he's lying – for some reason he found the Deed, but is not telling us that?? Think about it. If – (*aside to FRANK*) Sorry, dude, talking about you like –

FRANK: No, go.

NOAH: Hon, think about it: if this is legally sound AND he has the Deed, why would he even show you that? (*pointing at the map*) He'd just say, "Hey! Want some dinner? I'll get out of your hair, see ya!" Think about it. Why would he even show us this if he already has it? Or if he knew how to find it? Clearly he's just as baffled as we are.

FRANK: Clearly.

NOAH: Except he happened to need a place to stay – don't we all? – so now he's caught up in all this.

A beat.

FRANK: Rock Star's making sense to me. Abbey, listen, you want me outta here, I'll go. You wanna search my stuff, be my guest. But I ain't here to take anything from you. I just want what's right. (*beat*) Cuz I feel you. If he were my dad, I'd be pissed at him too. You think something's yours, you think you deserve it … then (*blowing: "It's gone!"*). So yeah, take another look. Cuz I sure as hell don't want this land going to the Queen. Whatever happens, screw *that*.

ABBEY: Okay … Thank you. I'm sorry for all this. (*beat*) Okay, can you guys just … give me a second to … look at this? Maybe there is something we're missing.

FRANK: Sure. And that means I can … stay, m'lady?

> *She looks at him … nods. He nods back.*

> *Before FRANK goes into the kitchen:*

FRANK: (*to ABBEY*) Good luck there. I mean that.

> *And he goes. ABBEY scours the map, but her demeanour has changed, her guard is down, she's vulnerable now. The enormity of this hits her, and she holds back tears.*

> *After a moment, NOAH hovers over her, touches her back.*

NOAH: You okay?

> *ABBEY suddenly starts to cry – frustrated but trying to keep quiet.*

ABBEY: Why would he do this?! We agreed. Sure he had some questions, but we agreed.

NOAH: Questions?

ABBEY: I thought it was just cold feet.

> *She cries and he comforts her … but she works to stay focused on the map, studying it.*

ABBEY: I'm okay. Thanks. I'm okay.

> *NOAH gets the hint and backs off. But he lingers.*
> *Then hovers.*

> *Once again takes a look at the bloodstain on the floor.*

FRANK: (*from off*) Either of you want dessert? Fresh saskatoon berries!

> *A beat while NOAH and ABBEY look at each other.*

FRANK: (*from off*) Yo. Saskatoon berries and cream, you want?

NOAH: (*looking to Abbey and shrugging*) … Sure.

SCENE 3F.1

FRANK and NOAH sit outside on the porch, both with a bowl of saskatoon berries and cream. NOAH is working on another Hey Y'all.

Inside: ABBEY, also eating a bowl of saskatoon berries and cream, sits at the table. As she goes over the map, checking distances with her dad's directions, her work is also projected behind her. This entire scene plays with the Map of the Land as a backdrop.

NOAH: This is great too, man. Right combo of tartness and sweetness. Perfect.

FRANK nods.

NOAH: Oh. (*looking up to the Creator*) Thank *you.*

They all take another bite.

NOAH: And hey, look, I'm sorry, man. For her. She's not usually ... Usually she's really nice. You just caught her at a ... you know ...

FRANK: It's fine, Rock Star. I've dealt with a lot worse.

NOAH: But she's not ... she's not like ... I hope you don't think she's like ... "racist."

FRANK laughs.

NOAH: What, it's just when it comes to personal stuff, and her family ... she gets protective. "Emotional." She can only see it from her perspective. Isn't everyone like that? Aren't you?

FRANK: Emotional?

NOAH: No, you know ... see things from your own "side."

FRANK: Mn, pretty used to seeing things from your side actually. Pretty used to them being shoved down my throat. Look, Drummer Boy, me and my people live in an upside-down world. Everything we think to be right and true, in the real world is actually the other way round.

NOAH: (*feeling as if he understands*) Yeah ... we're trying though. Aren't we? I mean, we've come a long way since – you know. There's obviously a big movement to rectify all that.

FRANK: A big movement?

NOAH: Sure. Reconciliation. It's a national, you know, movement.

   FRANK snickers.

NOAH: You don't think so? You don't feel it? I'm honestly asking.

FRANK: (*making fun of the word "reconciliation"*) "Wrecked-'n-silly-nation"? (*beat*) You own property?

NOAH: Hm?

FRANK: In the city, where you two obviously live, you own property? A condo or something?

NOAH: Sure, barely.

FRANK: A "condominium"? (*making fun of the word*)

NOAH: Sure.

FRANK: Two-bedroom?

NOAH: No man, one-bedroom, no square footage, you don't even wanna know how much I paid and it still doesn't get more than a tiny one-bedroom.

FRANK: (*sarcastic*) Yeah man, that must suck. (*beat*) But you own it.

NOAH: Sure, well the bank does. And I was lucky, I got in before the market blew up.

FRANK: Great, so since there's this big movement going on, this really big "wrecked-'n-silly-nation" movement – does that mean my daughter could come live with you in your condominium?

NOAH: Ha ...

FRANK: No, I'm serious. She's real bright, she got into uni in the fall, but we can't find her an affordable place to live. I assume you have a couch. Could she come live with you?

NOAH: Uh ... well ... uh ... Are you sure you'd want her to live with *me*? Ha ha ... I mean I guess we could talk about it ...

FRANK: Oh, you'll consider it! Really?

NOAH: I don't know man – okay, I get it, it's not that easy to rectify things. We all gotta live together.

FRANK: No, no, that's not what I'm saying. What I'm saying is if this movement you're talking about was really BIG – then people would be willingly *offering* up their places – like they do to refugees. There would be news stories *every day* about conditions on reserves, how many people have to share single rooms, how we're not allowed to own the land our house is on, how I can't even afford to fix my mould-infested walls. When graves of Native kids are found, there wouldn't just be some boohoos and flags at half-mast, there would be some real change, as if they actually thought of us as human beings. But you people have the attention span of a fruit fly, so after spending a few days shaking your heads and saying, "How awful," and feeling something for a second, you quickly forget and move on, until it happens the next time and the next time … Wash, rinse, repeat. Sure, the word "reconciliation" is floating around, but it's not a "movement," it's at best "an idea" that people bandy about when it suits them. Or because it makes them feel better at a party or an art gallery.

NOAH: Hey man, that's not fair, okay? At least we're talking … that's a start. Even my parents are, like, reading books by residential school Survivors.

FRANK: Buddy, I got a guy giving this land to the Queen. "At least we're talking." "That's a start." There's only so many *years* we can hear that before –

A beat while FRANK tries to calm his emotions.

NOAH: Before what?

Beat.

Say it dude, before what?

Another beat.

FRANK: Nope. Too tired to get into this, kid. I'm goin' for a walk.

He goes off into the woods.

Projected: ABBEY's work on the map continues.

SCENE 3F.2

NOAH goes inside:

NOAH: How's it going? That thing making any sense?

ABBEY: Scale is good. Directions lead to the right coordinates.
He knows what he's doing obviously, he's been making maps for years. All
I can think is either Frank got it wrong, or my dad didn't get a chance to
leave it there ...

Beat. NOAH leans over the map.

NOAH: C'mon, Danny Mitchell, what happened out here?

ABBEY: (*an idea*) Wait. Mitchell ... Abbey ...? Mitchell ...? Oh my
God ... Bottom right-hand corner.

The projection pushes in on the bottom right-hand corner,
where is written: "FORARM."

NOAH: (*reading*) "FOREARM," but it's missing the E. (*sounding it out*)
"Fo-rarm"? "Fo-rar-mm"?

ABBEY: My initials ...

NOAH: "*For* Abbey R. Mitchell."

ABBEY: That's why he couldn't find anything. I think this map is
coded. For me.

Beat.

ABBEY starts gathering her stuff to go. She grabs the rifle.

ABBEY: Come on. Let's go. I don't want to find the Deed with
him around.

NOAH: I still don't see why we don't just go back into cell range first.

NOAH grabs his stuff too, and they start exiting the house.

ABBEY: I hate that you won't trust me on this.

NOAH: What, I still think you'd have a case to contest this – like maybe
your dad's finally lost it. Giving it to the Queen?? A map coded for you??
I guarantee this can't even be legal. We could also call the cops and get
some / help out here.

ABBEY: No cop's gonna arrive for another two, three hours, and I can't wait for that.

NOAH: Still, we should confirm this is even legally sound! Before we go risking our lives ...

ABBEY: Are you scared of going off into the woods, is that what this is?

NOAH: No. Not scared. I mean, he did say there was a bear around here. So it doesn't seem like the smartest –

ABBEY: We have a gun. I've got ammo for it. Packed everything we need.

NOAH: Holy ... Babe. Did you see how he reacted when I wanted to call this in? Basically who knows what happened out here. So I agree with you about the time crunch. But I am expressing my *feelings.* I am expressing my feelings of fear. My big ol' bundle of fear feelings.

ABBEY: Cool. That's great. I validate your feelings. I feel them too. But can we try to be practical?

NOAH: Sure. Just wanted to express my feelings ...

FRANK: (*from behind them*) Hey there, friends!

    He's holding a rifle.

ABBEY and **NOAH:** ... Hey, hi, yeah, hi ...

FRANK: (*looking up at the sky*) Nice night.

SCENE 4

FRANK is looking up at the night sky.

FRANK: There's a story my grandma used to tell us. About the time before people came. Grizzly Bear and Coyote were fighting: Grizzly wanted the world to always be dark, so he could sleep, but Coyote wanted it to always be light so he could find food. So they fought and fought. Coyote would make it light out, the Bear would make it dark again ... until finally they made a deal. They agreed that it would be dark half the time, and light the other half. And that's why we have night and day.

NOAH: ... Huh. Neat.

FRANK: Yeah, some idiots think it's got to do with the earth revolving or something. (*smirking*) Point is, we were taught we aren't superior to Mother Nature. The Creator made the earth, and then came the animals. Humans were the last to arrive and we had to learn from the animals. How to hunt, how to live, how to protect ourselves. So we have to care for Mother Earth and learn from all living things.

NOAH: ... Totally, yeah. That's why when you, you know, hunt an animal, you thank it for giving its life. I don't do that enough. (*beat*) I don't hunt, but. You know, when I cook, or. Shop.

FRANK: Right ... So look, Abbey, I know how you feel here. Your future in the hands of some coded map and stranded with some guy you don't know. An Indian to boot.

ABBEY: That has nothing to do with it.

FRANK: Sure, sure. But listen – how well you know the history of this land here? This river. Those hills. How well you know it?

ABBEY: Sorry, do we have time for this?

FRANK: Humour me.

ABBEY looks at the gun in his hand.

ABBEY: Okay ... Well ... on my dad's side, I know my great-grandparents homesteaded here. I know my grandpa and his brother died in a mining accident upriver. And I'm told my grandparents actually had good relations with the ... First Nations people around here.

FRANK: That's nice. And when did they first get here?

ABBEY: Um … late 1800s?

FRANK: And what about the history before they came?

ABBEY: Look, I don't have time for this, Frank. On my mom's side, we came here as refugees, okay? This country provided a safe haven for that side of my family, so I'm not just –

FRANK: 1862. That mean anything to you guys? (*beat*) Course not. 1862, James Douglas, your first colonial governor here, also head of the Hudson's Bay Company – you know the one, with the smallpox-infected blankets? He signed an agreement with our Chief for this Land right here to be almost a million acres. For our nation's use only. But then without our consent, that million acres was gradually reduced – often by homesteaders like your family – down to seven thousand acres. That's ZERO POINT SEVEN percent of what was agreed. That, specifically, is the situation you've inherited. Right here.

ABBEY: That's horrible, Frank. I didn't know that, and if that's true –

FRANK: Oh it's true. They just don't write it in your history books.

ABBEY: Then that's totally awful. I didn't know that. But … it can't really be that simple, can it? I mean, come on, how did *thousands* of people move here without a fuss? / There must –

FRANK: A "fuss"?

ABBEY: Yes. There must have been lots of space for everyone.

FRANK: Oh / right –

ABBEY: And if your people really didn't want us here, our technology and stuff, then why didn't they do anything about / it?

FRANK: Ahhhhh, YES, the ol' "but there's so much land" and "why didn't you fight back?" I love those ones. Same time, 1862, smallpox spread through here – literally wiped out half our Bands – sometimes up to 90 percent of our people – thousands upon thousands of my Ancestors – gone. And it wasn't like there wasn't a cure. Your people had a vaccine, to prevent smallpox and also to cure it, but did they give that to us? Nope. Instead, they intentionally infected us. So think about it: 90 percent of the people where you live: gone, within a year. Do you have the heart, the sheer numbers, to try and fight back?

ABBEY: Okay –

FRANK: But despite that, we *did* fight back. And that's why Governor Douglas made that deal with us. So we'd stop fighting. And that's why we allowed you here, because things were reciprocal at first. But we *didn't* agree to have the stakes to our own Territories knocked down, to start being fenced and locked out of our rivers and hunting grounds.

NOAH: That – it – / okay –

FRANK: And you know, a lot of it's gotta be just plain shock. Like – "Wait, what? We had an agreement and now you're doing WHAT?" That's how I feel a lot of the time, just, "What??" When you add it all up, I'm totally dumbfounded that anyone's ever racist toward me. That racism should actually be the other way around.

ABBEY: No one's / being –

NOAH: That's / not –

FRANK: So SURE, if you want to boil it down to "Might equals right" or "Survival of the fittest," then sure, you guys won that battle. By giving us smallpox –

ABBEY: Hey, come on, you're not being –

FRANK: Sterilizing our women. Enforced poverty. Jail time if we didn't send our kids away to get their identity beaten out of them.

NOAH: Frank –

FRANK: Stealing children for forced adoption. Making our culture illegal. We didn't even get the right to vote until the 1960s.

ABBEY: You can't blame all that on –

FRANK: So tell me. Is genocide simply a matter of "Might equals right"? Would you say to a Holocaust Survivor, "Well gee, survival of the fittest, why didn't your family fight back"?

    A long pause.

ABBEY: Did you tell my dad all that?

FRANK: ... Sure.

ABBEY: How did he take it?

FRANK: He ... He's a frickin' hard man, your dad. But he was listening.

ABBEY: Did you guys fight at all?

FRANK: … We were just talking.

ABBEY: You mean, like this? (*nodding to the gun in his hand, if he has one*)

FRANK: Listen, I'm not here to perpetuate this "Might equals right" crap –

ABBEY: No?

FRANK: No. I'm just telling it like it is. And you seem like a practical woman, Abbey, a business woman. So I'm gonna make you a deal. Like Coyote and the Bear. Okay? I get this map is some weird stuff between you and your dad, and I respect that. I even respect your family's history on this land, short as it may be, as a safe haven. But one thing I don't respect is this "giving it to the Queen" thing. Screw that. So I'd like to come along, make sure you find that Deed. I'll dig if I have to, do my part, bring some dried moose meat. Be your guide. You need a fire, I'll build it. Need a shelter, done. And I'll keep an eye out. Like I said, I've seen a grizzly wandering around here …

> *NOAH winces.*

FRANK: And if we do find that Deed and get you back safely on time, then all I ask in return is this: You sign 50 percent of the land over to me. To my Band.

> *Pause.*

NOAH: Uh. Ha ha. You're joking, right?

FRANK: The half that you intend to sell anyway? That's the half we need.

> *Pause.*

ABBEY: Sorry … half the land?

NOAH: You're serious??

> *Pause.*

ABBEY: Frank … I can't just give you … Selling half the land is the only way we can afford the eco-resort. Giving you half, for free, means you cripple us. I've invested everything I have in this. In case you haven't noticed, my dad's losing it – I can't leave him alone … And my mom needs to be close. I have to pay for someone to be with her when I'm not, cuz her arthritis. I need money and I need help. And this land is all we have. I'm sorry.

>Beat.

FRANK: Have Rock Star sell his condo and move back here.

NOAH: Frank, you can't just tell us how to – I still have a mortgage. Selling my condo may give me enough to pay off the loan and then a bit of surplus, but not enough to sustain us. And we can't *work* out here without some development, a cell tower –

FRANK: So if you guys can't live out here, sustain yourselves, like we can, like we have to, every day – then piss off – move your dad into the city –

ABBEY: "Piss off"? Really …

FRANK: Give us back half the land, sell the other half, and live off the proceeds.

ABBEY: My dad won't move, okay, he can't live in a condo, in the city, he's lived here all his life, he grew up here – you realize what you're saying, right? You're basically saying, "Get out, go back where you came from." We're *from* here. / We're *from* here.

FRANK: No you're not, *we* are from here. And your people had no issue removing us illegally from our homes. And no one offered *us* halfsies.

NOAH: Okay / okay –

ABBEY: I'm not … Look, I understand. It's not fair. Your family fought. It was war, and they lost. And it's awful – I understand –

FRANK: No, you don't.

ABBEY: My mother and grandmother came here from Lebanon in the seventies during the war … After losing everything – their home, their men, their country – everything. They came with nothing. Left behind their culture, their land, their lives … But my mom made a life for herself here. And now you want to take it all away again?

NOAH: Okay, / can we –

FRANK: I can't believe how easy it is for you people to see yourselves as victims, / as broke. You are land-fricking-RICH.

ABBEY: "You people?"

NOAH: Okay. Dude. You can't make assumptions either, okay? That works both ways. We need this. We do. Abbey hasn't been able to find a job, man, no one'll hire her cuz she filed a ... harassment suit against her dickhead boss. So now everyone's too scared to hire her. She stood up for herself and others like her, and it's basically, like, ruined her career. And I'm ... The music industry is changing, it's all free streaming ... seriously, Frank. You'd break us, our potential future, everything we've been working toward. That's what you're asking us here.

> *Beat.*

ABBEY: Look Frank, I understand where you're coming from, I do. And I'm not unreasonable. I feel for the cause of your people, obviously, it's awful. But I didn't – you know – cause it. And I'm just as much a cog in the machine as you are.

> *FRANK scoffs.*

ABBEY: There are systems, that are already set up. And when you move to this country, you are required to fit into them. You have absolutely no choice but to meld into them. And that's what my family did.

FRANK: You were required to fit into systems? Oh, I'm so sorry ... Well if we didn't fit in the residential school *system*, we died. Every political process here was *systematically* set up to terminate our very existence or undermine it. The Indian Act makes us wards of the state. Legally children for our entire lives. It's deep-rooted, systemic racism, when they can create laws to govern an entire genocide of Peoples. The Indian Act made it illegal to hire lawyers to deal with our Land issue, lawyers would get disbarred for representing us, we were outlawed from selling our goods. Couldn't even leave the reserve without a pass. Even today, we can't sell our reserve Lands, can't get loans to start businesses as easily. We aren't given a fraction of the services everyone else gets – education, healthcare, water ... We weren't even recognized as human beings until recently. But you can just waltz onto our land – that you don't even technically own – and start a business that disrupts our Traditional hunting and fishing Territories. The only thing that keeps a lot of our people from starving to death. It must be nice to benefit from the "systems" that we reserve Indians can't even participate in. So forgive me if I don't seem a little more supportive of *your* real-estate needs. And forgive me if I'm not in the mood to play everyone's favourite game show "Who's more oppressed?" Cuz the system was built for people like you. You're not a slave to the Indian Act.

Beat.

ABBEY: No, but I am a slave to the law and that means it's not easy to just transfer land. Anything we want to do requires an entire Master Plan, which costs money – I am three years and $80,000 in the hole over this process, and it *just* got approved. So I'm not about to –

FRANK: Wait. Your plans got approved?

ABBEY: Got the notice last month. It's been through community consultation and everything – to which a total of five people showed up.

FRANK: What consultation? When?

ABBEY: An email went out. A sign was posted, / there was a meeting –

FRANK: An EMAIL?

ABBEY: It went through the proper process, Frank, and yeah, it's now approved. (*beat*) That's why we're out here, to get my dad's signature so I can handle the rest of it. We plan to break ground this summer.

Beat.

FRANK: Except now you need a new plan. Cuz now you gotta deal with that map.

He points at the map.

Listen, if you guys don't think you need my help out there, try your luck on your own. As you say, it's not "my land," so it's no skin off my back. But if you can't find the Deed and get back in time, all your "master plans" are for nothing. The entire property goes to the Queen.

If FRANK is not holding a gun: he grabs his pack and hunting rifle, preparing to go.

FRANK: Oh I've also set bear traps out there. Wild animal traps. Take your leg right off. Which reminds me, there's wild animals out there. Cougars, that hunt at night. Coyotes. So, up to you: find a way to give us half, or risk losing it all. Your call.

FRANK smiles. ABBEY considers, then looks at the gun in FRANK's hand.

NOAH: Okay, Jesus. Wild animals? Bear traps? Sorry but before we do *anything*, we are going back into range and calling this in. Make sure this is even – *legal*.

ABBEY: He's obviously just lying about a bear, he's trying to scare us.

NOAH: Well, cool! It's working! (*beat*) So you're fine just risking our *lives* out there, all because of some map that we can't even be sure wasn't written at gunpoint? Think about it. (*If ABBEY has seen the bloodstain, add:*) **Blood on the floor.** No phone, his cell just sitting there. And this guy just *happens* to be here, toting a *lethal weapon*, / now suddenly proposing he –

FRANK: It's a hunting rifle.

NOAH: Whatever, whatever, suddenly proposing he can "help us" find it? Seems a bit … convenient. To say the frickin' least. (*beat*) Babe, let's go back. Talk to your lawyer, and IF it's remotely legal to give your land to the Queen, then we say your dad wasn't in his right mind – or was coerced.

ABBEY: That's a gamble. Trying to prove that. Especially if he's no longer alive.

> *NOAH looks between ABBEY and FRANK – who are looking at each other. A pause.*

ABBEY: What happened out here, Frank?

> *Beat.*

FRANK: No matter what I say, you don't believe me anyway. So go on. Head out there. Go ahead.

NOAH: Oh my God, this is insane. Babe – it's only an hour back into cell range, we make some calls, and if this is legal, we go searching then! (*beat*) Babe – Dude – guys …?

> *ABBEY and FRANK stare at each other …*

NOAH: This is insane. This is like … This is INSANE!

CHOICE-POINT 4

THE HOST: Choice-Point:

    A.   Should Noah and Abbey go call this in?

    B.   Should Abbey refuse the deal?

    C.   Should Frank obtain the deal?

Make sure your device is on. You have fifteen seconds.

    The clock ticks down fifteen seconds. Then:

Your answers will be revealed in fifteen minutes. Intermission.

    The house lights rise, with the choices still projected on the screen.

    INTERMISSION.

Act Two

The choices are still projected on the screen. The audience is seated. The house lights fade.

THE HOST: Welcome back. I hope you enjoyed your time away and are eager to see what happens next. Let's find out. You chose ...

The results are displayed and ***THE HOST*** *says the choice.*

If the audience picks A: ***NOAH*** *and* ***ABBEY*** *go call this in.*

THE HOST: Noah and Abbey go call this in. Okay, looks like we've got a lot of practical scaredy-cats in the room ... All right then. Enjoy the show of your own choosing. And I'll be back.
▶ **Go to Scene 4B, page 104**

If the audience picks B: ***ABBEY*** *refuses the deal.*

THE HOST: Abbey refuses the deal. Okay, looks like a lot of you want her to refuse, even though you have no idea what will happen when she does ... All right then. Enjoy the show of your own choosing. And I'll be back.
▶ **Go to Scene 4C, page 114**

If the audience picks C: ***FRANK*** *obtains the deal.*

THE HOST: Frank obtains the deal. Okay, looks like a lot of you want to get out there on the land, and would like to see Frank's Band get half of it ... at least. All right then. Enjoy the show of your own choosing. And I'll be back.
▶ **Go to Scene 4A, page 88**

SCENE 4A

Frank obtains a deal for 50 percent of the land, and they all search ...

The map of the property is projected on the screen.

A VOICE-OVER (VO) plays:

FRANK: (*VO, reading*) "And it is the loss of our land that is the precise cause of our impoverishment. Indigenous Lands today account for only 0.2 percent of Canada. The settler share is the remaining 99.8 percent. With this distribution, you don't have to have a doctorate in economics to understand who will be rich and who will be poor."

ABBEY, FRANK, and NOAH appear silhouetted in front of the projected map. They're leaning over a table, the map in front of them. ABBEY is reading a contract, while FRANK draws a line down the map.

Simultaneously onscreen: A line is drawn diagonally down the centre of the map, dividing the property in half.

FRANK: (*VO*) "And when we speak of reclaiming a measure of control over our lands, we obviously do not mean throwing Canadians off of it. All Canadians have acquired a basic human right to be here. At present, we are asking for the right to protect our Aboriginal Title Land, to have a say on any development on our lands, and when we find the land can be safely and sustainably developed, to be compensated for the wealth it generates."

FRANK then labels his half of the property: "FRANK'S HALF."

ABBEY places the contract on the table, and she signs her name.

The lights fade on them, leaving the map projected.

SCENE 4A.1

A new line on the map begins to show the route they're hiking. The land is expansive. The trees massive.

ABBEY hikes, with a GPS and compass in hand. NOAH and FRANK follow close behind. NOAH is trying to keep up. ABBEY and FRANK both have a rifle.

As they hike, FRANK, overlapping with the voice-over, reads aloud from a book. It's Arthur Manuel and Grand Chief Ronald M. Derrickson's Unsettling Canada: A National Wake-Up Call.

FRANK: "... for the wealth it generates. There is room on this land for all of us, and there must also be, after centuries of struggle, room for justice for Indigenous Peoples." Boom! Mic drop! End of chapter one. I'm getting good at this, reading and walking.

NOAH: Okay: you've already read this book, now you're just reading it to us?

FRANK: That's right. I wouldn't read you a bad book! What do you think?

NOAH: It's cool. I think a lot of people are ... mystified, you know. About what Indigenous people actually *want*. Like, practically. And that states it pretty clearly. It's cool.

FRANK: Cool.

NOAH: Cuz you know, like, what's really wrong with Indigenous people getting some control? It's like when the owner of an apartment building changes, nothing has to change for the *tenants*. It's just that First Nations would have agency, finally, over how it's all managed. I think that's a *good* thing. Especially for, like, climate change and all that.

FRANK: Cool. So does that mean I can have your condo?

> *NOAH chuckles.*

FRANK: I'd still let you live there. But instead of paying a mortgage to a bank, you pay me rent.

NOAH: ... Ha, yeah yeah, no no, that's different. I give you my condo, I lose my investment. It's not just a place to live, it's ... No, what I'm talking about is the development companies, the real-estate companies, I'd love it if they were all First Nations.

FRANK: Oh yeah, why's that?

NOAH: Like, justice? Balance of scales? And maybe they'd all have, like, compost pickup. Energy-efficient windows.

FRANK: Right, because they're managed by Indians? It really does amaze me how naive you are.

ABBEY: Guys, come on.

As they hike off ...

NOAH: How come you always say "Indians" and I'm not allowed?

SCENE 4A.2

Deeper in the forest, on the bank of a stream ...

ABBEY stops, consults her map, then waits for them.
FRANK and NOAH bring up the rear.

FRANK: Rock Star's slowing down back here ...

NOAH: Sorry, babe, this pack is killing me. One sec.

He dumps it down. ABBEY and FRANK exchange a look.

ABBEY: Raided MEC* like it was going out of business.

NOAH: I was excited. Haven't even got to use my spork yet. Ooh, do you think we could stop for a bit? I'm starving. And I could use my spork!

FRANK: How we doing for time?

ABBEY: Little behind.

NOAH: Sorry. If I get some food in me I'll be faster. I'm starving.

FRANK: You're not "starving" ... Few minutes here? Nice spot.

ABBEY: Let's make it quick.

They sit and distribute food and water. NOAH reveals his
spork – FRANK smiles. (Throughout, they ad lib if need
be: "Want some?" or "Thanks" when some is shared.)
After a beat:

ABBEY: So neighbour ... you have a daughter, huh?

FRANK: Two. The youngest, Rain, is about to have a child of her own.

NOAH: No! Really? (*beat*) Cool. Grandpa.

FRANK: Don't even. Adoption, huh?

ABBEY: ... Yeah we uh ... never happened for us. So yeah. That's the plan.

FRANK: (*nodding*) How long you been together?

NOAH / ABBEY: Seven / Two ... (*looking at each other*) Two / Seven ...

---

*   Mountain Equipment Co-op (or, since 2020, the Mountain Equipment
    Company), a popular outdoor-gear retail store in Canada.

NOAH: Basically, ha – We were together for a while, but then – we weren't. Really. Then we, like, got – back together. So yeah, all in all, about seven years, but yeah two on this side of the uh … / yeah.

FRANK: And this your first time out here?

NOAH: Yeah, yeah. She uh … yeah. I'd be out here all the time if I could though, I love it.

FRANK: (*to ABBEY*) How often *you* come out?

ABBEY: Couple times a year. Depends. Much as I can.

FRANK: Grew up in that house?

ABBEY: Yeah, till I was fourteen. Then moved away with my mom. Would come back in the summers though. It's beautiful here.

> *She offers some food, and FRANK takes it.*

FRANK: Let's hope it stays that way. Doesn't it get your goat that if the government wants to, say, build a pipeline through here, there's nothing you can actually do about that?

NOAH: … What do you mean?

ABBEY: He means that if the government wants to build something here, we can ask for fair compensation, but we can't actually stop them.

NOAH: Wait. What? So you don't really own it?

ABBEY: Sure we do, it's just like zoning. It's like your condo. The government regulates what can happen. So you do own it, but …

FRANK: With reservations.

NOAH: … Huh. Wait, so is that the same on reserve? Or are you guys able to, like, just say no.

FRANK: Are you kidding? Bands supposedly have "controlling interest" over their reserve, but the government will just railroad 'em. Some Bands understand they have no power to "just say no," so they make sure to get compensated instead. Same thing. But then people complain that Bands are "milking the government."

NOAH: … Frickin' government. Hey, anyone mind if I smoke?

NOAH has pulled out a joint. FRANK doesn't mind.
ABBEY gives NOAH a look, which he tries to ignore. He
lights up.

ABBEY: It does make sense though, if the government is looking out for the public good.

FRANK: But who determines "good" is the question. And which "public." For the longest time we couldn't even vote for your government or else we'd have to give up our Indian Status. So the "public good" has never, ever meant the original people of this land.

It's clear ABBEY is holding her tongue.

NOAH: But ... I mean, it's starting to, though, right? Like with "wrecked-'n-silly-nation"? I mean, *we* just handed you a buttload of reconciliation, Frank. *If* we find the Deed. And part of the reason we did that is because we understand things do have to change. They have to. The "public good" means *all* of us.

Beat.

FRANK: Let me ask you: Before I walked up here and entered your life, what were you doing to reconcile?

NOAH: ... Okay, I don't need to ... defend my life choices to you.

FRANK: No, no. I'm just curious. No judgment. You seem like a well-intentioned, upstanding citizen. I'd like to know.

NOAH: Okay. Well, I always, like, give money on the street, particularly when I see a First Nations person –

FRANK: Ha ha. Good, good. And you always know what we look like?

NOAH: No ... whatever. Look, I'm trying to help and you bite my hand? And I've been to some rallies when I can, I read, I vote Green! I even wrote a song about ... whatever, I don't know, man, I'm just me, I have no real power.

FRANK: You mean you don't recognize your power. Until someone walks up and asks you for some of it. (*beat*) I think we all have more power than we care to admit.

NOAH considers the meaning of that, then looks at
ABBEY. Her silence. He offers her a toke again.

NOAH: Just one ...? May take the edge off.

ABBEY decides to take it and has a tiny little toke. NOAH has another one, then puts it out.

Beat. They sit. NOAH munches on some food.

ABBEY: I used to play "ferries" in this stream when I was a kid. We'd build tiny little rafts and houses for them, entire villages.

Beat.

ABBEY: My dad would take us on these adventures. Camping out. Capture the flag. It was great.

Beat.

NOAH: Oh right, I could use my water-filter thing!

He springs up, gets his water bottle and filter.

ABBEY: We should get going.

NOAH: Yeah, yeah, just gonna fill my water bottle.

NOAH is off.

FRANK: I remember playing those games. Ferries in the stream. Capture the flag … You don't remember me? I played with you back then. Me and my family would be on the other side of the river, fishing. We used to play together.

ABBEY: Oh my God …

FRANK smiles.

ABBEY: Oh my God … You're Frankie …

FRANK: Frank 'n Beans. Yours truly.

They share a moment. It's potentially even romantic … they obviously liked each other when they were kids.

NOAH re-enters with his water bottle.

NOAH: Ha HA! Awesome. Look at that. It's so *clear*. I can't see anything. And yet I can see … everything.

ABBEY: We should go.

NOAH: Yeah. Okay. Glad we stopped. Get some sustenance. I'll be good now. I was frickin' starving.

FRANK: Okay, that's the third time you've said "starving." I'd appreciate if you just said "hungry."

NOAH: O-kay ... C'mon, I think political correctness has a line, I think. We can't say "starving" anymore? It's just an exaggeration.

FRANK: Over a thousand kids in residential schools had malnutrition experiments done on them. Kept on starvation-level diets – fed a flour mixture that was illegal in the rest of Canada – so – you complain about "starving"; I think about those kids. My mom and dad. Or the ones who didn't make it. So it's not about being "politically correct," it's about recognizing your privilege.

NOAH: Okay, man. I didn't know. I'm sorry. (*beat*) Really? Jesus ...

FRANK: ... Whatever, get your pack on, come on. We going up that mountain?

ABBEY: Think so.

FRANK: That bridge doesn't look safe. I'll go test it.

> *He goes off.*

> *ABBEY and NOAH connect.*

NOAH: Geez ... You okay?

ABBEY: Yeah ... yeah.

> *But ABBEY looks up at the mountain, unsure.*

ABBEY: I don't know what we're gonna find up there.

NOAH: What do you mean?

> *ABBEY shrugs, then looks up at the mountain again.*

NOAH: You're just paranoid. It's the weed.

> *But they both stare up at the mountain ... The lights fade.*

SCENE 4A.3

On a ridge, twenty minutes away ...

The gentle sound of drumming. They're hiking up an incline now: ABBEY in front, following her map and compass, rifle still in hand. FRANK second, rifle still in hand. NOAH third, drumming on his canteen. To the beat of NOAH's drumming, FRANK starts singing to the tune of Pink Floyd's "Another Brick in the Wall (Part 2)":

FRANK: "We don't need no ... bears around here."

NOAH: Ha, nice.

FRANK: "We don't need no ... coyotes."

NOAH: Coyotes? Jesus ...

FRANK: "No bad run-ins with a cougar."

NOAH: Geez, man, making it worse ...

FRANK: Traditional safety song, here, very traditional – "Hey! Creatures! Please leave us alone."

NOAH: "Creatures" instead of "teachers," nice.

FRANK: Everybody!

NOAH and **FRANK:** "Hey! Creatures! Please leave us alone ..."

NOAH starts beat-boxing to the rhythm. FRANK joins in, drumming.

FRANK: Abbey, the more noise we make the safer we are. Second verse, Abbey: "We don't need no ..." Sing it, Abbey! "We don't need no ..."

ABBEY: ... "dad who's crazy."

NOAH: Nice.

FRANK: Noah! –

NOAH: Uhh, "Crazy's probably not that PC."

FRANK: Nope! "No reserves, no IA Agents."

NOAH: IA?

ABBEY: Indian Affairs.

FRANK: "IA, leave them kids at home."

The song dies out ...

FRANK: We used to sing that as a protest song.

NOAH: Right, yeah. Yeah, of course. (*beat*) I can't believe I forgot my Bluetooth speaker, that thing makes a lot of noise.

FRANK: (*stopping*) Shh-shh.

NOAH: (*scared*) What? (*really, really scared*) Where, what is it, what, where??

FRANK: Squirrel.

NOAH: Oh ... Jesus ...

ABBEY: Uhh ... Looks like we have to scramble up these rocks.

They stand and look at the land around them. NOAH's pack is off right away, and he proceeds to get out binoculars.

NOAH: Oh wow, look at this view. Sweet.

FRANK: Where we headin' there?

ABBEY: Just up, over that a ways.

She busies herself with putting down her pack – keeping the rifle in hand.

Beat.

FRANK, making sure to stay congenial, looks at his watch.

FRANK: Made up some time. All goes well, could still make it.

ABBEY: Yup.

FRANK: You doing okay?

ABBEY: I'm fine.

NOAH is looking at the view.

NOAH: Whoa. What's that? Looks like a camp. Like, teepees? A Longhouse, maybe? Cool. Is that your reserve?

FRANK looks ... but doesn't answer.

ABBEY: Where?

She looks through the binoculars. Projected, we see what she's seeing: a small camp of teepees and wooden structures on the flatlands.

ABBEY: No, that's not on reserve. That's on our property. (*to FRANK*) What is all that?

FRANK: It's uh ... Yeah, we uh ...

ABBEY: Have you guys set up camp on our property? Is that what I'm seeing?

FRANK: Okay, Abbey, / calm down –

ABBEY: Frank, *please* tell me that's not what I'm seeing. Please tell me you haven't *already* occupied a portion of land that I haven't even given to you yet.

FRANK: Let me explain. We've been using those flatlands for thousands of years / and –

ABBEY: Oh spare me the history. *Now*, Frank, now. What are you doing there *now*.

FRANK: Your dad gave us permission –

ABBEY: Did he.

FRANK: He said we could set up a site out there –

ABBEY: Okay, and do you have that in writing somewhere?

FRANK: I have a handshake deal –

ABBEY: And why am I just learning about this now?

FRANK: I didn't wanna ... fan the flames.

ABBEY: I'm guessing that's where my dad would find you guys trespassing all the time.

FRANK: Here we go ... trespassing ... on our own / land.

ABBEY: I remember. He said you guys would go out there trying to find evidence of an old village site. Because if you proved there was one, that'd help your case for a land claim. Your claim to *all* the land around here; the town, *our* property – everything.

NOAH: This doesn't / sound good, dude –

ABBEY: My dad would call the cops, but you'd eventually come back. So is that what I'm seeing out there? An excavation, a camp?

FRANK: ... We're not – Okay, we're not just there to prove – These are our traditional hunting and gathering grounds. And your dad understood that.

ABBEY: Really. So why'd he leave this – coded for *me*? (*beat*) So just to be clear, you just made a deal with me in which *if* we find the Deed, I *give* you that entire half of the land, just give it to you, out of the kindness of my *heart* – but now I see that you're already taking it? And are threatening to take ALL of it with a land claim? Please tell me I'm wrong here. Please tell me how not to see this whole thing as, like, extortion.

NOAH: Hey, whoa, whoa ... If I may? Perhaps you could both put down your ... like, *weapons*? And if you want to talk, then just, you know, talk. Cuz this is obviously getting pretty revved up.

ABBEY: I'm not putting this down. He should put his down.

> *A violent pause.*

NOAH: Abbey ...

ABBEY: I don't trust him. There's no way I can trust him now. He's hiding things in order to get what he wants. Frank, I'm pretty sure I could say our "deal" was signed under duress, that I was coerced.

FRANK: I frickin' knew it ... So no matter what, you're the Boss and I'm the Bitch, eh?

ABBEY: You're the one who lied.

> *Beat.*

FRANK: Abbey, what exactly is your fear here? What's changed? Sure, we're camped out on "your" land, you never noticed before.

ABBEY: That doesn't matter ...

FRANK: And sure we're attempting to gain some agency, some –

ABBEY: Agency?

FRANK: – control over our lands. Considering all this was stolen in the first place –

ABBEY: Oh, don't –! *I* didn't / steal it –

FRANK: And how much has been taken from / us –

ABBEY: That was hundreds of years ago! What about all the things you've been given? BILLIONS OF DOLLARS in compensation for the residential schools. Hundreds of millions for healing projects, / not to mention the HUGE payouts from industry –

FRANK: Those numbers PALE in comparison –

ABBEY: All paid by taxpayers. Like me and my dad. But now you're asking us to pay even / more?

NOAH: Abbey, you do know that Native people pay tax, right?

ABBEY: Kind of –

FRANK: No, not "kind of"! Personal income made *on reserve* is the only thing eligible for tax exemption. All other income is taxed. I pay tax on the pittance your dad pays me out here.

ABBEY: Okay. But when my family came here – my mom – do you know what they were given? Nothing. They had to learn a new language and work their asses off, they weren't handed –

FRANK: Because they moved to a foreign land. Our land! And those numbers you just quoted me? They PALE in comparison to the wealth Canada makes off our land, every year; the lakes, resources, the mines, those numbers are a *fraction.* And anyway throwing money around doesn't make up for "Compulsory Sterilization," having your rights revoked, your name / changed –

ABBEY: But those things –

FRANK: – and talk about language? Ours was beaten out of us at residential school, if we didn't die first. We have the highest rate of suicide, the highest rate of unemployment, hundreds of reserves with unsafe drinking water –

ABBEY: Those things were not my doing – they are not my problem!

NOAH: I think they are, Abbey, they actually / are –

ABBEY: And don't pretend to snub your nose at financial compensation when that is exactly what you're looking for right now! / What's the difference?

FRANK: No – the difference is control, Abbey, *agency* over our lives. Not wards of the state, not "You're the Boss and I'm the Bitch," but *partners* in a shared future. Can you deny that that's owed to us?

ABBEY: Fine, fine, but why does it have to be ME who gives it to you?

FRANK: Why not? Why not you too? (*to NOAH*) Why not anyone who can? Gotta do what's in our power to do.

> *Beat.*

NOAH: Ab. I think he does have a bit of a –

ABBEY: Noah, you have the luxury of this not affecting you at all.

NOAH: That's not true. That's actually not true.

ABBEY: Oh, really? – Hey, Frank, Noah's condo in the city, it's got a bit of a view – Wanna go halfsies with him on that too?

FRANK: Love to.

NOAH: Guys. Guys. Christ! So what it sounds like is needed here in order to move forward is, Frank, you need to agree that if you still want us to give you half the land, then any future Land Claim leaves this property out of it. Simple.

> *Beat.*

NOAH: Abbey? Would that satisfy you? We keep going as planned, so long as their Band leaves your property totally out of their claim.

ABBEY: ... It's a start.

NOAH: See? We can just talk this out.

FRANK: Look at this guy. The negotiator. But hold up, Rock Star, there's no way I can agree to that. I can't speak on behalf of that many people. It's not my Band's claim, it's our entire Nation, our entire Territory, all of the different Bands. If we win a claim, all of the Councils aren't gonna listen to one little guy who says, "Oh wait, I actually promised these guys we'd leave their property out of it."

NOAH: Jesus Christ ... why not??

ABBEY: Fine so, here's my counter: In light of this new encroachment on our land, the deal we made is off –

FRANK: I knew it, I knew / you'd –

ABBEY: You put down your gun so I can feel safe. We all continue on, and if we do get the Deed, *then* we discuss what the hell to do with the property. But we do so one step at a time.

FRANK: Discuss.

ABBEY: That's right.

FRANK: Consult.

ABBEY: Yeah.

FRANK: Decide at a later date.

ABBEY: Yes.

    Beat.

FRANK: Is she like this? Is this ... what she's like?

NOAH: I don't know, kinda.

FRANK: I put this down and there's nothing stopping you from "accidentally" pulling your trigger.

NOAH: Whoa – dude! Dude, there's NO way she would EVER do ANYTHING like that!

FRANK: She'll never give up, will she? We'll make a deal and she'll always find some way to break it. Just like her ol' man. Just like all you people.

ABBEY: Enough, Frank! I don't know how many racist comments we have to endure. Put that thing DOWN and let's get on with this!

FRANK: Don't raise that thing at me.

ABBEY: Don't.

NOAH: Guys, don't.

ABBEY: Put it down!

NOAH: Hey, we can work this out!

ABBEY: Put it down! Now!

    Their guns are raised –!

CHOICE-POINT 4A.3

THE HOST: Choice-Point:

    A.   Should Noah convince them to work it out?
       ▶ **Go to Scene 5A, page 123**

    B.   Should Abbey get Frank to drop his weapon?
       ▶ **Go to Scene 5B, page 127**

    C.   Should Frank take Noah hostage?
       ▶ **Go to Scene 5C, page 129**

Turn your clicker on. And you have fifteen seconds.

The timer starts ...

Votes are in.

You chose ...

The results are projected and **THE HOST** *says the choice.*

SCENE 4B

Noah and Abbey go call this in

Lights rise on the lakeside. We hear the sound of a motor boat in the distance. FRANK is seated in the bush, looking through binoculars.

The sound of the motor boat cuts out. FRANK chews at some jerky, watches. And waits, like an experienced hunter.

His phone buzzes.

Projected: RAIN would like FaceTime ...

FRANK accepts the call. His daughter RAIN appears projected on a video call:

RAIN: Hey Dad, how's it going? You're in range.

FRANK: Yeah, yeah, for – How are you?

RAIN: Oh you know ... still here. Is everything okay?

FRANK: Yeah – yeah, things are fine. How's it going there?

RAIN: Seriously? Dad, I can't handle this anymore. There's *mushrooms* growing out of the bathroom floor. I'll bet the fetus is loving all the mould. I'm sharing a bed with Linda who snores. There's hardly any food here, we're starving.

FRANK: Over a thousand kids in residential schools had malnutrition experiments done on them. Kept on starvation-level diets – fed a flour mixture that was illegal in the rest of Canada – so – you complain about "starving"; I think about those kids. Your grandma and grandpa.

RAIN: I know, Dad. You've told me this. I know it's not as bad as they had it. But I gotta get outta here, I been calling around and I'm just getting on everyone's nerves with all this.

FRANK: I know, Rain. I'm trying. Between finding a place for your sister in the city and trying to get you out of that mould trap, I'm stretched to my limit with housing options. The DIA doesn't care if we die in their death-trap houses so I gotta take care of things on my own. I'm really trying to make this right.

RAIN: I know. I don't mean to nag but – you didn't say it'd be this long and I have nowhere else. I should just move in with Debbie when she gets a place. Then you wouldn't have to worry about us. We wouldn't be such a burden.

FRANK: You're not a burden, Rain. And you can't move in with your sister. Her budget can barely afford a place just for her. And how is she supposed to go to school and do her assignments with you and a baby living with her?

RAIN: Great, I'd be a burden for her too.

FRANK: Stop it. You're not a burden for anyone.

RAIN: Well, what then? You say you want me to stay on the rez and raise my baby in the traditional way and then you say that I can't live on the rez because it's unsafe. What am I supposed to do?

FRANK: I know. I know. I'm sorry. It's not your fault. I've let you down. Just let me ... just let me figure it out, okay? Can you handle another night there?

RAIN: ... Sure, whatever.

> *The distant sound of the motor boat starts up again.*
> *FRANK looks through the binoculars.*

FRANK: All right. Well, let me figure it out. You hang in there. We got this. There's a very real possibility that I may be able to seal up the land situation here. Maybe more.

RAIN: What do you mean?

FRANK: Just let me handle it, okay? You hang in there. Keep fighting the good fight ...

RAIN: Dad, what are you up to?

FRANK: Just trust me. I love you.

RAIN: Okay ...? I love you too.

FRANK: Bye.

> *FRANK hangs up. Through the binoculars, he follows the*
> *trail of the boat ... back the way it came.*

FRANK: They're headin' back. Guess this whole thing is legit.

> *Then, binoculars down, he thinks. Takes a bite of jerky.*

> *A moment later, he silently screams to himself.*

*Then calmly: FRANK reaches behind himself and pulls
out his rifle. He stares at it. A long beat. A long breath out.
Then, finally, he shakes his head, and:*

FRANK: Screw it.

He dials his phone.

FRANK: Ben. Where are you right now? ... Good. Grab your truck and
a few of the guys. I need you to block the road out to Danny Mitchell's.
I'll explain tomorrow, but I promise, it'll be worth it.

Blackout.

The map is projected on the screen.

SCENE 4B.1

The projected map tracks ABBEY and NOAH's progress as they search for the Deed. It's clear they are now crossing a bridge over a stream.

Offstage, NOAH yelps in pain.

NOAH: Ah – ah! I can't – I can't –

ABBEY enters, helping NOAH – he's limping. His pant leg is torn up, his leg is bleeding profusely, and he clearly can't put weight on his foot. He's in tons of pain.

ABBEY: Here, sit down, sit down. Lemme see.

NOAH: (*making pain noises*) What the hell, man! Just fell right through.

ABBEY: It's an old bridge.

NOAH: No, man, that was ... I don't know what that was. (*pain noise*)

ABBEY: (*wincing*) Must'a sliced it on the wood, all the way up.

More sounds of pain from NOAH while ABBEY tries to nurse him. She gets out a first-aid kit and gauze bandage.

NOAH: I swear, it fell through like it was just – (*pain noise*) Oh man ... I can't look ...

ABBEY: Then don't.

She starts wiping his leg, then wrapping it in gauze. NOAH howls.

NOAH: Ah, piss ... I'm sorry, babe.

ABBEY: It wasn't your fault. Could've happened to me ...

NOAH: Yeah, but it didn't. (*pain noise*) We got any painkillers?

ABBEY: Yeah, just let me do this first. Can you – put weight on it?

NOAH: Ab ... just –

ABBEY: Did you sprain it or is it just cut?

He stands a bit, tries to put weight on it – yelps in pain, and falls back down.

NOAH: I'm sorry, I'm sorry. I twisted it or – (*more pain noises*)

ABBEY: Okay, lift your leg, here. That okay?

NOAH: Yeah ... (*pain noise*)

She finishes wrapping his leg, and as they wait for the bleeding to stop, she looks around, thinking.

ABBEY: Dammit ...

A beat. ABBEY stands, considering her options, then looks at her map.

NOAH: Painkillers?

ABBEY: Right, yeah, yeah.

She gets him painkillers.

NOAH: Can you grab me a drink too? I got cans in my bag.

ABBEY: You brought Hey Y'alls?

NOAH makes more pain sounds. She gets him a Hey Y'all.

ABBEY: They're warm.

He reaches for the can, pops it, and gulps almost the whole thing back.

ABBEY takes the map and GPS to the river, looking out. She takes a big stress breath.

NOAH: How far are we?

She looks at the map and GPS.

NOAH: Do you know where we are? (*pain noise*) Babe, do you even know where we are?!

ABBEY: Yes! Yes. I haven't done this since I was a kid, and now doing it by code while I haven't slept? It's not easy.

NOAH: Okay, roughly: are we halfway, more than half, what?

ABBEY: Roughly ... another hour there? Three back? And that's at a good clip.

NOAH: ... I'm sorry.

ABBEY: It's not your fault.

NOAH: Maybe I can –

He tries to stand – yelps.

NOAH: No, no.

ABBEY: You sprained it, you can't walk on it.

NOAH: I could use a crutch or something, like a branch as a crutch.

ABBEY: We have to climb a mountain, scramble up rocks ...

NOAH: Well, what do we do?

> *NOAH continues to wince in pain. He checks if his bleeding has stopped, which it hasn't.*

ABBEY: I have to go by myself.

NOAH: You're gonna leave me? There's bears and coyotes out here!

ABBEY: Oh ... they're not gonna do anything.

NOAH: Jesus – you don't know that!

ABBEY: They're not like sharks, they don't smell blood.

NOAH: I really don't find that funny.

ABBEY: I didn't mean it to be funny. I'd leave you the gun.

NOAH: Oh my God, this is ... Oh God, this is ... NOT how I pictured this trip! Let's go back, babe. I'm way over my head here. This is ... I gotta go back. You gotta take me back. I need anaesthetic, I need enough gauze to stop this – I need ice. / I need a doctor.

ABBEY: Calm down –

NOAH: I haven't slept, / I'm panicked, we have no idea where Frank even is anymore, and now I'm, I'm –

ABBEY: Honey, calm down, calm down, you're in shock, but you're gonna be / okay.

NOAH: No – can I just say? SCREW your dad. SCREW him. And screw THIS. AAAAAAAAGGHH! *Screw* this land. (*beat*) And this is my *kick foot*, I play bass drum with this foot. It better not be permanently damaged!

> *Beat.*

ABBEY: You done?

ABBEY kneels down to NOAH, gentle now, caring.

ABBEY: Listen, going back to the boat took, like, two and a half hours. I'm worried about time. If I bring you back, I'd be cutting it really close.

NOAH: This is ridiculous.

ABBEY: So either I leave you here, or you go back on your own.

NOAH: I can't go back on my own! I can't walk! I have no idea where I am!

ABBEY: I'll draw you a map.

NOAH: Draw me –? Christ, I'll just stay here. Babe, I'll just stay here. It's fine. It's fine.

> *But it's clearly not fine. ABBEY looks at her watch, then the map. She considers, shakes her head – mad and frustrated. She paces. She takes up the rifle again. Pacing. Thinking.*
>
> *A light now rises on FRANK: he is nearby, hiding behind a tree, watching and listening to this unfold. He is holding his rifle.*

ABBEY: I can't let this land go. I can't. It's in my family. My blood.

NOAH: Babe, I know it's important. Worth a helluva lot of money but ... I don't know, maybe this is ... like ... a / sign.

ABBEY: I don't believe in signs.

NOAH: Maybe you should just – *think* about letting it go.

ABBEY: To the Queen?

NOAH: That's gotta be – reversible somehow. Maybe you could, you know, convince your dad.

ABBEY: If I see him again. (*beat*) I gotta think worst-case scenario.

> *FRANK silently reacts to this – gritting his teeth.*

ABBEY: But we're not there yet. And it's gonna be easy for me. We used to camp out all the time, go on adventures. So what I really hope is he's just testing me. It's a test of whether I *deserve* the land I think. (*beat*) And if I bring you back and then go search on my own, I'm also taking the chance that Frank's there, and he follows me.

NOAH: (*rolling eyes*) Follows you? Well, so what, so what? Say he does follow you, say we do have to give him half the land ... Is that really so bad?

Beat.

ABBEY: Say he wants all of it. What do I do then?

Beat.

NOAH: And that's more important to you than, say ... I don't know ... my *life*?

ABBEY: Honey ...

NOAH: No, that's fine. At least I know where I stand. That's good cuz I was actually thinking of ...

ABBEY: ... What?

NOAH: Oh no, I was just actually thinking of *asking you something* on this trip – but now? Ho ho, not so sure! Now that I know where your priorities really lie.

ABBEY: ... You were?

He motions a gesture of frustrated defeat. A beat.

ABBEY: But hon. I'm trying to be practical. For us. Do you really think your tours are gonna sustain us? Retirement, adoption, kids' education?

NOAH: I can't have this conversation / right now.

ABBEY: I've put all my eggs into this basket.

NOAH: I know.

ABBEY: We have legal bills, what's gonna cover that – your new / album?

NOAH: I know, / I know.

ABBEY: I love you, of course I do. And I wouldn't leave you stranded. I'd leave you the gun. I'd show you how to shoot it. You'd have food, water. Alcohol. I'd be back in like two hours. We'd be in town and into a clinic before you know it. Jacuzzi in a hotel tonight even ...

NOAH: Jesus. Jesus. Jesus! Whatever, there's no winning with you. Okay, *if* you do this, won't *you* need the gun?

She pulls out a knife. He shakes his head.

NOAH: And here I thought coming out here would be ... romantic.

ABBEY stands over NOAH, still not quite sure.

NOAH sits with the rifle and his hurt leg, looking up at ABBEY.

FRANK sits perched, hidden, considering his options.

CHOICE-POINT 4B.1

THE HOST: Choice-Point:

    A. Should Frank step out of hiding and offer his assistance?
       ▶ **Go to Scene 5D, page 131**

    B. Should Abbey leave Noah and forge on toward the Deed?
       ▶ **Go to Scene 5E, page 135**

    C. Should Noah propose to Abbey?
       ▶ **Go to Scene 5F, page 142**

Turn your clicker on. And you have fifteen seconds.

    The timer starts ...

    Votes are in.

You chose ...

    *The results are projected and **THE HOST** says the choice.*

SCENE 4C

Abbey refuses the deal and suggests an alternative ...

They're all now back in the house. ABBEY is standing with the map in her hands. FRANK is seated on a chair in the middle of the living room. He no longer has his gun. NOAH is standing next to FRANK – looking at him. NOAH has a long length of rope.

FRANK: Go ahead, Rock Star. Go ahead.

NOAH: Guys ... this is ... can't we all just sign a truce or a peace treaty or something?

FRANK: Cuz we all know how much those get honoured.

NOAH: Well, we can't just –! We can't! (*to ABBEY*) You're only seeing this from – Okay, I understand you're worried if we go out there on our own, he could – follow us, or ambush us at the boat and take the Deed, but why don't we just go call the cops? They could, like, detain him –

FRANK: That's even worse, man!

ABBEY: Not enough time! And you think he's just gonna sit here waiting for the cops?

NOAH: Well, we'll have to untie him eventually and – what's he gonna frickin' do then?

ABBEY: He's agreed to this, Noah, it's his choice.

FRANK: *My* choice??

NOAH: Hon, you're acting crazy. Of course he agreed to it, what choice did he have?

FRANK: Drummer Boy, I'll explain it to you in city-boy language. Your lady has agreed that if she gets that Deed we'll have a good-faith negotiation about my interests in this land. So in exchange, and to ease her fears, I'm willing to let you guys tie me up.

NOAH: No, I get that – but that is crazy!

FRANK: But remember: I want my fingers free so I can read my book. And: I don't want my mouth covered. I hate that part.

NOAH: You hate that part? Man, we live in different worlds.

FRANK: So yeah ... tie me up, so long as I'm free to talk and neither of you *ever*, ever, EVER shut me up. That's the deal, right, Abbey?

ABBEY: That's the deal.

NOAH: Okay, so just let me: We tie you up, she decodes that thing, we go find the Deed, you sit here reading (which – weird), we bring the Deed into town, and then we come back, untie you ... and all is *good*? Like all is ... totally okay?

FRANK: Well, then – as your lady said: We have a good-faith negotiation about this land. That's the only thing I'm after here.

NOAH: ... This seems so weird.

FRANK: Rock Star, a cop once handcuffed me to a fence for an entire day cuz he didn't like the look of my steel-toed boots. I'm used to this crap. We do what's in our power to do, and right now, I don't have much.

NOAH: I'm sorry, dude. I'm so sorry, for ... basically *perpetuating ...*

ABBEY: Noah, can you just do it?

> *FRANK holds out his hands to be tied up. NOAH and ABBEY – awkwardly – tie FRANK to the chair. FRANK even helps. It's actually kind of funny. Ad lib things like "Here?," "Here's better," and "That okay?" are exchanged.*

FRANK: What *was* your dad thinking, eh? Setting us up here like this.

ABBEY: Maybe he was testing you, see what you'd do.

FRANK: Or maybe he's seeing what *you'd* do. (*beat*) Hey, if he happens to come back early, this'll be a funny sight for him, eh?

NOAH: I don't find this funny. At all. Jesus, did he even know I was coming? Cuz if he did – what a dick move. Involving *me* in all this? I haven't even met him yet. Total dick.

> *FRANK tests the ties. So does ABBEY. They're good. FRANK's hands are free but his arms are tied. His ankles are tied to the chair.*
>
> *Now that it's done, it's actually really awful. But FRANK's in a good mood, at least.*

FRANK: My book?

NOAH: Oh yeah yeah, where is it?

FRANK: In my bag in my truck.

NOAH: Okay.

A moment, then NOAH goes off.

ABBEY opens the map, lays it on the table, and tries to decipher her dad's code. The map is projected, so her work can be seen on the screen.

FRANK: You'd really dig this book, Abbey. It's called *Unsettling Canada*. Written by a former Chief of a nearby rez. Did talks at the United Nations.

ABBEY: Neat.

FRANK looks at himself tied up.

FRANK: Amazing, you know ... Our land's been occupied; our rights, culture, our language stripped. I'm speaking *your* language, can't even speak my own. I've been beaten, jailed, shot at. But if we ever fight back or simply try to protect ourselves, then *we're* the savages.

ABBEY looks at him. FRANK smiles at her.

— + —

▶ **If it was Frank who figured out the map was coded, add:**

FRANK: Nice of me to point out that was coded, wasn't it? Wonder if you'd have ever figured that out.

— — —

FRANK: Ah, silent treatment. Not unlike your government, turn a deaf ear when the conversation doesn't suit you.

Beat.

FRANK: So speaking of our deal for you to never shut me up: how much you know about the Royal Proclamation? Never heard of it? Perfect. King of England, 1763. Stated that Indians should not be "molested or disturbed" on their Lands. (*looking at his hands*) Hm. Hmmmm ...

ABBEY: Frank, I'm sorry, but this technically isn't your land.

FRANK: Oh really! I'm so glad you brought that up because the same Proclamation also said that until a *lawful purchase* of lands is made, then "that land is reserved for the use of Indians." I'd put that in air quotes if my hands weren't tied up. And *there was no purchase* here. Sodbusters like your family just moved right in. And you say this isn't my land ... Your own Constitution recognizes this is ALL Aboriginal Land! But your government still doesn't *act* that way. Canada is consistently on the list of United Nations' Human Rights violators.

ABBEY: I understand it's unjust, Frank, of course I do, but I didn't invent the system. I'm just a cog in it, like you.

ABBEY exits to gather supplies.

FRANK: Ha! We may have both inherited this "unjust" world. But you're the one who can easily, so easily do something about it.

NOAH comes back in with the book. He's not sure what to do. He ... hands it to FRANK.

The book's cover page is projected:

Unsettling Canada:
A National Wake-Up Call
by Arthur Manuel and Grand Chief Ronald M. Derrickson
Foreword by Naomi Klein

NOAH: This looks neat, man.

FRANK: Neat? It's great. I'll read you some in a bit. Right now, I was giving your lady a lesson on human-rights violations. Have a listen if you want. (*calling to ABBEY*) Abbey, the Canadian government lets in all these refugees, while its own Indigenous people, who it *swore* to protect, "unmolested and undisturbed," are actually given starvation wages. You know our Band Chief makes six hundred bucks a month? A MONTH! And that's normal. So is 175 bucks a month for social assistance on reserve; 175 A MONTH. People think, "Oh, they get so much money, free trucks, free housing" – no, no, no. Lies, lies, lies. That's what they *want* you to believe so they keep the status quo.

NOAH: Okay, but wait, I've driven past reserves near the city and they often do have big houses and fancy cars.

FRANK: Right. You white folks always have an example of a rez that disputes the Native poverty statistics, or a magical Indian friend whose behaviour somehow confirms every Native stereotype you want confirmed.

NOAH: But come on, do you deny those places or people exist?

FRANK: Absolutely not. Look. America elected a Black president, does that mean racism is dead? There are black millionaires, does that mean that African American poverty is a myth? No. But when it comes to Native people, one example is supposed to represent the entire race. The one or two reserves you've "driven past" have probably had to lease reserve land to a Walmart or something and are a tiny fraction compared to the hundreds of reserves that were put in the middle of nowhere in an attempt to kill off its residents. One Native in a big house does not an entire Nation make. So many times I've heard, "We're living off your backs." We're not. (*calling to ABBEY*) You're living off ours!

NOAH: Okay, man, I think we need to just let her –

FRANK: (*continuing his rant*) And when we simply try to *protect* our Land? We get slapped with court injunctions. Cops come in with their batons and pepper spray, sometimes even the military – the Canadian military against its own people! People it swore to protect, unmolested, / undisturbed –

NOAH: But we can't help that. What can we do? – / That's not –

FRANK: What can you DO? Well for starters, you kids are sitting on a helluva lot of compensation. Everyone is, anyone who lives and even just *rents an apartment* in this country is doing so on land that has been ripped out or coerced from under its original Peoples, while a lot of those people starve, get addicted, are jailed, or kill themselves. Did you know that before settlers came, suicide was practically unheard of in our culture? And now? Our youth kill themselves at a rate that's more than five times higher than the rest of Canadians. We're Third – no *Fourth* World citizens in a First World country. So what can you *do*, you ask?

ABBEY enters with a rifle and puts ammo in her bag.

FRANK: I'll tell you, Abbey! You need our Band's free and informed *consent* before you develop this property in any way. And we want 50 percent of the profits. If you don't want to transfer half the land, then let's share it ALL. That's what my Ancestors did: shared the land. Consenting partners!

ABBEY: We already have the community's consent, Frank.

FRANK: No you don't, you have "consultation." It's ticking a box.

ABBEY: This is how you enter a good-faith negotiation?

FRANK: What exactly is your fear here? You lead a pretty good life, you got a nice guy – /

NOAH: Thanks man /

FRANK: No problem – You have your ups and downs, but how much do you really need? And my offer is reasonable, considering all this was stolen in the first place.

ABBEY: Oh, don't –! *I* didn't / steal it –

FRANK: And how much has been taken from / us –

ABBEY: That was hundreds of years ago! What about all the things you've been given? BILLIONS OF DOLLARS in compensation for the residential schools. Hundreds of millions for healing projects, / not to mention the HUGE payouts from industry –

FRANK: Those numbers PALE in / comparison –

ABBEY: All paid by taxpayers. Like me and my dad. But now you're asking us to pay even / more?

NOAH: Abbey, you do know that Native people pay tax, right?

ABBEY: Kind of –

FRANK: No, not "kind of"! Personal income made *on reserve* is the only thing eligible for tax exemption. All other income is taxed. I pay tax on the pittance your dad pays me out here.

ABBEY: Okay – But when my family came here – my mom – do you know what they were given? Nothing. They had to learn a new language and work their asses off, they weren't handed –

FRANK: Because they moved to a foreign land. Our land! And those numbers you just quoted me? They PALE in comparison to the wealth Canada makes off our land, every year; the lakes, resources, the mines, those numbers are a *fraction*. And anyway throwing money around doesn't make up for "Compulsory Sterilization," having your rights revoked, your name / changed –

ABBEY: But those things –

FRANK: – and talk about language? Ours was beaten out of us at residential school, if we didn't die first. We have the highest rate of suicide, the highest rate of unemployment, hundreds of reserves with unsafe drinking water –

ABBEY: Those things were not my doing and are not my problem!

NOAH: I think they are Abbey, they actually / are –

ABBEY: And don't pretend to snub your nose at financial compensation when that is exactly what you're looking for right now! / What's the difference?

FRANK: No – the difference is control, Abbey, *agency* over our lives. Not wards of the state, not "You're the Boss and I'm the Bitch," but *partners* in a shared future. Can you deny that that's owed to us?

ABBEY: Fine, fine, but why does it have to be ME who gives it to you?

FRANK: Why not? Why not you too? (*to NOAH*) Why not anyone who can? Gotta do what's in our power to do.

> *Beat.*

NOAH: Ab. I think he does have a bit of a –

ABBEY: Noah, you have the luxury of this not affecting you at all.

NOAH: That's not true. That's actually not true.

ABBEY: Oh, really? – Hey Frank, Noah's condo in the city, it's got a bit of a view – Wanna go halfsies with him on that too?

FRANK: Love to.

NOAH: Okay – guys – we don't have all night here. Literally! ... Jesus. Time is ticking, babe, you decoded that frickin' thing?

ABBEY: I think so.

FRANK: Abbey, this isn't what I was asking of your old man, it's not even what I set out for here with you. But yeah, total consent and 50 percent of profits is what I'm asking now, because ... well, because of who you are. Because you insist your privilege is righteous.

ABBEY: Privilege –

FRANK: And worse, that you "can't do anything about it." And because I refuse to be bullied anymore. *We* won't be bullied anymore.

ABBEY: Who's bullying who here?

FRANK: Who's the one tied up? And believe me, young lady, you have not seen ANYTHING yet. You're lucky I'm only asking this much.

ABBEY: Shut up – You have no leverage here. Without me, without this map, you've got nothing.

FRANK: So now you're telling me to shut up? I thought we had a deal. Typical!

ABBEY: Seriously, drop it or you'll get nothing but a jail term or worse.

FRANK: Jail term? For what?

ABBEY: You come into my home, wielding a weapon. You should know that the law is on my side here, no matter what. No matter *what.*

> *Beat.*

FRANK: Do you want to see your dad again?

> *Utter silence. The air turns icy cold.*

ABBEY: Excuse me?

FRANK: If you ever want to see your dad again, you'll untie me, give me the gun, and take me to that Deed.

> *Another long beat.*

NOAH: I knew it. Holy man. (*beat*) Abbey. Let the cops handle this. We're way over our heads here.

ABBEY: (*to FRANK*) You're bluffing. If that were true, you'd have played that card a long time ago.

> *FRANK shrugs, up to her. Beat.*

NOAH: Abbey. Stop. Think. We need to deal with this in the right way.

> *ABBEY walks right up to FRANK, leans into his face ...*
> *inspects him.*

ABBEY: You're bluffing.

FRANK: (*shrugging*) You and your dad have stated your case. I've stated mine. Unless you want to believe that's just rabbit blood?

> *ABBEY looks at the stain on the floor ... then looks back*
> *at FRANK. She's shaking.*

CHOICE-POINT 4C.

THE HOST: Choice-Point:

A. Should Frank get his way, and they untie him?
    ▶ **Go to Scene 5G, page 151**

B. Should Noah and Abbey involve the authorities?
    ▶ **Go to Scene 5H, page 158**

C. Should they leave Frank tied up, and search for the Deed themselves?
    ▶ **Go to Scene 5I, page 166**

Turn your clicker on. And you have fifteen seconds.

The timer starts ...

Votes are in.

You chose ...

*The results are projected and **THE HOST** says the choice.*

SCENE 5A

Noah convinces them to work it out ...

Replay the last few moments ...

FRANK: She'll never give up, will she? We'll make a deal and she'll always find some way to break it. Just like her ol' man. Just like all you people.

ABBEY: Enough, Frank! I don't know how many racist comments we have to endure. Put that thing DOWN and let's get on with this!

FRANK: Don't raise that thing at me.

ABBEY: Don't.

NOAH: Guys, don't.

ABBEY: Put it down!

NOAH: Hey, we can work this out!

ABBEY: Put it down! Now!

Their guns are raised –!

NOAH steps right in between!

NOAH: Abbey, STOP!

Beat.

NOAH: Frank, CHRIST.

Pause.

NOAH: Can we just stick to the original agreement here? (*to ABBEY*) I understand your principles, babe, I understand your mom came here with nothing, how hard your dad's family worked, and how you're looking out for your future – our future – I understand all that.

ABBEY: I don't think / you do.

NOAH: And I understand you feel threatened. I understand you *are* threatened. That every day is a fight. And your struggle is valid. It is. But it's not enough. (*beat*) Whatever justification you have, it's not enough. Think about it. (*beat*) I know you want to win, babe, I know you never feel like you win and you want to win here. But, you already did. We already did. We won at birth. This country was set up for us. For our parents. Even your mom. Was your mom forced to give up her language, her culture? No. *They* were. (*beat*) We gotta lose something here.

ABBEY: We? That's so easy for you to say. You can retreat at any time. Back to your condo, and all will be fine for you. This struggle is not *yours*.

NOAH: Okay: Ouch. Um. I'm actually out here to – to try and change that. I was planning to … But you're right, it's not mine. And I know it hurts even more when *you* gotta give something up, and others don't. (*beat*) So look, yeah, if there's a way that I can … you know, give something up too then – sure. I mean, (*to FRANK*) maybe your daughter needs a place to crash when she's in the city, maybe we talk about – staying with me.

ABBEY: Oh cuz that's exactly the same!

NOAH: I don't know –

ABBEY: No, you know what's exactly the same? His daughter crashing on your couch without permission and then having to sell your condo and giving 50 percent of it to him.

NOAH: But – sharing this land doesn't make you homeless, Abbey.

ABBEY: Neither would selling your condo.

NOAH: Ugh, God, my condo is not even on the table!

FRANK: Who says?

> *NOAH is caught off guard. Looks at FRANK. And his weapon. Beat.*

ABBEY: He's right. Tell you what, hon, you give up half your condo, and I'll keep this deal with Frank. Now whose side are you on?

NOAH: (*squirming*) Okay, you know what? Okay – it's not about sides, Abbey. And I don't think someone's kindness should depend on *others* being kind too. It shouldn't work like that. I don't think you should give money to a person on the street only if *others* are doing it.

FRANK: Hey, no one's *giving* anything to anybody – you are *returning* what your parents stole for you.

NOAH: Okay. Okay –

FRANK: Either you do that, or you are guilty of thievery yourself.

NOAH: Christ, man. And Frank: You gotta see this from our perspective, okay? You gotta recognize how bullying will only be met with – with ... And I get it: you may *feel* vulnerable if you put that down, but you gotta see how much power you carry too. You're a hunter, you know the terrain, you'd obviously take *all* the land if you could, you did already search for the Deed, so. You gotta see that from our perspective. (*beat*) Really, I just wish you guys would talk. And *listen* to each other. And maybe we could stop thinking about what we might *lose*. Or what we've *lost*. And instead think about what we might *gain*. A neighbour. A business partner, maybe. A friend.

Beat.

And fine. Yeah. You can – your Band can have half my condo too. I was gonna invest any profit from the sale into this venture here anyway, so yeah. I'm in. I'm in for the three of us working *together*. (*beat*) Everyone happy? We keep our deal on half the land. (*pointing to FRANK's gun*) You put that down, I offer half my condo, and *if* we find this fricking stupid fricking Deed, then we all live happily ever after.

Pause.

FRANK: Kid grew some balls.

NOAH: I've ... always had balls, I just ... don't like to flaunt them all over.

Beat.

FRANK: I honour you, Rock Star. Thank you, for your grace, and respect.

NOAH: Abbey. You good?

Beat.

ABBEY: On one condition –

FRANK: Here we go ...

ABBEY: You're not convicted of any wrongdoing toward my dad.

Beat.

FRANK: Interesting. I've been beaten, jailed, shot at ... But if we ever fight back or simply try to *protect* ourselves – then *we're* the savages.

Beat.

Abbey, if I'm not convicted of any wrongdoing against your dad, our agreement stands.

> *Deal? Deal. They move toward each other and shake hands.*

FRANK: And even now, even with all this ... you're still the Boss and I'm the Bitch.

ABBEY: Frank, we're *giving* you – just *giving* you half of our lives. How does that make you the Bitch?

FRANK: Because it's still your *choice*. Inherently that makes you the Boss. But I thank you, Boss. Thank you.

> *The handshake ends and FRANK puts down his weapon.*

> *Lights fade.*

▶ Go to Scene 6A, page 175

SCENE 5B

Abbey gets Frank to drop his weapon ...

Replay the last few moments ...

FRANK: She'll never give up, will she? We'll make a deal and she'll always find some way to break it. Just like her ol' man. Just like all you people.

ABBEY: Enough, Frank! I don't know how many racist comments we have to endure. Put that thing DOWN and let's get on with this!

FRANK: Don't raise that thing at me.

ABBEY: Don't.

NOAH: Guys, don't.

ABBEY: Put it down!

NOAH: Hey, we can work this out!

ABBEY: Put it down! Now!

Their guns are raised –! NOAH jumps in between.

NOAH: Whoa, whoa, whoa. You guys, this is crazy! You're being crazy – let's just TALK.

FRANK: There's no talking with *this* one.

NOAH: Hon, come on ... no one wants to end up on the front page news here, okay?!

ABBEY: I will not be *forced* into anything, Frank.

FRANK: No, no, of course not. You need to call all the shots.

ABBEY: Listen, without me, without that map, you got nothing. Less than nothing. And may I remind you that *you're* the one standing on *my* property? Pointing a gun at me?

FRANK: And you have a weapon pointed in my face.

ABBEY: I'm simply protecting myself here, Frank. If you pull that trigger, you're going away for life. If I pull the trigger, it's self-defence. I have an armed trespasser on my property.

Beat. FRANK seethes under the weight of this reality. Then, finally, he lowers his weapon. Puts it down.

ABBEY: Noah ...

ABBEY indicates for NOAH to get rid of FRANK's gun. NOAH throws it over the ledge.

FRANK: You see the way this always plays out, Drummer Boy? No matter what, I'm her bitch.

ABBEY turns to look at FRANK a moment.

ABBEY: You can't punish me for things that happened before I even existed. We can try to figure out a way to repair what happened a century ago, but attacking me now does nothing to fix what happened then. And withholding things from me only makes it worse. (*beat*) We find the Deed and we go from there.

FRANK: We had a deal.

ABBEY: You lied to me.

FRANK: Indian Giver.

Beat.

ABBEY: Let's go.

She looks up at the mountain and starts off.

Beat.

NOAH: Sorry, man. Guess I shouldn't have said anything. I just thought those teepees were cool.

Then NOAH sheepishly follows after ABBEY.

FRANK stands there a moment, re-evaluating. He takes a deep breath and looks after them.

Lights fade.

▶ **Go to Scene 6A, page 175**

ACT TWO: SCENE 5B

SCENE 5C

Frank takes Noah hostage ...

Replay the last few moments ...

FRANK: She'll never give up, will she? We'll make a deal and she'll always find some way to break it. Just like her ol' man. Just like all you people.

ABBEY: Enough, Frank! I don't know how many racist comments we have to endure. Put that thing DOWN and let's get on with this!

FRANK: Don't raise that thing at me.

ABBEY: Don't.

NOAH: Guys, don't.

ABBEY: Put it down!

NOAH: Hey, we can work this out!

ABBEY: Put it down! Now!

Their guns are raised –! NOAH jumps in between.

NOAH: Whoa, whoa, whoa. You guys this is crazy! You're being crazy – Let's just TALK.

FRANK: There is no talking with *this* one.

NOAH: Hon, come on ... No one wants to end up on the front-page news here, okay?!

FRANK suddenly has a knife up to NOAH's neck.

NOAH: Oh God! Oh God, oh my God ...

FRANK: So what is it you value more, Abbey? The land? Or your boyfriend here?

ABBEY: You're bluffing. You're not gonna do anything.

NOAH: Abbey?? Please!

FRANK: Which is it?

ABBEY: He's not gonna hurt you, Noah, he's not that stupid.

FRANK: Well, Rock Star, we know where *you* stand.

NOAH: Abbey ...!?

FRANK: And what about your dad? Where does he stand? You value *him*?

Beat.

ABBEY: Excuse me?

FRANK: You want to see him again?

Beat.

ABBEY: What are you saying?

FRANK: I'm saying if you ever want to see your dad again, you'll drop the weapon, grab the map, and take me to that Deed.

Stunned, ABBEY lets the rifle slide from her hand.

FRANK pushes NOAH aside as he picks it up.

FRANK: Now let's do this.

ABBEY stands there looking at FRANK.

ABBEY: I knew it. I knew it.

FRANK: I'd start moving if I were you.

She looks to NOAH, pulls out the map, and starts walking.

NOAH stands there trying to compose himself. He rubs his hands over his face, taking a deep breath.

NOAH: ... Frank, man ... What did you ...? How could some land be worth all of this?

FRANK: For you, land is something to be bought and sold, so you can have a nice life. For us, we are of the land. You take away our land, we cease to exist. Everything we are is connected to the land. Our language, our culture, our history, food, oxygen. That's not something you can just buy and sell. (*beat*) It's also something you'll never understand.

FRANK gives NOAH a nudge, and he follows behind ABBEY. And FRANK follows ...

▶ Go to Scene 6B, page 186

SCENE 5D

Frank steps out of hiding and offers his assistance ...

Repeat the last few moments ...

NOAH: Okay, *if* you do this, won't *you* need the gun?

ABBEY pulls out a knife. He shakes his head.

NOAH: And here I thought coming out here would be ... romantic.

ABBEY stands over NOAH, still not quite sure. NOAH sits with the rifle and his hurt leg, still in pain, looking up at ABBEY.

FRANK sits perched, hidden, considering his options.

ABBEY kneels down to NOAH.

ABBEY: I hoped it would be too.

FRANK makes a decision and walks out of the forest into the open, holding his rifle.

NOAH: What the hell?

ABBEY grabs the rifle from NOAH and points it at FRANK.

NOAH: Abbey! Don't!

FRANK does not point back.

FRANK: Easy there, little lady. Aren't you getting tired of pointing firearms at me?

ABBEY: Aren't you getting tired of being where you're not wanted?

FRANK: I may not be wanted but I'm needed. He's injured and you're racing time. (*to NOAH*) How's your leg? (*taking a look*) Oh man, that's nasty!

NOAH: The bridge fell right through!

FRANK: (*laughing*) I know, I saw.

NOAH: You saw??

FRANK: I was tailing you.

NOAH: ...?

FRANK: Here, let's clean that up ... (*off NOAH's reaction*) What?

NOAH: Nothing. Just felt like it was ... booby-trapped man.

FRANK: (*laughing*) Booby-trapped? Ha haaa, you think I ...? (*laughing again*) I like you, man. You're so ... I like you.

> *FRANK sets down his rifle and reaches into his backpack.*

ABBEY: Slowly, Frank.

FRANK: I just put down my gun. What do you think, I'm reaching for a grenade? I'm getting pine pitch. Stops the bleeding like that. Or would you rather he passes out from loss of blood?

> *ABBEY lowers her rifle.*

FRANK: Thank you.

> *FRANK sets to work on NOAH's wound.*

ABBEY: How do we know you *didn't* rig that bridge? To take us out of commission?

FRANK: Right. I don't want this land going to the Queen but you're the only one who can find the Deed. So naturally, I'm going to plunge you to your deaths before you find said Deed. Yep, I'm a criminal mastermind.

ABBEY: Fine, so you've been following us all this time just to, what, make sure we'll be okay, Florence Nightingale? What are you really after here?

FRANK: I'm concerned about your well-being. Because the quicker we get your boyfriend all fixed up, the quicker you and I can get that Deed.

NOAH: Wait, you're still going to leave me here by myself?

FRANK: Well, she can't take you with her, not in your condition.

ABBEY: I don't need to take *you* with me either.

FRANK: I don't know, Abbey. You see how dangerous it is out here. You haven't been on this land since you were a teenager. I spend every day out here. I know every nook and cranny with my eyes closed. My interests are the same as yours. I just want you to get that Deed.

ABBEY: Right, and what happens when we get there and you decide to take it at gunpoint. You want to come along, you have to leave your gun behind.

NOAH: Great, so whatever happens you *are* just leaving me here.

FRANK: Sorry, little lady, I'm afraid I don't have much reason to trust you. I think I'll hold on to my gun.

ABBEY: I have just as much reason not to trust you.

FRANK: So what were you gonna do? Just leave him here on his own? That's cold.

ABBEY: No ... I don't know ... I'm running out of time.

FRANK: (*to NOAH*) She's right, Rock star. She can't stay with you or her time runs out. She can't take you with her, you'll slow her down, and her time runs out.

NOAH: Yep, I get it, we're leaving me here.

FRANK: Nope, can't leave you here either. The bears will get you and YOUR time runs out.

NOAH: What?

FRANK: Yeah, I don't know what she's talking about – bears can smell blood from miles away.

NOAH: Wait, what!!

FRANK: Oh yeah. Their sense of smell is like two thousand times better than ours. You're like a rotting carcass right now just waiting to be eaten.

NOAH: Dude! Be serious!

FRANK: I am! Google it.

NOAH: Holy ... Christ. (*suddenly packing up*) Well get me outta here then!

FRANK: All right, Abbey. Someone needs to take Noah back and we both know it can't be you, so let's compromise. I take the Rock Star back, you get the Deed, and we rendezvous at the house. Deal?

ABBEY: Okay ... deal. Thank you ... Noah, is that okay?

NOAH: Do I have a choice?!

    A beat.

ABBEY: I'd say yes. If you ... you know ... I'd say (*nodding*).

NOAH: ... Good to know.

Beat. But **NOAH** *definitely doesn't ask now.* **ABBEY** *grabs her pack and heads off down the trail.*

FRANK: (*looking at* **NOAH**) She's a tough nut to crack, isn't she?

NOAH: She's ... different out here, that's all.

FRANK: More herself maybe. Here.

FRANK helps NOAH up and hangs his own canteen around NOAH's neck.

FRANK: Bang on that.

NOAH: Right, right, they don't like noise.

NOAH drums on his canteen as FRANK helps him hobble.

FRANK: Good, louder.

NOAH drums louder.

FRANK: (*laughing*) Good stuff, clobber that thing!

NOAH drums louder. As they exit, FRANK sings to the tune of Pink Floyd's "Another Brick in the Wall (Part 2)."

FRANK: "We don't need no ... bears around here!"

NOAH: Nice ...

FRANK: "We don't need no ... coyotes."

NOAH: Coyotes? Jesus ...

FRANK: "No bad run-ins with a cougar."

NOAH: Holy Christ ...

FRANK: "Creatures, please, leave us alone."

NOAH: Nice, "creatures" instead of "teachers."

They're off, but still singing:

FRANK: Everybody! "Hey!"

NOAH and **FRANK:** "Creatures! Please leave us alone ..."

They're gone.

▶ Go to Scene 5F.2, page 145

SCENE 5E

Abbey forges on, alone ...

Repeat the last few moments ...

NOAH: Okay, *if* you do this, won't *you* need the gun?

ABBEY pulls out a knife. He shakes his head.

NOAH: And here I thought coming out here would be ... romantic.

ABBEY stands over NOAH, still not quite sure. NOAH sits with the rifle and his hurt leg, still in pain, looking up at ABBEY.

FRANK sits perched, hidden, considering his options.

ABBEY kneels down to NOAH.

ABBEY: I hoped it would be too.

NOAH: ... Just go.

Beat.

ABBEY: You'll be fine.

NOAH: Famous last words.

ABBEY: (*showing NOAH the gun*) That's the safety. Only take it off if – you know. Trigger there.

NOAH: I know what a trigger is.

Beat.

ABBEY: Okay.

She stands ... but then stops.

ABBEY: I'd say yes. If you ... you know ... I'd say (*nodding*).

NOAH: ... Good to know.

Beat. But NOAH definitely doesn't ask now.

ABBEY: Okay. I love you.

NOAH: You too. Go if you're going. I'll be fine.

Sheepish, she goes.

After she's gone … NOAH begins to cry. And not just because his leg is in pain, which it still is. He whimpers.

FRANK – still hidden behind the tree – bows his head, not wanting to hear this.

NOAH tries to stop crying by guzzling a Hey Y'all. But then he starts crying again.

FRANK rolls his eyes and is not sure what to do. Follow ABBEY? Stay and help NOAH?

Crossfade to …

SCENE 5E.1

Abbey, hiking, sees an encroachment ...

Hiking quickly, ABBEY comes to a stop ... catching her breath, on a bit of a lookout. She looks back. Should she really continue on? She's having second thoughts. Should she go back? She consults her watch, then the map. She's suddenly confused.

ABBEY: This seems like a detour ... Why would you lead me this way?

She gets out her binoculars and scans her surroundings. Then – she sees something. She focuses in.

ABBEY: Are you kidding me?

Projected onscreen, we see what she's seeing: on a plateau in the distance, there are wooden structures, canvas tents, and teepees.

ABBEY: Now who's encroaching on who? Asking half the land ... looks like you're already taking it.

She puts her binoculars away, shakes her head, and consults her map again.

Come on, Dad; what's going on out here?

She forges onward ...

SCENE 5E.2

Frank helps Noah ...

Back by the stream. NOAH's crying has subsided. He just hugs the rifle and works on a Hey Y'all.

Still hidden behind a tree, FRANK starts to get up – making a noise in the bushes. NOAH reacts! Scared, he points the gun, thinking it's a bear.

NOAH: Oh man, oh man ... Abbey! ABBEY!!

He fumbles trying to take the safety off the gun.

Still hidden, and having some fun, FRANK intentionally makes more noise in the bushes.

NOAH: Oh man ...

FRANK now imitates the sound of a bear, huffing and gruffing, making NOAH freak out even more! But FRANK can't keep it up for laughing.

FRANK: Hey, Rock Star.

NOAH: (*blanching*) ... What the ... hell?!

FRANK: Just me.

NOAH: What the – hell! You total dick!

FRANK: (*laughing*) You done over there?

NOAH: Done? Done what? What are you –? (*embarrassed*) Yes, I'm done. How long you frickin' been there?

FRANK: (*enjoying this*) Oh ... a while.

NOAH: What the hell, man! Scared the piss outta me ...

FRANK: It's good for you. We need a little dose of fear once in a while, keeps us grounded.

>   *Beat.*

NOAH: How much did you hear?

FRANK: Oh ...

NOAH: Everything? You heard everything??

FRANK: I was following you guys.

NOAH: Oh my – what the hell, man!

FRANK: I plugged my ears when you started crying though.

NOAH: Oh man ... why didn't you –? Oh man ...

FRANK: Hey, hey. It's okay. I feel you. Your heart hurts. I feel you, dog.

> *Beat.*

FRANK: She's a tough nut to crack, isn't she?

NOAH: She's ... different out here, that's all.

FRANK: More herself maybe.

> *NOAH sulks.*

FRANK: How's your leg? (*taking a look*) Oh man, that's nasty!

NOAH: The bridge fell right through!

FRANK: (*laughing*) I know, I saw.

NOAH: You saw??

FRANK: I was tailing you.

NOAH: ...?

FRANK: Here, c'mon ... (*off NOAH's reaction*) What?

NOAH: Nothing. Just felt like it was ... booby-trapped man.

FRANK: (*laughing*) Booby-trapped? Ha haaa, you think I ...? (*laughing again*) I like you, man. You're so ... I like you. Here. C'mon, let's get you back to the house.

> *FRANK is picking up NOAH's stuff.*

NOAH: Wait. What? Why?

FRANK: Gotta tend to that foot.

NOAH: But – I'm – no, she's coming back here.

FRANK: So we'll leave her a note, you can't leave your leg like that, it's still bleeding. Also I don't know what she's talking about – bears can smell blood from miles away.

NOAH: What!!

FRANK: Oh yeah. Their sense of smell is like two thousand times better than ours. You're like a rotting carcass right now just waiting to be eaten.

NOAH: Dude! Be serious!

FRANK: I am! Google it.

NOAH: Holy ... Christ. (*suddenly packing up*) Well get me outta here then!

> *FRANK helps NOAH up. NOAH then stops.*

NOAH: Oh. Gotta leave a note.

> *NOAH bends over, writes.*
>
> *It's also projected:*
>
> GONE BACK TO HOUSE
>
> FRANK GOT ME

NOAH: Wait. "FRANK GOT ME?" Sounds like you got me hostage or something.

> *NOAH crosses out* FRANK GOT ME.
>
> *Projected:* ~~FRANK GOT ME~~

FRANK: That looks worse.

NOAH: Agh.

> *NOAH writes:* I'M FINE

FRANK: I could've forced you to write that.

NOAH: What?

FRANK: If I took you hostage, I'd *make* you write "I'M FINE" so she wouldn't panic.

> *NOAH adds:* I'M NOT HIS HOSTAGE
>
> *They look at the note.*

NOAH: Ah, man, that's worse ... Screw it, let's go.

> *FRANK helps NOAH up and hangs his own canteen around NOAH's neck.*

FRANK: Bang on that.

NOAH: Right, right, they don't like noise.

NOAH drums as FRANK helps him hobble.

FRANK: Good, louder.

NOAH drums louder.

FRANK: (*laughing*) Good stuff, clobber that thing!

NOAH drums louder. As they exit, FRANK sings to the tune of Pink Floyd's "Another Brick in the Wall (Part 2)."

FRANK: "We don't need no ... bears around here!"

NOAH: Nice ...

FRANK: "We don't need no ... coyotes."

NOAH: Coyotes? Jesus ...

FRANK: "No bad run-ins with a cougar"

NOAH: Holy Christ ...

FRANK: "Creatures, please, leave us alone."

NOAH: Nice, "creatures" instead of "teachers."

They're off, but still singing:

FRANK: Everybody! "Hey!"

NOAH and **FRANK:** "Creatures! Please leave us alone ..."

They're gone.

▶ Go to Scene 5F.2, page 145

SCENE 5F

Noah proposes to Abbey ...

Repeat the last few moments ...

NOAH: Okay, *if* you do this, won't *you* need the gun?

ABBEY pulls out a knife. He shakes his head.

NOAH: And here I thought coming out here would be ... romantic.

ABBEY stands over NOAH, still not quite sure ...

NOAH sits with the rifle and his hurt leg, still in pain, looking up at ABBEY ...

FRANK sits perched, hidden, considering his options ...

ABBEY: I hoped it would be too.

ABBEY looks at her watch. The map. Out at the land. Then down at NOAH.

ABBEY: (*to herself*) Ya know what?

She suddenly bends down and kisses NOAH. It turns into quite a passionate kiss – long awaited, some anger in there, and some desperation. The desire for abandon. To forget the worries of the world.

And then NOAH's injured leg gets in the way – and he YELPS in pain! Which stops the kiss. He wriggles around in pain and self-pity.

ABBEY looks at her watch. The map. Out at the land. Then down at NOAH.

ABBEY: Here, babe.

NOAH: What.

ABBEY: I'm taking you back.

NOAH: What??

ABBEY: Of course, of course, come on.

But that hits NOAH, and he gets all emotional. He doesn't know what to say, but he's happy.

ABBEY: C'mon.

NOAH: Babe? You're the bomb! I love you, baby.

ABBEY: I know. I love you too. Come on ...

> *She helps him and they start to hobble back ... but then*
> *NOAH stops, still emotional. He can't quite believe it. He*
> *starts looking in his backpack.*

ABBEY: What?

NOAH: One sec.

> *He roots around and then finds what he's looking for. He*
> *looks at ABBEY. Looks at their surroundings. Then a*
> *big breath.*

NOAH: Abigail Raneen Mitchell?

> *He (painfully) starts to get down on one knee –*

ABBEY: WHAT!?! Not HERE! Not NOW!

NOAH: (*painfully getting up*) No, no, yeah, yeah totally –

ABBEY: Well no, you can if ... you can if .../ Yes, sure, now!

NOAH: No, no. / No, no. It's not –

ABBEY: It's fine, it's fine!

NOAH: NO, you're RIGHT. We don't want the story of – our ... / you know, to be ...

ABBEY: Yeah. Yeah, totally. Right? Yeah?

NOAH: Yeah, yeah, it's totally dumb.

> *An awkward beat. Then she chuckles.*

ABBEY: ... I love you.

> *And she kisses him. A tender moment between them – in*
> *which she essentially says, "Yes."*

> *The lights crossfade to reveal FRANK, still spying on*
> *them: he gives a big roll of the eyes and shakes his head.*
> *But smiles.*

SCENE 5F.1

Abbey takes Noah back to house ...

Back at the house. ABBEY helps NOAH crutch into the house. They're both in darker moods now. NOAH in pain and exhausted. ABBEY's really anxious.

ABBEY: You okay? There's stuff in the bathroom, antiseptic and bandages.

NOAH: Okay, thanks, babe.

NOAH crumples onto a chair.

ABBEY: You can get it, right? And make sure to wrap it tight, and keep it elevated and iced. I'll be back as soon as I can.

NOAH: Wait ... You really think there's still time?

ABBEY: I have to try!

NOAH: Okay, okay. Bye. Be ... Be safe.

ABBEY: ... You too.

ABBEY has the rifle. She goes to leave, but then takes a breath – and turns back. She suddenly (weirdly) gets down on one knee in front of NOAH. Looks up at him.

He takes her in. She says nothing. They just stare at each other. And he gets it. And nods for her to leave.

She gets up and at the door says, intentionally:

ABBEY: I'll see you soon.

NOAH: I know.

She's gone. He watches her leave. A long breath out. He shakes his head, whimpers a bit. Then hobbles in pain off to the bathroom.

The place is unoccupied. The sound of birds.

Outside: FRANK appears near the house. He considers following ABBEY into the woods ... But then doesn't. He turns back toward the house.

SCENE 5F.2

Abbey searching alone ...

ABBEY enters, having just finished a scramble up a steep embankment. Her backpack is gone. She's tired and breathing heavily. She takes a moment to catch her breath – and looks at her watch.

A voice-over plays:

FRANK: (*VO*) "And it is the loss of our land that is the precise cause of our impoverishment. Indigenous Lands today account for only 0.2 percent of Canada. The settler share is the remaining 99.8 percent. With this distribution, you don't have to have a doctorate in economics to understand who will be rich and who will be poor."

ABBEY consults her equipment. It looks like she's close to the spot. She tries to narrow it down.

She finds and inspects a moss-covered section of an embankment. She reaches and grabs at it. She opens a sort of large cellar door that's been camouflaged with moss, vines, and branches. The door reveals the opening to a cave or tunnel that goes into the side of the mountain.

ABBEY: Jesus ...

FRANK: (*VO*) "And when we speak of reclaiming a measure of control over our lands, we obviously don't mean throwing Canadians off of it and sending them back to the countries they came from. All Canadians have acquired a basic human right to be here."

ABBEY looks in, gets out a flashlight. She looks in with the light, then is about to enter the darkness – but hears a caw from above. She looks up at some birds. Then she disappears inside the tunnel with the flashlight ...

The land is unoccupied. Birds caw above.

SCENE 5F.3

Frank and Noah (injured) back at the house

Back at the house: FRANK is standing at the window, looking out, gun in hand.

FRANK: (*VO*) "At present, we're asking for the right to protect our Aboriginal Title Land, to have a say on any development on our lands, and when we find the land can be safely and sustainably developed, to be compensated for the wealth it generates ..."

NOAH is seated, leg up on ice, reading aloud from FRANK's book:

NOAH: "... wealth it generates. There is room on this land for all of us and there must also be, after centuries of struggle, room for justice for Indigenous Peoples."

FRANK: Boom! Mic drop!

Startled, NOAH jumps out of his seat! FRANK laughs.

FRANK: End of chapter one.

NOAH: Okay: you've already read this book, now you're just having me read it?

FRANK: That's right. I wouldn't make you read a bad book! What do you think?

NOAH: It's cool. I think a lot of people are ... mystified, you know. About what Indigenous people actually *want*. Like, practically. And that states it pretty clearly. It's cool.

FRANK: Cool.

NOAH: Cuz you know, like, what's really wrong with Indigenous people getting some control? It's like when the owner of an apartment building changes, nothing has to change for the *tenants*. It's just that First Nations would have agency, finally, over how it's all managed. I think that's a *good* thing. Especially for, like, climate change and all that?

FRANK: Cool. So does that mean I can have your condo?

NOAH chuckles.

FRANK: I'd still let you live there. But instead of paying a mortgage to a bank, you pay me rent.

NOAH: ... Ha, yeah, no no, that's different. I give you my condo, I lose my investment. It's not just a place to live, it's ... No, what I'm talking about is the development companies, the real-estate companies, I'd love it if they were all First Nations.

FRANK: Oh yeah, why's that?

NOAH: Like, justice? Balance of scales? And maybe they'd all have, like, compost pickup. Energy-efficient windows.

FRANK: Right, because they're managed by Indians? It really does amaze me how naive you are.

FRANK looks out the window again.

FRANK: She's cutting it close out there.

NOAH: You think she's okay? Should we go ...?

FRANK: Where?

Beat. NOAH crutches over to the window too, looks out, anxious.

NOAH: And where are the cops? It's been at least a few ... hours. (*catching himself*)

FRANK: It's a long journey. Maybe they got ... held up.

NOAH: Christ, this frickin' place.

Beat.

FRANK: So what's your angle out here, Rock Star? You really the type to live this far away from the action?

NOAH: Yeah, I'm ... considering it. We're getting priced out of the city. My plan was actually – if all went well out here – to propose to Abbey this week, then sell my condo to invest in the resort. Cuz she still doesn't know how she's gonna pay for all of it, and take care of her parents.

FRANK: So you're invested too then.

NOAH: Well ... not technically yet.

Beat.

NOAH: And you? What are *you* really aiming for? I mean, you already said you want *half* the land. Why?

FRANK: *Why?*

NOAH: Yeah, what would you ... like, do, with it. If you had it.

FRANK: Can't it just simply exist?

NOAH: ... Come on, man. It's worth a ton of money, what would you do with it?

FRANK: We'd sell a portion to make a quick buck so we can get some housing repairs on our rez. My daughter has lung problems cuz of the mould in our place and now she's pregnant and my grandkid's gotta live with that. So, crucial housing renos – which the government is *not* paying for, by the way. Despite the stereotype that we get "free houses." And then some cash for the Band's education fund. Like, for my other daughter who got accepted into uni but can't afford to live there – again, despite the stereotype that our schooling is "paid for." Then we'd try to rent some of the land so we have sustainable, long-term income. And then some of it we keep for wildlife.

NOAH: Like a preserve?

FRANK: Sure.

NOAH: Sounds kinda colonial. Dividing land, some for money, some for wildlife.

FRANK: Yeah well, what choice do we have?

NOAH: Okay, so ... if you had your *ideal* situation. What would it be?

FRANK: Ideally? We're so far away from that, Rock Star ... ideals are for dreamers.

NOAH: What, you can't dream?

FRANK: ... Okay. Yeah, okay: ideally ... you and everyone like you *disappear*, cease to exist – poof! (*snapping his fingers*) – and all the land goes back to me and my people.

NOAH: *All* of it?

FRANK: Ideally, yeah. That's reconciliation, Rock Star.

NOAH: We can't just disappear.

FRANK: Why not?

NOAH: You think –? Abbey's not gonna do that, man. She'd fight you, all the ranchers would fight you. You're a smart guy – you know we're not going anywhere. For better or worse this country is way past the point of no return. So what would your ideal be for ALL concerned.

FRANK: Oh, for ALL concerned. You should've said so! Then yeah, ideally, she comes back with that Deed and you two are honourable and trustworthy. We work out a land-sharing agreement where we're all just happy and hunky-dory and seeing rainbows. Bla bla bla.

Beat.

NOAH: Land-sharing agreement? Neat. (*beat*) See? That wasn't so bad. That's actually kind of ... good. Right? Cuz it means we'd be committed to making *each other* happy. That's like ... *that's* ...

FRANK: But in that scenario we'd have to let go of over 150 years of occupation and genocide, Rock Star. We don't get our languages back, our ceremonies, our kids, our way of life. We just ... forgive it all.

Beat.

NOAH: But isn't that ... when it comes down to it ... the only way?

FRANK: Only if that forgiveness is earned. For centuries we've been told to "forgive and move on," "assimilate," "you have to get over it, that's the only way." "Forget your cousin who went missing." "Forgive the guy who punched your kid in the side of the head." "Forgive centuries worth of genocide"? No – you want us to *forgive*? You need to *earn* that forgiveness.

NOAH: But I ... me and Abbey, her dad? ... we weren't there, we didn't do all of that. I'm just me. I was just ... born.

FRANK: Hey, me too, man. Like you, I was just ... born. I didn't ask for this.

Beat.

FRANK: Do me a favour. You wanted to know my solution. I want to know yours. What you think is the appropriate response to genocide.

NOAH: Frank ... I can't answer that ... I know we have to start somewhere, but –

FRANK: Right. And isn't this property somewhere?

ABBEY is in the doorway.

ABBEY: Frank.

FRANK turns. A tense beat. She comes into the house. Slowly puts down her bag. Looks at them. At the situation. They watch her, unsure of what she found out there. Then:

ABBEY: Is this what you did to my dad too?

FRANK: ... What do you mean?

Beat.

FRANK: What happened out there?

Beat.

FRANK: Did you find the Deed? Cuz if you did, you've got about twenty minutes before you have to leave.

ABBEY: Have a seat.

FRANK: (*a skeptical beat*) What'd you find out there?

ABBEY has – or grabs – the rifle. Not pointed. But she has it.

ABBEY: Have a seat, Frank, please.

NOAH: Um, Ab. We *were* just talking and actually he said something really neat. This term "land-sharing" –

She suddenly slams the gun into the side of FRANK's head.

FRANK: Agh –!

NOAH: Ho – whoa!

ABBEY: I said, sit down! (*forcing FRANK into the chair*)

FRANK: Okay, okay!

NOAH: Abbey – Abbey – Jesus Christ! What the / hell!?

ABBEY: Back off, Noah!

NOAH: Okay, okay. Okay, okay ... oh my God ...

She stands over FRANK – seething with anger and pain – holding herself back from either collapsing in tears or beating FRANK to death.

▶ Go to Scene 6C, page 196

SCENE 5G

Frank gets his way, and they all search for the Deed ...

Repeat the last few moments ...

ABBEY: You're bluffing.

FRANK: (*shrugging*) You and your dad have stated your case. I've stated mine. Unless you want to believe that's just rabbit blood?

Beat. ABBEY looks at the stain on the floor ... then looks back at FRANK. She's shaking.

She suddenly grabs the rifle – and holds it to FRANK's head.

NOAH: Abbey!!

FRANK: Do it! And you'll never see your dad again.

A violent pause.

NOAH: Abbey. This is our future. Please think about our future. This is a human life.

Another beat.

FRANK: You know there's only one way out of this.

NOAH: Shut up. There's never just one way to handle anything.

Then ABBEY suddenly howls in anger. She hoists the rifle over her head to hit him – but can't.

Blackout. A voice-over:

FRANK: (*VO*) "And it is the loss of our land that is the precise cause of our impoverishment. Indigenous Lands today account for only 0.2 percent of Canada. The settler share is the remaining 99.8 percent. With this distribution, you don't have to have a doctorate in economics to understand who will be rich and who will be poor ..."

SCENE 5G.1

All search, Frank with the gun

The map is projected on the screen. It shows the route the trio has travelled so far.

FRANK: (*VO*) "And when we speak of reclaiming a measure of control over our lands, we obviously do not mean throwing Canadians off of it and sending them back to the countries they came from. All Canadians have acquired a basic human right to be here."

Lights rise on the land. Expansive. The trees massive.

"At present, we are asking for the right to protect our Aboriginal Title Land, to have a say on any development on our lands, and when we find the land can be safely and sustainably developed, to be compensated for the wealth it generates."

ABBEY hikes with GPS and compass in hand. She is flanked by NOAH and FRANK following close behind. FRANK has his rifle. As they hike, NOAH reads aloud from FRANK's copy of Unsettling Canada.

NOAH: "... for the wealth it generates. There is room on this land for all of us and there must also be, after centuries of struggle, room for justice for Indigenous Peoples."

FRANK: Boom! Mic drop! End of chapter one. You're getting good at that, reading and walking.

NOAH: Okay: you've already read this book, now you're just making us read it?

FRANK: That's right. I wouldn't make you read a bad book!

They're hiking up an incline now: ABBEY in front, following her map and compass; NOAH second; and FRANK third, gun still in hand.

FRANK: Shh-shh. (*stopping*)

NOAH: (*scared*) What? (*really, really scared and hiding behind FRANK*) Where, what is it, what, where??

FRANK: ... Squirrel.

NOAH: Oh ... Jesus ...

FRANK stands looking at the squirrel. Silence. Then the squirrel chitters.

ABBEY: (*confused*) Uhh ... looks like we have to scramble up these rocks.

FRANK: Where we headin' there?

He goes to look at the map, but ABBEY moves it –

ABBEY: Just up, over that a ways. But this seems like a detour.

ABBEY stands on a ledge, looking out.

NOAH's bag is off right away, and he proceeds to dig into his pack. FRANK raises his gun.

FRANK: Ah ah –

Scared, NOAH slowly pulls from his backpack ... a Hey Y'all. FRANK relaxes on the gun. Making sure to stay congenial, FRANK looks at his watch.

FRANK: Making good time. Depending what happens up there. (*to ABBEY*) You doing okay?

ABBEY: I'm fine.

FRANK: All right, ready when you are.

ABBEY: (*pointing over the horizon*) What's that?

FRANK looks. NOAH takes the binoculars. We see projected what he's seeing: a small camp of teepees and wooden structures on the flatlands.

NOAH: Looks like a camp. Like, teepees? A Longhouse maybe? Is that your reserve?

FRANK looks ... but doesn't answer.

ABBEY: That's not on reserve. That's on our property. (*to FRANK*) What is all that?

FRANK: It's uh ... Yeah, we uh ...

ABBEY: Have you guys set up camp on our property? Is that what I'm seeing?

FRANK: Okay, Abbey, / calm down –

ABBEY: Frank, *please* tell me that's not what I'm seeing. Please tell me you haven't *already* occupied a portion of our land.

FRANK: We've been using those flatlands for thousands of years / and –

ABBEY: Oh spare me the history. *Now*, Frank, now. What are you doing there *now*.

FRANK: Your Dad gave us permission –

ABBEY: Did he.

FRANK: He said we could set up a site out there –

ABBEY: Okay, and do you have that in writing somewhere?

FRANK: I have a handshake deal.

ABBEY: And why am I just learning about this now?

FRANK: I didn't wanna … fan the flames.

ABBEY: I'm guessing that's where my dad would find you guys trespassing all the time.

FRANK: Here we go … trespassing … on our own / land.

ABBEY: I remember. He said you guys would go out there trying to find evidence of an old village site. Because if you proved there was one, that'd help your case for a land claim. Your claim to *all* the land around here; the town, *our* property – everything.

NOAH: This doesn't / sound good dude –

ABBEY: My dad would call the cops, but you'd eventually come back. So is that what I'm seeing out there? An excavation, a camp?

FRANK: … We're not – Okay, we're not just there to prove – These are our traditional hunting and gathering grounds. And your dad understood that.

ABBEY: Really. So why'd he leave this – coded for *me*?

> Beat. **ABBEY**, now confident, has a new idea.

ABBEY: So what's the plan, Frank?

NOAH: Uhhhh, Abbey ... don't, we don't need to know his plan. I'd rather be blissfully unaware actually.

FRANK: The plan is: You grab that map and keep walking. Now.

ABBEY: And then what?

NOAH: Abbey, don't.

ABBEY: Even if we do find the Deed and you get back safely and end up with the rights to all of our land, I don't see how there's any way you're not spending the rest of your life in prison. And if you've done something to my dad ... You don't see, I don't know, an angry mob of ranchers taking some sort of vigilante justice?

FRANK: Oh sure. The battle will rage on. But I'll have secured this land. That'll be final. I won't have waited for some frickin' land claim to be "approved." For "permission" to have access to our own land. But taken it. Back. What is rightfully ours.

ABBEY: Taking one for the team then, are ya? So you're a hero?

FRANK: I never said that.

ABBEY: Gotta make your daughters proud? Haven't done one thing in your life to make them proud? Something like that?

FRANK: Start walkin', Abbey, and shut the hell up.

ABBEY: Oh, wasn't aware that was part of the deal. Or here's a deal: Equal partnership. Fifty-fifty. A true collaboration, that's what your book said, didn't it?

FRANK: Ahhh, so the tables have turned and now *you're* begging for half. Nice. And that's what you think you deserve, do ya? You think that's what all settlers, your colonial government – the bringers of *genocide* – that's what they deserve? Fifty-fifty? Really??

ABBEY: Don't make it – It's just me and you here, Frank.

NOAH: ... And me.

FRANK: It's not, though, sister. We bring with us everyone that came before, all our Ancestors. They're with us here, right now. And we set the table for everyone to come.

ABBEY: It's just you and me here.

Beat.

NOAH: And ...

ABBEY: And far as I can tell: you need me, "your guide." Without me, without this map, you get nothing. Less than nothing.

Beat.

NOAH: She does have you there, man. I think she's got you there.

FRANK: You're willing to give up your dad for some land? Then yeah, I guess it depends what you value more. The land ... or your loved ones.

He points the gun at NOAH.

NOAH: Whoa, whoa! Holy – whoa, back up here ... Holy man. Dude. Frank. Abbey? Dude.

Beat.

NOAH: Abbey? Abbey, hon, please, obviously, just do as he says.

FRANK: Walk.

ABBEY stays put.

NOAH: Abbey!

ABBEY: He's not gonna do anything, Noah. He's bluffing about my dad, and he's bluffing –

Gunshot. NOAH screams!

NOAH: Ah Christ! Oh Christ! Holy ...!

The bullet has ricocheted off the ground at NOAH's feet.
FRANK takes aim at NOAH again.

ABBEY: Okay! Okay! Stop! I'll go. I'll go.

And ABBEY starts walking. FRANK lowers his gun.
NOAH cries a little.

NOAH: Jesus, man. I think I peed my pants. (*beat*) I think I peed my pants, man.

FRANK: Let's go.

NOAH walks ... but then turns back, grows some balls.

NOAH: ... Frank, man ... Jesus ... How could some land be worth all of this?

FRANK: For you, land is something to be bought and sold, so you can have a nice life. For us, we are of the land. You take away our land, we cease to exist. Everything we are is connected to the land. Our language, our culture, our history, food, oxygen. That's not something you can just buy and sell. (*beat*) It's also something you'll never understand.

FRANK motions with his gun, and NOAH starts walking.

▶ Go to Scene 6B, page 186

SCENE 5H

Abbey and Noah go to the boat ...

Repeat the last few moments ...

ABBEY: You're bluffing.

FRANK: (*shrugs*) You and your dad have stated your case. I've stated mine. Unless you want to believe that's just rabbit blood?

ABBEY looks at the stain on the floor ... then looks back at FRANK. She's shaking.

She suddenly grabs the rifle – and holds it to FRANK's head.

NOAH: Abbey!!

FRANK: Do it! And you'll never see your dad again.

A violent pause.

NOAH: Abbey. This is our future. Please think about our future. This is a human life.

Another beat.

FRANK: You know there's only one way out of this.

NOAH: Shut up. There's never just one way to handle anything. (*beat*) Abbey, let's go. We need to call this in, call the authorities, and deal with this in the right way. (*beat*) Come on. This is our future we're talking about, babe. Whatever's happened out here, we're not – vigilantes.

NOAH goes over, and slowly takes the gun from ABBEY.

Lights fade over the sound of a motor boat.

SCENE 5H.1

The riverbank ...

We hear the sound of the motor boat getting closer and closer, then cutting out. Lights snap up.

ABBEY and NOAH are on the boat, docked at the riverside. NOAH has the rifle.

ABBEY holds the map. She gets out of the boat, back onto land.

NOAH: I'm so sorry, hon. I'm so sorry.

ABBEY: Stop apologizing, it's not your fault.

NOAH: But it is, though! It was *me* who wanted to spend a couple nights in a hotel first. It was *me* who wanted to make sure this was even legal and go call this in. So now what was supposed to take three days we have to do in less than, like, twelve hours!

ABBEY: Right. So can we stop wasting time and go?

But NOAH doesn't leave the boat.

ABBEY: What.

NOAH: It's just ... When the cops get here, what are they gonna, like, do to him?

ABBEY: Noah, we just found out he was one of the guys who put my dad in a coma, now he's probably got him tied up somewhere – or worse – and you're worried what the cops are gonna do?

NOAH: No, I'm worried about all this ... escalating. I mean, "Eye for an eye makes ..." – you know.

ABBEY: Do you want me to go without you? Is that what you want? Cuz I can. I will.

NOAH: What? No. Well ... No, no I can't let you go out there alone.

ABBEY: Then let's go.

She puts down the rifle to help him with his pack.

ABBEY: And God, what do you have in here? You better not be bringing Hey Y'all. We need to travel light.

FRANK quickly steps out of the woods – with his own rifle in hand.

NOAH: Holy … Christ …!! Oh man. Oh man, oh my God –

FRANK: Hey, hey, HEY –

He has the rifle trained on ABBEY, who was attempting to retrieve her own rifle. But she's pinned.

Beat.

FRANK: Hey, Drummer Boy: next time you tie someone up, don't leave their hands free so they can "read." No matter how good the book might be.

NOAH: Oh my God, it *is* all my fault! Frank, I'm begging you … she's all I have, man … Take anything you want, just don't hurt her, please, I'm begging you! I'm begging you …

ABBEY: He's not gonna hurt me, Noah. He's not that stupid. He needs me. He needs this map.

Beat.

ABBEY: So what's your plan, Frank?

NOAH: Abbey … don't, we don't need to know his plan. I'd rather be blissfully unaware actually.

FRANK: The plan is: You take that map, and start walking. Now.

ABBEY: And then what?

NOAH: Abbey, don't.

ABBEY: Even if we do find the Deed and you get back safely and end up with the rights to our land, I don't see how you're not spending the rest of your life in prison. And if you've done something to my dad, you don't see, I don't know, an angry mob of ranchers taking some sort of vigilante justice?

FRANK: Oh sure. The battle will rage on. But I'll have secured this land. That'll be final. I won't have waited for some frickin' land claim to be "approved." For "permission" to have access to our own land. But taken it. Back. What is rightfully ours.

ABBEY: Taking one for the team then, are ya? So you're a hero?

FRANK: I never said that.

ABBEY: Gotta make your daughters proud? Haven't done one thing in your whole life to make them proud? Something like that?

FRANK: Start walkin', Abbey, and shut the hell up.

ABBEY: Shut up? Sure thing. Wasn't aware that was part of the deal ...

ABBEY grabs the map and starts walking. FRANK motions with his gun, and NOAH starts walking ...

As lights fade, a voice-over:

FRANK: (*vo*) "And it is the loss of our land that is the precise cause of our impoverishment. Indigenous Lands today account for only 0.2 percent of Canada. The settler share is the remaining 99.8 percent. With this distribution, you don't have to have a doctorate in economics to understand who will be rich and who will be poor ..."

SCENE 5H.2

All searching, Frank with gun

The map is projected on the screen. It shows the route the trio has travelled so far.

FRANK: (*VO*) "And when we speak of reclaiming a measure of control over our lands, we obviously do not mean throwing Canadians off of it and sending them back to the countries they came from. All Canadians have acquired a basic human right to be here."

Lights rise on the land. Expansive. The trees massive.

"At present, we are asking for the right to protect our Aboriginal Title Land, to have a say on any development on our lands, and when we find the land can be safely and sustainably developed, to be compensated for the wealth it generates."

ABBEY hikes with GPS and compass in hand. She is flanked by NOAH and FRANK following close behind. FRANK has his rifle. As they hike, NOAH reads aloud from FRANK's copy of Unsettling Canada.

NOAH: "… for the wealth it generates. There is room on this land for all of us and there must also be, after centuries of struggle, room for justice for Indigenous Peoples."

FRANK: Boom! Mic drop! End of chapter one. You're getting good at that, reading and walking.

NOAH: Okay: you've already read this book, now you're just making us read it?

FRANK: That's right. I wouldn't make you read a bad book!

They're hiking up an incline now: ABBEY in front, following her map and compass; NOAH second; and FRANK third, gun still in hand.

FRANK: Shh-shh. (*stopping*)

NOAH: (*scared*) What? (*really, really scared and hiding behind FRANK*) Where, what is it, what, where??

FRANK: … Squirrel.

NOAH: Oh … Jesus …

FRANK stands looking at the squirrel. Silence. Then the squirrel chitters.

ABBEY: (*confused*) Uhh ... looks like we have to scramble up these rocks.

FRANK: Where we headin' there?

He goes to look at the map, but ABBEY moves it –

ABBEY: Just up, over that a ways. But this seems like a detour. Why would he lead me this way?

ABBEY stands on a ledge, looking out.

NOAH's bag is off right away, and he proceeds to dig into his pack. FRANK raises his gun.

FRANK: Ah ah –

Scared, NOAH slowly pulls from his backpack ... a Hey Y'all. FRANK relaxes on the gun.

ABBEY: (*to FRANK, pointing over the horizon*) What's that?

FRANK looks. NOAH takes the binoculars. We see projected what he's seeing: a small camp of teepees and wooden structures on the flatlands.

NOAH: Looks like a camp. Like, teepees? A Longhouse, maybe? Cool. Is that your reserve?

FRANK looks ... but doesn't answer.

ABBEY: That's not on reserve. That's on our property. (*to FRANK*) What is all that?

FRANK: It's uh ... Yeah, we uh ...

ABBEY: Have you guys set up camp on our property? Is that what I'm seeing?

FRANK: Okay, Abbey, / calm down –

ABBEY: Frank, *please* tell me that's not what I'm seeing. Please tell me you haven't *already* occupied a portion of our land.

FRANK: We've been using those flatlands for thousands of years / and –

ABBEY: Oh spare me the history. *Now*, Frank, now. What are you doing there *now*.

FRANK: Your dad gave us permission –

ABBEY: Did he.

FRANK: He said we could set up a site out there –

ABBEY: Okay, and do you have that in writing somewhere?

FRANK: I have a handshake deal –

ABBEY: And why am I just learning about this now?

FRANK: I didn't wanna … fan the flames.

ABBEY: I'm guessing that's where my dad would find you guys trespassing all the time.

FRANK: Here we go … trespassing … on our own / land.

ABBEY: I remember. He said you guys would go out there trying to find evidence of an old village site. Because if you proved there was one, that'd help your case for a land claim. Your claim to *all* the land around here; the town, *our* property – everything.

NOAH: This doesn't / sound good, dude –

ABBEY: My dad would call the cops, but you'd eventually come back. So is that what I'm seeing out there? An excavation, a camp?

FRANK: … We're not – Okay, we're not just there to prove – These are our traditional hunting and gathering grounds. And your dad understood that.

ABBEY: Really. So why'd he leave this – coded for *me*?

> *Gunshot! ABBEY and NOAH jump with fear. But FRANK has simply shot his gun into the air. He cocks it again.*

FRANK: Clock is ticking, Abbey. You wasted time going back on that boat, let's not waste anymore. Shall we?

> *And ABBEY starts walking. FRANK lowers his gun. NOAH cries a little …*

NOAH: Jesus man. I think I peed my pants. I think I peed my pants, man.

FRANK: Let's go.

NOAH walks ... but then turns back, grows some balls.

NOAH: What *is* all this for? Really. How could some land be worth all of this?

FRANK: For you, land is something to be bought and sold, so you can have a nice life. For us, we are of the land. You take away our land, we cease to exist. Everything we are is connected to the land. Our language, our culture, our history, food, oxygen. That's not something you can just buy and sell. (*beat*) It's also something you'll never understand.

FRANK motions with his gun, and NOAH starts walking.

▶ **Go to Scene 6B, page 186**

SCENE 5I

Abbey and Noah leave Frank tied up and search for the Deed themselves

Repeat the last few moments ...

ABBEY: You're bluffing.

FRANK: (*shrugging*) You and your dad have stated your case. I've stated mine. Unless you want to believe that's just rabbit blood?

Beat. ABBEY looks at the stain on the floor ... then looks back at FRANK. She's shaking.

ABBEY: Nope. You didn't convince me.

NOAH: Uh ... I'm a little convinced. We should maybe *consider* he knows where your dad is.

ABBEY: No. This is the last-ditch effort of a desperate man. If he knew where my dad was he would have played that card ages ago.

FRANK: You're willing to take that chance? I gotta hand it to you, Abbey. You're more cold-hearted than I thought. I feel for ya, Rock Star.

ABBEY: I'm not cold-hearted. I just know a liar when I see one. Noah, let's go.

ABBEY starts packing her stuff. NOAH starts packing as well. He turns to FRANK while he packs.

NOAH: I'm really, very sorry. She isn't normally like this. It must be the stress of the whole dad gone thing ... (*beat*) But really, do you know where he is?

FRANK, tied up, lifts his book and begins reading.

NOAH: Right, you wouldn't tell me if you did ... Man, I hope you *are* bluffing ... Cuz if not ... (*a threatening pose, then*) Are those ropes too tight? Like, is your circulation okay?

ABBEY: Noah!!

NOAH jumps and grabs his pack and follows ABBEY out the door.

FRANK reads for a moment more ... until he's sure they're gone. Then he drops his book on the floor and starts trying to shimmy out of the ropes.

SCENE 51.1

Wind in the trees.

*The map is projected, and it tracks **ABBEY** and **NOAH**'s progress as they search for the Deed. It's clear that they are now crossing a bridge over a stream.*

*Offstage, **NOAH** yelps in pain –*

NOAH: Ah – ah! I can't – I can't –

*ABBEY enters, helping **NOAH** – he's limping. His pant leg is torn up, his leg is bleeding profusely, and he clearly can't put weight on his foot. He's in tons of pain.*

ABBEY: Here, sit down, sit down. Lemme see.

NOAH: (*making pain noises*) What the hell, man! Just fell right through.

ABBEY: It's an old bridge.

NOAH: No, man, that was ... I don't know what that was. (*pain noises*)

ABBEY: (*wincing*) You must've sliced it all the way up.

*More sounds of pain from **NOAH** while **ABBEY** tries to nurse him. She gets out a first-aid kit and a gauze bandage.*

NOAH: I swear, it fell through like it was just – (*pain noise*) Oh man ... I can't look ...

ABBEY: Then don't.

She starts wiping his leg, then wrapping it in gauze. NOAH howls.

NOAH: Ah, piss ... I'm sorry, babe.

ABBEY: It wasn't your fault. Could've happened to me ...

NOAH: Yeah, but it didn't. (*pain noise*) We got any painkillers?

ABBEY: Yeah, just let me do this first. Can you – put weight on it?

NOAH: Ab ... just –

ABBEY: Did you sprain it or is it just cut?

He stands a bit, tries to put weight on it – yelps in pain, and falls back down.

NOAH: I'm sorry, I'm sorry. I twisted it or – (*more pain*)

ABBEY: Okay, lift your leg, here. That okay?

NOAH: Yeah … (*pain noise*)

She finishes wrapping his leg, and as they wait for the bleeding to stop, she looks around, thinking.

ABBEY: Dammit …

A beat. ***ABBEY*** *stands, considering her options, then looks at her map.*

NOAH: Painkillers?

ABBEY: Right, yeah, yeah.

She gets him painkillers.

NOAH: Can you grab me a drink too? I got cans in my bag.

ABBEY: You brought Hey Y'all?

NOAH *makes more pain sounds. She gets him a Hey Y'all.*

ABBEY: They're warm.

He reaches for the can, pops it, and gulps almost the whole thing back.

ABBEY *takes the map and the* GPS *to the river, looking out. She takes a big stress breath.*

NOAH: How far are we?

She looks at the map and the GPS.

NOAH: Do you know where we are? (*pain noise*) Babe, do you even know where we are?!

ABBEY: Yes! Yes. I haven't done this since I was a kid, and now doing it by code while I haven't slept? It's not easy.

NOAH: Okay, roughly: are we halfway, more than half, what?

ABBEY: Roughly … another hour there? Three back? And that's at a good clip.

NOAH: ... I'm sorry.

ABBEY: It's not your fault.

NOAH: Maybe I can –

He tries to stand – yelps.

NOAH: No, no.

ABBEY: You sprained it, you can't walk on it.

NOAH: I could use a crutch or something, like a branch as a crutch.

ABBEY: We have to climb a mountain, scramble up rocks ...

NOAH: Well, what do we do?

NOAH continues to wince in pain. He checks if his bleeding has stopped, which it hasn't.

ABBEY: I have to go by myself.

NOAH: You're gonna leave me? There's bears and coyotes out here!

ABBEY: Oh ... they're not gonna do anything.

NOAH: Jesus – you don't know that!

ABBEY: They're not like sharks, they don't smell blood.

NOAH: I really don't find that funny.

ABBEY: I didn't mean it to be funny. I'd leave you the gun.

NOAH: Oh my God, this is ... Oh God, this is ... NOT how I pictured this trip! Let's go back, babe. I'm way over my head here. This is ... I gotta go back. You gotta take me back. I need anaesthetic, I need enough gauze to stop this – I need ice. / I need a doctor.

ABBEY: Calm down –

NOAH: I haven't slept, / I'm panicked, and now I'm, I'm –

ABBEY: Honey, calm down, calm down, you're in shock, but you're gonna be / okay.

NOAH: No – can I just say? SCREW your dad. SCREW him. And screw THIS. AAAAAAAAGGHH! *Screw* this land. (*beat*) And this is my *kick foot*, I play bass drum with this foot. It better not be permanently damaged!

Beat.

ABBEY: You done?

ABBEY kneels down to NOAH, gentle now, caring.

ABBEY: If I bring you back, hon, I'd be cutting it really close.

NOAH: This is ridiculous.

ABBEY: So either I leave you here, or you go back on your own.

NOAH: I can't go back on my own! I can't walk! I have no idea where I am!

ABBEY: I'll draw you a map.

NOAH: Draw me –? Christ, I'll just stay here. Babe, I'll just stay here. It's fine. It's fine.

But it's clearly not fine. ABBEY looks at her watch, then the map. She considers, shakes her head – mad and frustrated. She paces. She takes up the rifle again. Pacing. Thinking.

ABBEY: I can't let this land go for nothing. I can't. It's in my family. My blood.

NOAH: Babe, I know it's important. Worth a helluva lot of money but … I don't know, maybe this is … like … a / sign.

ABBEY: I don't believe in signs.

NOAH: Maybe you should just – *think* about letting it go.

ABBEY: To the Queen?

NOAH: That's gotta be – reversible somehow. Maybe you could, you know, convince your dad.

ABBEY: If I see him again. (*beat*) I gotta think worst-case scenario. But – we're not there yet. And it's gonna be easy for me. We used to camp out on the land all the time, go on adventures. So what I really hope is he's just testing me. It's a test of whether I *deserve* the land I think.

NOAH: And that's more important to you than, say … I don't know … my *life*?

ABBEY: Honey …

NOAH: No, that's fine. At least I know where I stand. That's good cuz I was actually thinking of …

ABBEY: ... What?

NOAH: Oh no, I was just actually thinking of *asking you something* on this trip – but now? Ho ho, not so sure! Now that I know where your priorities really lie.

ABBEY: ... You were?

He motions a gesture of frustrated defeat. A beat.

ABBEY: But hon. I'm trying to be practical. For us. Do you really think your tours are gonna sustain us? Retirement, adoption, kids' education?

NOAH: I can't have this conversation / right now.

ABBEY: I've put all my eggs into this basket.

NOAH: I know.

ABBEY: We have legal bills, what's gonna cover that – your new / album?

NOAH: I know, / I know.

ABBEY: I love you, of course I do. And I wouldn't leave you stranded. I'd leave you the gun. I'd show you how to shoot it. You'd have food, water. Alcohol. I'd be back in like two hours. We'd be in town and into a clinic before you know it. Jacuzzi in a hotel tonight even ...

NOAH: Jesus. Jesus. Jesus! Whatever, there's no winning with you. Okay, *if* you do this, won't *you* need the gun?

She pulls out a knife. He shakes his head.

NOAH: And here I thought coming out here would be ... romantic.

ABBEY stands over NOAH, still not quite sure.

NOAH sits with the rifle and his hurt leg, looking up at ABBEY.

ABBEY kneels down to NOAH.

ABBEY: I hoped it would be too.

NOAH: ... Just go.

Beat.

ABBEY: You'll be fine.

NOAH: Famous last words.

ABBEY: That's the safety. Only take it off if – you know. Trigger there.

NOAH: I know what a trigger is.

Beat.

ABBEY: Okay.

She stands ... but then stops.

ABBEY: I'd say yes. If you ... you know ... I'd say (*nodding*).

NOAH: ... Good to know.

Beat. But he definitely doesn't ask now.

ABBEY: Okay. I love you.

NOAH: You too. Go if you're going. I'll be fine.

Sheepish, she goes.

After she's gone ... NOAH begins to cry. And not just because his leg is in pain, which it still is. He whimpers.

NOAH tries to stop crying by guzzling a Hey Y'all. But then he starts crying again.

Crossfade to ...

SCENE 51.2

Abbey finds the spot ...

ABBEY enters, having just finished a scramble up a steep embankment. Her backpack is gone. She's tired and breathing heavily. She takes a moment to catch her breath – and looks at her watch.

FRANK: (*VO*) "And it is the loss of our land that is the precise cause of our impoverishment. Indigenous Lands today account for only 0.2 percent of Canada. The settler share is the remaining 99.8 percent. With this distribution, you don't have to have a doctorate in economics to understand who will be rich and who will be poor."

ABBEY consults her equipment. It looks like she's close to the spot. She tries to narrow it down.

She finds and inspects a moss-covered section of an embankment. She reaches and grabs at it. She opens a sort of large cellar door that's been camouflaged with moss, vines, and branches. The door reveals the opening to a cave or tunnel that goes into the side of the mountain.

ABBEY: Jesus ...

FRANK: (*VO*) "And when we speak of reclaiming a measure of control over our lands, we obviously don't mean throwing Canadians off of it and sending them back to the countries they came from. All Canadians have acquired a basic human right to be here."

ABBEY looks in, gets out a flashlight. She looks in with the light, then is about to enter the darkness – but hears a caw from above. She looks up at some birds. Then she disappears inside the tunnel with the flashlight ...

The land is unoccupied. Birds caw above. The wind shakes the leaves.

SCENE 51.3

Back at the cabin

FRANK: (*VO*) "At present, we're asking for the right to protect our Aboriginal Title Land, to have a say on any development on our lands, and when we find the land can be safely and sustainably developed, to be compensated for the wealth it generates."

> *FRANK is sitting in the chair, still tied up. He waits, patiently, happily reading his book.*

> *ABBEY and NOAH enter, NOAH hobbling, with his arm around ABBEY's shoulder. They see FRANK exactly where they left him.*

FRANK: Well?

> *NOAH sits himself down at the table to nurse his leg.*

> *ABBEY slowly puts down her bag, then looks at FRANK.*

FRANK: What happened out there? Did you find the Deed?

> *She walks over to FRANK and just stares at him, rifle in hand.*

FRANK: Cuz if you did, you've got about twenty minutes before you have to leave.

> *Beat.*

ABBEY: What did you do to my dad?

> *Beat.*

FRANK: Do you have the Deed or not?

> *She suddenly slams the gun into the side of FRANK's head.*

▶ Go to Scene 6C, page 196

SCENE 6A

They all find the spot ...

The trio arrives at a clearing beside a very steep incline.
FRANK is in the lead, weaponless. ABBEY follows behind
him with the rifle and the GPS. NOAH trails.

ABBEY motions for them to stop. So they do. She consults
the map and the GPS. FRANK and NOAH look at each
other, and look around.

ABBEY: Looks like it's ... around here.

She looks at her watch.

FRANK: Made good time.

ABBEY: Yeah. (*breathing out*) Hey uh. I gotta ... Okay, when I was in
my teens, I ... whatever, I was friends with these Native girls but they ...
Anyway, I was at a bush party with them, and they were talking about
Vision Quests, so I asked, interested, what a Vision Quest was like. I was
fourteen. And they – they took me on one. Kind of. Basically they took
me to this big rock quarry in the middle of nowhere and left me there,
drunk and stoned. I had no idea where I was. I was down there for I don't
know how long, I couldn't get out. Then they just came back, laughing.
I was humiliated. Crying and puking ... everyone was laughing ...
I thought they were my friends. – And I'd just been *interested*, you know,
interested in their – And growing up next to your reserve ... I was the
only kid on the school bus, on a bus full of Native kids. My dad pressed
charges against those girls, but then their dads paid a visit to us, and ...
it was just. Ugly. One of the reasons my mom and I left. So – I'm sorry if ...
(*beat*) Maybe I got it from my ... Maybe I learned it through experience.
But it's part of me. And there's a lot at stake here, so ... that's my deal.

Beat.

FRANK: Okay.

ABBEY: Okay?

FRANK shrugs: whatever. That wasn't the reaction
ABBEY was looking for. But whatever.

ABBEY: Okay, well, looks like we're close. Gimme a sec.

ABBEY wanders, getting the exact spot on the GPS.
NOAH and FRANK stand awkwardly.

FRANK: Hey, so: Two gold prospectors are coming home from a really good dig. They're all excited about their haul, whole bunch of nuggets and stuff. But then one of them suddenly falls to the ground. Doesn't seem to be breathing, eyes rolled back in his head. So the other guy quickly picks up his phone, dials 911, and gasps to the operator: "My friend, my friend is dead! What should I do?" The operator says: "Just take it easy. I can help. First, let's make sure he's dead." There's a silence, then a shot is heard. BANG! The guy's voice comes back on the line, says: "Okay, now what?" – Hahaaaaaa. Gets me every time ...

> *Beat.*

FRANK: Wrong crowd?

> *Beat.*

NOAH: Yeah, interestingly enough, I always kinda wanted to be a gold prospector.

FRANK: Really?

NOAH: Yeah, but it didn't pan out.

FRANK: Oh man, that's bad. That's a groaner.

NOAH: I know, I know ...

ABBEY: Okay ... It's here somewhere.

> *FRANK and NOAH go over to her. They inspect a moss-covered section of an embankment, reaching and grabbing at it.*

ABBEY: Looks like it's ... like a door or ...?

NOAH: Here. Here's an edge.

FRANK: Here's another edge. Oh here. Here. There's a ... (*uncovering a handle of sorts*) Stand back.

> *FRANK pulls – and opens a sort of large cellar door that's been camouflaged with moss, vines, and branches. The door reveals the opening to a cave or tunnel that goes into the side of the mountain.*

ABBEY: Jesus, Dad ...

NOAH: Cool.

ABBEY looks in. FRANK hands her his flashlight. A beat. She takes it.

ABBEY: Thanks.

ABBEY looks in with the light.

NOAH: Can't see anything ...

ABBEY: I have to go in.

NOAH: You uh ... you okay, alone?

ABBEY: Yeah. (*considering*) Yeah.

She thinks about handing the rifle to NOAH, but thinks better of it and keeps it. And she enters the cave ...

NOAH and FRANK stand outside awkwardly. NOAH looks in, but can't see anything.

FRANK: So what's your angle out here, Rock Star? You really the type to live this far away from the action?

NOAH: Yeah, I'm ... considering it. We're getting priced out of the city. My plan was actually – if all went well out here – to propose to Abbey this week, then sell my condo to invest in the resort. Cuz she still doesn't know how she's gonna pay for all of it, and take care of her parents.

FRANK: So you're invested too, then.

NOAH: Well ... not technically yet.

Beat.

NOAH: And you? What are *you* really aiming for? I mean you want *half* the land. Why?

FRANK: *Why?*

NOAH: Yeah, what would you ... like, do, with it. If you had it.

FRANK: Can't it just simply exist?

NOAH: ... Come on, man. It's worth a buttload of money, what would you do with it?

FRANK: We'd sell a portion to make a quick buck so we can get some housing repairs on our rez. My daughter has lung problems cuz of the mould in our place and now she's pregnant and my grandkid's gotta live with that. So, crucial housing renos – which the government is *not* paying for, by the way. Despite the stereotype that we get "free houses." And then some cash for the Band's education fund. Like, for my other daughter who got accepted into uni but can't afford to live there – again, despite the stereotype that our schooling is "paid for." Then we'd try to rent some of the land so we have sustainable, long-term income. And then some of it we keep for wildlife.

NOAH: Like a preserve?

FRANK: Sure.

NOAH: Sounds kinda colonial. Dividing land, some for money, some for wildlife.

FRANK: Yeah well, what choice do we have?

NOAH: Okay, so … if you had your *ideal* situation. What would it be?

FRANK: Ideally? We're so far away from that, Rock Star … ideals are for dreamers.

NOAH: What, you can't dream?

FRANK: … Okay. Yeah, okay: ideally … you and everyone like you *disappear*, cease to exist – poof! (*snapping his fingers*) – and all the land goes back to me and my people.

NOAH: *All* of it?

FRANK: Ideally, yeah. That's reconciliation, Rock Star.

> *The caw of a bird. NOAH and FRANK look up and watch some birds circle overhead.*

NOAH: Cool, eagles?

FRANK: Vultures.

> *They watch them circling.*

> *NOAH, suddenly nervous, leans into the tunnel:*

NOAH: Ab … how you doing? Ab …? What happened?

> *NOAH moves away from the entrance. ABBEY steps out – rifle in hand, visibly shaken and distraught. A beat. She hands FRANK a handwritten note. FRANK reads:*

FRANK: (*reading*)
    "Forgive me, Abbey, my daughter, my blood
    Please forgive me
    I've come to be
    uncomfortable, with the idea of
    owning things
    This land, this lake, can you really own a tree?
    Met Frank and haven't been the same
    Got in my head
    People like me, best we can do is disappear
    poof
    white dust
    There is no Deed
    Never even seen it, just passed down
    No hidden deed, no giving it to the Queen
    I just wanted you to walk the land again
    This unceded land
    our curse
    our inheritance
    which according to the current rule of law
    transfers to you, honey
    After this"

    ABBEY holds up an empty bottle of pills. FRANK reacts ...
    but ABBEY motions for him to keep reading.

FRANK: (*reading*)
    "Didn't know what else to do
    All I know is
    you can't choose what you inherit
    But you can choose
    what you do with it
    I love you
    Dad"

    Pause.

    ABBEY still has the gun, but it's drooped in her hands and
    pointed at the ground.

    NOAH looks into the cave.

NOAH: He's ... in there? He's gone?

FRANK: I'm sorry, Abbey. I really am. That is not what I intended at all.

NOAH: No? Best we can do is disappear?

FRANK looks down ... A long pause.

Then ABBEY gets out the map, lays it out, and looks at it. Looks at them.

NOAH: Ab. Even if this is your dad's handwriting, who says he didn't write it with a gun to his head?

ABBEY looks at the note. Then at FRANK.

CHOICE-POINT 6A

THE HOST: Choice-Point:

    A. Frank's Band gets all of the land ...
       ▶ **Go to Scene 6A.1, page 182**

    B. They each get 50 percent of the land ...
       ▶ **Go to Scene 6A.2, page 183**

    C. Abbey just returns the old Village Site to Frank's Band ...
       ▶ **Go to Scene 6A.3, page 184**

    D. Abbey keeps all of the land ...
       ▶ **Go to Scene 6A.4, page 185**

Turn on your device. You have fifteen seconds.

The timer starts ...

Votes are in.

You've chosen ...

The results are projected and ***THE HOST*** *says the choice.*

SCENE 6A.1

Frank gets all the land

ABBEY looks at the map, which is also projected. She takes a pen and crosses out the dividing line.

She also crosses out "ABBEY'S HALF" and replaces it with: "ALL TO FRANK'S BAND."

NOAH: Holy ...

ABBEY looks at FRANK. FRANK nods to her, with respect ...

▶ Go to Scene 7, page 206

SCENE 6A.2

They each get 50 percent

ABBEY looks at the map, which is also projected. She looks at "FRANK'S HALF" and "ABBEY'S HALF" – considers. She then looks up at FRANK, and holds out her hand to shake.

A beat.

FRANK looks at NOAH, who gives a slight shrug. FRANK, reluctantly, shakes ABBEY's hand.

▶ Go to Scene 8, page 211

SCENE 6A.3

Abbey just returns the old Village Site to Frank's Band

ABBEY looks at the map, which is also projected. She takes a pen and crosses out the dividing line.

She also crosses out "FRANK'S HALF."

She draws a new line, around the area of the old Village Site. Inside that line, she writes: "TO FRANK'S BAND."

She looks up at FRANK, who stares back at her. He looks at NOAH, who looks down at his feet. Finally, FRANK nods, accepting his fate. For the moment.

▶ Go to Scene 9, page 216

SCENE 6A.4

Abbey keeps the land

> *ABBEY looks at the map, which is also projected. She takes a pen and crosses out the dividing line. She also crosses out "FRANK'S HALF." She looks up at FRANK.*

> *FRANK stares back, then looks at NOAH, who looks down. Finally, FRANK nods, accepting his fate. For the moment.*

> *ABBEY sighs and takes a deep breath.*

ABBEY: It's a real shame, after sending my dad to his grave, that you'd try to attack us now too ...

FRANK: The hell you talking about?

> *ABBEY looks at NOAH, then cocks the rifle.*

NOAH: Abbey ...

ABBEY: All for some stupid land.

> *ABBEY raises the gun and points it at FRANK.*

FRANK: Jesus Christ ...

NOAH: ABBEY!!

> *Blackout. A loud gunshot.*

▶ Go to Scene 10, page 221

SCENE 6B

They arrive at the spot, Frank has the gun ...

*The trio arrives at a clearing beside a very steep incline.
ABBEY motions for them to stop. So they do ... and catch
their breath.*

*ABBEY consults the map and the GPS. FRANK and
NOAH look at each other, and look around. FRANK still
has the rifle.*

ABBEY: Okay, well, looks like it's around here. Gimme a sec.

FRANK: She's in good shape.

NOAH: (*out of breath*) She's always going to some ... different ... spin
class or something ...

ABBEY paces, getting the exact spot on the GPS.

*NOAH looks down over the steep embankment they just
climbed up.*

FRANK: Hey, so: Two gold prospectors are coming home from a really
good dig. They're all excited about their haul, whole bunch of nuggets
and stuff. But then one of them suddenly falls to the ground. Doesn't
seem to be breathing, eyes rolled back in his head. So the other guy
quickly picks up his phone, dials 911, and gasps to the operator: "My
friend, my friend is dead! What should I do?" The operator says: "Just
take it easy. I can help. First, let's make sure he's dead." There's a silence,
then a shot is heard. BANG! The guy's voice comes back on the line, says:
"Okay, now what?" – Hahaaaaaa. Gets me every time ...

Beat.

FRANK: Wrong crowd?

Beat.

NOAH: Yeah, interestingly enough, I always kinda wanted to be a gold
prospector.

FRANK: Really?

NOAH: Yeah, but it didn't pan out.

FRANK: Oh man, that's bad. That's a groaner.

NOAH: I know, I know ...

ABBEY: Okay ... It's here somewhere.

> *FRANK and NOAH go over to her. They inspect a moss-covered section of an embankment, reaching and grabbing at it.*

ABBEY: Looks like it's ... like a door or ...?

NOAH: Here. Here's an edge.

FRANK: Here's another edge. Oh here. Here. There's a ... (*uncovering a handle of sorts*) Stand back.

> *FRANK pulls – and opens a sort of large cellar door that's been camouflaged with moss, vines, and branches. The door reveals the opening to a cave or tunnel that goes into the side of the mountain.*

ABBEY: Jesus, Dad ...

NOAH: Cool.

> *ABBEY looks in. FRANK hands her his flashlight. A beat. She takes it.*

ABBEY: Thanks.

> *ABBEY looks in with the light.*

NOAH: Can't see anything ...

ABBEY: I have to go in.

NOAH: You uh ... you okay, alone?

ABBEY: Yeah. (*considering*) Yeah.

> *And she enters the cave ... NOAH and FRANK stand outside awkwardly.*

FRANK: So what's your angle out here, Rock Star? You really the type to live this far away from the action?

NOAH: Yeah, I'm ... considering it. We're getting priced out of the city. My plan was actually – if all went well out here – to propose to Abbey this week, then sell my condo to invest in the resort. Cuz she still doesn't know how she's gonna pay for all of it, and take care of her parents.

FRANK: So you're invested too, then.

NOAH: Well ... not technically yet.

    Beat.

NOAH: And you? What are *you* really aiming for? I mean you want the land. Why?

FRANK: *Why?*

NOAH: Yeah what are you gonna, like, do with it.

FRANK: Can't it just simply exist?

NOAH: ... Come on, man. It's worth a buttload of money, what are you gonna do with it?

FRANK: Sell a portion to make a quick buck so we can get some housing repairs on our rez. My daughter has lung problems cuz of the mould in our place and now she's pregnant and my grandkid's gotta live with that. So, crucial housing renos – which the government is *not* paying for by the way. Despite the stereotype that we get "free houses." And then some cash for the Band's education fund. Like, for my other daughter who got accepted into uni but can't afford to live there – again despite the stereotype that our schooling is "paid for." Then we'd try to rent some of the land so we have sustainable, long-term income. And then some of it we keep for wildlife.

NOAH: Like a preserve?

FRANK: Sure.

NOAH: Sounds kinda colonial. Dividing land, some for money, some for wildlife.

FRANK: Yeah well, what choice do we have?

NOAH: Okay, so ... if you had your *ideal* situation. What would it be?

FRANK: Ideally? We're so far away from that, Rock Star ... ideals are for dreamers.

NOAH: What, you can't dream?

FRANK: ... Okay. Yeah, okay: ideally ... you and everyone like you *disappear*, cease to exist – poof! (*snapping his fingers*) – and all the land goes back to me and my people.

NOAH: *All* of it?

FRANK: Ideally, yeah. That's reconciliation, Rock Star.

The caw of a bird. NOAH and FRANK look up and watch some birds circle overhead.

NOAH: Cool, eagles?

FRANK: Vultures.

They watch them circling.

NOAH, suddenly nervous, leans into the tunnel:

NOAH: Ab ... how you doing? Ab ...? What happened?

NOAH moves away from the entrance – and FRANK instinctually does too, getting distance from them, and pointing the rifle at the tunnel entrance.

ABBEY comes out of the tunnel, visibly shaken and distraught. A beat. She hands FRANK a note. FRANK reads:

FRANK: (*reading*)
"Forgive me, Abbey, my daughter, my blood
Please forgive me
I've come to be
uncomfortable, with the idea of
owning things
This land, this lake, can you really own a tree?
Met Frank and haven't been the same
Got in my head
People like me, best we can do is disappear
poof
white dust
There is no Deed
Never even seen it, just passed down
No hidden deed, no giving it to the Queen
I just wanted you to walk the land again
This unceded land
our curse
our inheritance
which according to the current rule of law
transfers to you, honey

After this"

> *ABBEY holds up an empty bottle of pills. FRANK reacts ...
> but ABBEY motions for him to keep reading.*

FRANK: (*reading*)
"Didn't know what else to do
All I know is
you can't choose what you inherit
But you can choose
what you do with it
I love you
Dad"

> *Pause.*

> *NOAH looks into the cave.*

NOAH: He's ... in there? He's gone?

> *FRANK puts down his gun (if he hasn't already).*

FRANK: I'm sorry, Abbey. I really am. That is not what I intended at all.

NOAH: No? Best we can do is disappear?

> *FRANK looks down ...*

FRANK: I was just bluffing. When I said I knew where your dad was.
You have to believe me. I just wanted to get you to the Deed safely and on
time. That's all I wanted. I had no idea about this.

> *A long pause.*

> *Then ABBEY gets out the map, lays it out, and looks at it.
> Looks at them.*

NOAH: Ab. Even if this is your dad's handwriting, who says he didn't
write it with a gun to his head?

> *ABBEY looks at the note. Then at FRANK.*

CHOICE-POINT 6B

THE HOST: Choice-Point:

    A.   Frank gets all of the land ...
        ▶ **Go to Scene 6B.1, page 192**

    B.   They each get 50 percent of the land ...
        ▶ **Go to Scene 6B.2, page 193**

    C.   Abbey just returns the old Village Site to Frank's Band ...
        ▶ **Go to Scene 6B.3, page 194**

    D.   Abbey keeps all of the land ...
        ▶ **Go to Scene 6B.4, page 195**

Turn on your device. You have fifteen seconds.

    The timer starts ...

    Votes are in.

You've chosen ...

    *The results are projected and **THE HOST** says the choice.*

SCENE 6B.1

Frank's Band gets all the land

ABBEY looks at the map, which is also projected.

▶ **If they already had an agreement for fifty-fifty:**

ABBEY takes a pen and crosses out the dividing line. She also crosses out "ABBEY'S HALF" and replaces it with: "ALL TO FRANK'S BAND."

NOAH: Holy ...

ABBEY looks at FRANK. FRANK nods to her, with respect ...

▶ **If they never had an agreement for fifty-fifty:**

ABBEY takes a pen and writes the following: "All land bequeathed to FRANK'S BAND."

NOAH: Holy ...

ABBEY looks at FRANK. FRANK nods to her, with respect ...

▶ **Go to Scene 7, page 206**

SCENE 6B.2

They each get 50 percent

ABBEY looks at the map, which is also projected.

▶ **If they already had an agreement for fifty-fifty:**

ABBEY looks at "FRANK'S HALF" and "ABBEY'S HALF." She considers. Finally, she looks up at FRANK and holds out her hand to shake.

A beat.

FRANK looks at NOAH. NOAH gives a slight shrug. FRANK, reluctantly, shakes ABBEY's hand.

▶ **If they never had an agreement for fifty-fifty:**

ABBEY takes a pen and draws a dividing line down the middle of the property. On one side she writes, "ABBEY'S HALF," and on the other, "FRANK'S BAND."

NOAH: Holy ...

ABBEY looks at FRANK. FRANK nods to her, with respect ...

▶ Go to Scene 8, page 211

SCENE 6B.3

Abbey just returns the old Village Site to Frank's Band

ABBEY looks at the map, which is also projected.

▶ **If they already had an agreement for fifty-fifty:**

ABBEY takes a pen and crosses out "FRANK'S HALF."

She draws a new line, around the area of the old Village Site. Inside that line, she writes: "TO FRANK'S BAND"

She looks up at FRANK, who stares back at her. He looks at NOAH, who looks down at his feet. Finally, FRANK nods, accepting his fate. For the moment.

▶ **If they never had an agreement for fifty-fifty:**

ABBEY takes a pen and draws a line around the area of the old Village Site. Inside that line, she writes: "TO FRANK'S BAND."

She looks up at FRANK, who stares back at her. He looks at NOAH, who shrugs a bit. Finally, FRANK nods. With respect, and a bit of defeat. For the moment.

▶ Go to Scene 9, page 216

SCENE 6B.4

Abbey keeps all of the land

ABBEY looks at the map, which is also projected.

▶ **If they already had an agreement for fifty-fifty:**

ABBEY takes a pen and crosses out "FRANK'S HALF" and replaces it with: "ALL ABBEY'S."

She looks up at FRANK. He stares back. FRANK looks at NOAH, who looks down. Finally, FRANK nods, accepting his fate. For the moment.

ABBEY picks up the gun.

▶ **If they never had an agreement for fifty-fifty:**

ABBEY considers the map. She looks at the land around her. Then looks at FRANK. Then at the map again. And, simply, rolls the map up. She looks at FRANK: tough luck.

FRANK nods, accepting his fate. For the moment.

ABBEY picks up the gun.

ABBEY: It's a real shame, after sending my dad to his grave, that you'd try to attack us now too ...

FRANK: The hell you talking about?

ABBEY looks at NOAH, then cocks the rifle.

NOAH: Abbey ...

ABBEY: All for some stupid land.

ABBEY raises the gun and points it at FRANK.

FRANK: Jesus Christ ...

NOAH: ABBEY!!

Blackout. A loud gunshot.

▶ **Go to Scene 10, page 221**

SCENE 6C

Showdown at the house ...

ABBEY: WHAT DID YOU DO?!

FRANK: I don't know what you're talking about!

ABBEY: Don't mess with me, Frank.

She lifts the gun and points it straight at him.

ABBEY: Five years ago my dad got into a fight and ended up in a coma.

FRANK: Yeah, okay, I know.

ABBEY: You were there?

FRANK: ... Yeah, I ... but I didn't do anything to him. I was there, but it wasn't me.

ABBEY: Why the fight?

FRANK: Cuz – your dad called in the cops when he saw us camping out on "your" land, and we spent a few nights in the slammer.

ABBEY: So you put him in a coma? (*beat*) And how'd you end up working for him? How'd you meet him?

FRANK: At this – road block. He spent the whole day there at the blockade, spoutin' his mouth off, but then – once he tired down – we, you know, started talking. For real.

ABBEY: How'd you start working for him?

FRANK: Then ... the rest you know. I saw him in town and asked if he had any work for me.

ABBEY: Why'd you ask *him*?

FRANK: Why not?

ABBEY: Why him, Frank!

FRANK: Cuz ... yeah he owns the land out here, and I figured I could try to talk some sense into him.

ABBEY: Try to work him, is that right?

FRANK: "Work" him?

ABBEY: Grind him down. Get him to give you the land – or at least some of it. The portion you're already on. I saw your camp out there. Teepees, a Longhouse. I'm guessing that's where my dad would find you guys trespassing all the time.

FRANK: Here we go … trespassing … on our own / land.

ABBEY: I remember. He said you guys would go out there trying to find evidence of an old Village Site. Because if you proved there was one, that'd help your case for a land claim. Your claim to *all* the land around here; the town, *our* property – everything.

FRANK: That's not – I needed a job and …

ABBEY: And?

FRANK: And yeah I figured I could talk some sense into him, get him to rethink your plans out here. He seemed / open to it –

ABBEY: You give him all these books –

FRANK: Sure.

ABBEY: Show him these articles, statistics, really grind him down –

FRANK: Loaning books is illegal now?

ABBEY: Take advantage of a lonely old man, make him feel guilty, ashamed, / worse than useless, like he's –

FRANK: That's not – what? That wasn't my –

ABBEY: No??

FRANK: What did you find out there??

    A beat.

    NOAH hands FRANK a note. FRANK reads:

FRANK: (*reading*)
  "Forgive me, Abbey, my daughter, my blood
    Please forgive me
    I've come to be
    uncomfortable, with the idea of
    owning things
    This land, this lake, can you really <u>own</u> a tree?
    Met Frank and haven't been the same
    Got in my head

People like me, best we can do is disappear
poof
white dust
There is no Deed
Never even seen it, just passed down
No hidden deed, no giving it to the Queen
I just wanted you to walk the land again
This unceded land
our curse
our inheritance
which according to the current rule of law
transfers to you, honey
After this"

ABBEY holds up an empty bottle of pills. FRANK reacts ...
but ABBEY motions for him to keep reading.

FRANK: (*reading*)
"Didn't know what else to do
All I know is
you can't choose what you inherit
But you can choose
what you do with it
I love you
Dad"

ABBEY: Found him in an old mine shaft. He's gone.

FRANK: I'm sorry, Abbey. I really am. That is not what I intended at all.

A pause.

ABBEY: No? Best we can do is disappear?

FRANK looks down ...

— + —

▶ **If FRANK is tied up, add:**

FRANK: I was just bluffing. When I said I knew where your dad was. You have to believe me. I just wanted to get you to the Deed safely and on time. That's all I wanted. I had no idea about this.

— — —

A long pause.

*Then ABBEY gets out the map, lays it out, and looks at it.
Looks at them.*

NOAH: Ab. Even if this is your dad's handwriting, who says he didn't write it with a gun to his head?

ABBEY looks at the note. Then at FRANK.

CHOICE-POINT 6C

THE HOST: Choice-Point:

    A.   Frank's Band gets all of the land ...
        ▶ **Go to Scene 6C.1, page 201**

    B.   They each get 50 percent of the land ...
        ▶ **Go to Scene 6C.2, page 202**

    C.   Abbey just returns the old Village Site to Frank's Band ...
        ▶ **Go to Scene 6C.3, page 203**

    D.   Abbey keeps all of the land ...
        ▶ **Go to Scene 6C.4, page 204**

Turn on your device. You have fifteen seconds.

    The timer starts ...

    Votes are in.

You've chosen ...

    *The results are projected and **THE HOST** says the choice.*

SCENE 6C.1

Frank's Band gets all of the land

ABBEY looks at the map, which is also projected. She takes a pen and writes: "All land bequeathed to FRANK'S BAND."

NOAH: Holy ...

ABBEY looks at FRANK. FRANK nods to her, with respect ...

▶ Go to Scene 7, page 206

SCENE 6C.2

They each get 50 percent

ABBEY looks at the map, which is also projected. She takes a pen and draws a dividing line down the middle of the property. On one side she writes, "ABBEY'S HALF," and on the other, "FRANK'S BAND."

NOAH: Holy ...

ABBEY looks at FRANK. FRANK nods to her, with respect ...

▶ Go to Scene 8, page 211

SCENE 6C.3

Abbey just returns the old Village Site to Frank's Band

ABBEY looks at the map, which is also projected. She takes a pen and draws a line around the area of the old Village Site. Inside that line, she writes: "TO FRANK'S BAND."

She looks up at FRANK, who stares back at her. FRANK looks at NOAH, who shrugs a bit. Finally, FRANK nods. With respect, and a bit of defeat. For the moment.

▶ Go to Scene 9, page 216

SCENE 6C.4

Abbey keeps all of the land

ABBEY looks at the map, which is also projected. She considers the map, then looks at everything around her. The land. The house. The phone gone. The stain of blood.

She looks at FRANK. Then at the map again. And, simply, rolls the map up again. She looks at FRANK: tough luck.

FRANK nods, accepting his fate. For the moment.

— + —

▶ **If FRANK is tied up, add:**

ABBEY: Untie him, hon.

NOAH: Geez, man ... Okay, yeah.

NOAH goes to untie FRANK ... but FRANK simply pulls his arms free, the ropes falling easily.

NOAH: What the ...?

FRANK smiles.

FRANK: I slipped out of these ropes five minutes after you left. Next time you tie someone up, don't leave their hands free so they can "read."

They stare at FRANK, unsure.

FRANK: Figured she'd show her true colours if she thought I was out of commission.

— — —

ABBEY sighs and takes a deep breath.

ABBEY: It's a real shame, after sending my dad to his grave, that you'd now try to attack us too ...

FRANK: The hell you talking about?

ABBEY looks at NOAH, then cocks the rifle.

NOAH: Abbey ...

ABBEY: All for some stupid land.

ABBEY raises the gun and points it at FRANK.

FRANK: Jesus Christ …

NOAH: ABBEY!!

Blackout. A loud gun shot.

▶ **Go to Scene 10, page 221**

SCENE 7

Frank gets all of the land ...

*The map of the land remains projected. Showing: Frank's Band's use of the land. **THE HOST** explains:*

THE HOST: The eco-resort plans are entirely scrapped.
The access road moves so that it enters from the Reserve instead.
A sale of half the land does NOT occur.
In order to solve their immediate housing needs on reserve, Frank's Band leases some land to a developer for a solar farm, and for a cell tower.
And a small section of land is set aside for a private buyer, but that sale has not yet occurred ...
They're permanently reoccupying their old Village Site, asserting their inherent Land Title, but are still waiting for news of their claim.
Meanwhile Frank has moved his family into Abbey's childhood home ...

Lights up on the porch of the house. It's raining. Inside, the sound of a family, talking loudly, sometimes arguing.

FRANK is on the phone in the living room.

FRANK: I can't hear you, one sec ... One second – Jesus!

He comes out onto the porch. He has a crying BABY in a snuggly.

Reception's still spotty out here ... that's better ... We did, we paid for the extra – "wandbidth" or whatever but it's still ... (*beat*) I don't know! You're the lawyer, you tell me what I should do ... Oh man ... Nothing! Nothing! I didn't do *anything* to him! ... Ben. I *know* I can be honest with you, as my lawyer. I *am* being honest.

He looks back into the house, making sure he keeps his voice down and no one's listening.

I'm aware of that ... I know it looks bad ... Look, Abbey and I made a deal, okay? I understand the circumstances around the land transfer were unusual, but Abbey and I have a deal. A written deal. We have to try to get her to talk to the neighbours, Ben. To the lawyers. To everyone!

If this gets out of control, we could have another Gustafsen Lake here. Or an Oka ... (*beat*) I don't know. She washed her hands of this. She's not answering my calls. Last I heard, they split up. He sold his condo, went to Thailand or something. Abbey blamed me for their breakup and is holed up in some crappy apartment with her mother somewhere. So, yeah, I'm not exactly her favourite person, but we have to try to get through to her ... (*beat*) *Because* she sets the tone for all the other ranchers around here. We need her on our side. She's the only one who can get them to drop all this. So find her, tell her we'll cut her in. We'll pay back her debts on her investment, whatever she needs ... If you have to ask, you obviously wouldn't understand. Just do it. Goodbye. Gotta go. Bye!

> *He hangs up.*

Christ all frickin' mighty ...

> *Then his phone immediately rings again.*

> **Projected:** RAIN would like FaceTime ...

> *FRANK's mood instantly improves, and he answers.*
> *RAIN appears projected.*

FRANK: Hey, Rain. What'd the doctor say?

RAIN: My lungs are clearing up, I'm heading home early.

FRANK: That's great news. Someone misses you.

> *He holds the phone up to the BABY, who stops fussing.*

FRANK: See ...

RAIN: Aww ... he just loves being with his –

FRANK: Don't say it.

RAIN: ... Grandpa.

FRANK: Ouch, I still can't get used to that.

> *A beat.*

RAIN: I hear Mahekan called you an Elder.

> *FRANK shakes his head and just gives his attention to the child.*

RAIN: It looks good on you.

Another beat. More yelling from inside.

RAIN: What're they all riled up about?

FRANK: Oh … nothing. Trying to come to consensus.

RAIN: Right. I don't wanna know.

FRANK: Lori's being stubborn. Now she's changing her mind on whether to develop the land. Kept us arguing for weeks on one point, then we started coming to consensus, and she started arguing the other point. But Lori's – (*biting his lip*) got a right to her opinion. We all gotta hear her out.

RAIN: You know, governing by consensus might have worked when this continent was just our people, but we're up against a white government that doesn't care if every voice is heard.

FRANK: If we're going to save this land for traditional use, then we're going to make those decisions the traditional way. We're not going to ignore any of our people's voices. We're not going to stoop to the white government's level.

A beat.

RAIN: Did you talk to Ben?

FRANK nods.

RAIN: What does he think?

FRANK just puts his attention toward the baby.

FRANK: Seems that no matter what we do with our land, we're going to get a fight. They steal it from us, we have to fight to get it back. We get it back legally, and we gotta fight to keep it. They lie, cheat, and murder to steal our land, without any legal document, and we have to prove it's ours. Now I have a legal document proving it's my land and they think I lied, cheated, and murdered to get it. Some things never change.

RAIN: Of course they change. Change is the only constant in life. Isn't that what you used to always tell me, Elder Frank?

FRANK: Look at you, using my words against me. Maybe you should be my lawyer instead of Ben.

RAIN: Maybe I will.

FRANK: Okay then, if you were my lawyer, what would be your legal advice?

RAIN: I would advise you to be patient. And believe that things will change. For the better. They have to get better for our people. They can't get worse. Keep believing and keep fighting for what's right. Otherwise, you'll end up like Abbey's dad. Holding on so tight to anger and mistrust that it ends up killing you. WE need you around for a long time, Dad ... Grandpa.

FRANK: Wow. Congratulations. You are now my new lawyer.

RAIN: Cool. That first part was free but from now on, I charge by the hour.

FRANK: Fair enough. And you're right. No matter what happens: they can't take away the land. We have it in writing. They may try to dispute it, that's their way, but nothing anyone can do about that. Just keep your mind on that.

RAIN: Sir, yes, sir.

FRANK: I'll keep fighting, but I won't be around forever. And then ...?

RAIN: And then I'll keep fighting.

FRANK: And maybe by then, things will be better.

RAIN: Maybe.

> FRANK coos to the BABY.

FRANK: (to BABY) That's right, (speaking Secwepemctsín) re imts* ... I've set the table for ya, haven't I? That's right ... I'll teach you all you need to know, re imts.

> FRANK sits on the porch, the BABY on his chest. A beat. Then, introspective:

FRANK: We're still here, aren't we. (beat) Aren't we, re imts? (with a complex mix of pride and fatigue) Still here.

> As the lights fade, the projected image of RAIN on the screen is replaced by an image of a BEAR, eating berries.

---

* My grandchild.

The lights are out on FRANK, and the bear can still be seen eating berries.

Then, on another screen: a COYOTE, standing at attention, looking around.

Then the light on the screens fade too.

THE END.

▶ **Go to Curtain Call / Post-Show, page 225**

SCENE 8

The land is shared fifty-fifty ...

*The map of the land remains projected, showing the following, while **THE HOST** explains:*

THE HOST:

On Abbey's half of the land:

She had to move the Lodge way downriver and downscale the plans considerably.

The eco-resort does not include hunting and will no longer disrupt the salmon run.

And the access road does NOT go through the old Village Site.

Additional costs to Abbey: $130,000 and growing ...

Plus the loss of $700,000 from the potential land sale.

On Frank's Band's half:

In order to solve their immediate housing needs on reserve, they've leased some land to a developer for a solar farm, and for a cell tower.

And they sold a small section of land to a private buyer.

They're permanently reoccupying their old Village Site, asserting their inherent Land Title, but are still waiting for news of their claim.

And the agreements:

If Frank's Band wins their Title claim, they agree to leave Abbey's portion of land alone.

Each side gets 10 percent of profits from each other's land.

Each side has consent on the other's business.

*Lights rise on **FRANK**, out on the land. He's got a **BABY** in a snuggly and is bouncing it gently, cooing to it.*

Projected on the map, a car drives along the new access road to near the old Village Site. The car eventually stops.

***FRANK**'s phone buzzes. He checks the text, which is projected:*

***NOAH**'s text:* Here, don't see you.

***FRANK** texts back:*

FRANK's text: Over the ridge, west side of the clearing, in the shade of some trees.

NOAH's text: Which way is west again?

FRANK's text: Ha ha.

FRANK drops a pin of his location on the map.

FRANK's text: All hail the new cell tower.

NOAH's text: LOL. All hail.

NOAH and ABBEY walk on, following NOAH's cellphone GPS.

FRANK: Morning.

ABBEY / NOAH: Hey, / good morning.

FRANK: Another beautiful day.

ABBEY / NOAH: Yeah, / yeah.

FRANK: Thanks to global warming.

A beat.

NOAH: (*noticing the BABY*) Awww ... hi again ... what a cutie ... (*to FRANK*) Grandpa.

FRANK: What did I tell you about calling me that.

NOAH: Look at you ...! Hey there ...

NOAH touches the baby – it starts crying. NOAH is disappointed.

FRANK: Rain's getting some rest. Not a good night last night. (*to the BABY, in baby-talk*) Was it? Not a good night ...

ABBEY: Looking nice out here. Is that a new teepee?

FRANK: Oh, that's Britta.

NOAH: The buyer from Germany?

FRANK: She's trying to fit in. She thinks this is Native housing.

They chuckle.

FRANK: How's it all going? Still on schedule?

ABBEY: All good. We break ground next month.

FRANK: Good to hear. Hope it all works out. And not just cuz we get 10 percent. But it helps.

They smile again.

ABBEY: Us too.

Beat.

FRANK: So, you wanted to meet?

NOAH: Yeah, a few bits of ... news and ...

FRANK: Sit.

> *FRANK has laid out some snacks on a blanket. A beat as they decide who will speak first. NOAH indicates for ABBEY to speak.*

ABBEY: Well ... first off: We wanted to ... invite you, and your family, to our wedding.

FRANK: Noooo! Really?

ABBEY: Yeah, June 9th. At our place.

FRANK: We'd be honoured. Thank you. June 9th?

NOAH: It's a Saturday.

FRANK: Ahh, I may have a council meeting. But I can try and get out of it.

NOAH: Cool, cool. Let us know. There's seats for four.

ABBEY: (*indicating FRANK's grandchild*) ... and a half.

Beat.

ABBEY: And ...

NOAH: Yeah. So. Right. Well uh ... Well, we've been talking about it. Not sure how to ... you know ... approach you about this. Or when. But.

FRANK: Hm-mn.

NOAH: We're wondering if ... since you're Chief now ... we're wondering ... you can totally say no, I mean, it's a big ask ...

FRANK: Spit it out, Rock Star.

NOAH: We're wondering if you'd say a few words at our ceremony.

Beat.

FRANK: Oh geez, Rock Star, you slay me! Ha ha ha haa.

NOAH: Well I don't know. Maybe you ... I don't know.

FRANK: What would you want me to say?

ABBEY: Well ... our family and friends will be there. Some local people too. We thought it would be a good chance to put a face to the name. They all know what happened out here. And they're curious.

FRANK: ... I see.

NOAH: Uh. But, uh. It's just ... with your land claim in the news now ... a lot of people are even more nervous. About what's gonna happen to their homes. Their lives. Should they sell their property now, before value goes ... y'know ... There's just a lot of uncertainty and you know how that affects the market.

FRANK: Hm-mn. Okay, I could do my best to explain how it benefits them.

NOAH: Okay, we don't want – no ... we wouldn't need you to ... calm anyone down. We just think it'd be a good chance to ... I don't know ... model, what's going on out here. Our wedding is a celebration of *us* ... but also a celebration of ... *this*.

Beat.

FRANK: What would I wear?

NOAH: Anything, whatever you want.

ABBEY: It's summer formal. Whatever that means to you.

Beat.

FRANK: I could wear my regalia.

NOAH: Sure, yes, of course, you wouldn't have to. Whatever you want.

FRANK: Abbey?

ABBEY: Okay ... up to you.

FRANK: I'm kidding. I'd wear a blazer.

ABBEY: And what you say would be up to you too. We might just put a time limit on it.

They chuckle.

FRANK: All right. I'll put it to the Council. See if they'd let me out of that meeting to do a little PR.

They chuckle again.

NOAH: Cool. Cool. Hey, I've always wondered actually. How do you ... you know ... how does your Band or Council, like ... decide things? Is it by vote or ...?

FRANK: Consensus. Some Bands do it other ways. But us? Always consensus. Your democracy always leaves some people out. Leaves some people unhappy.

NOAH: Totally ...

FRANK looks down to his grandchild.

FRANK: But what do *you* think, (*speaking Secwepemctsín*) re imts.* Is this part of the table I'm settin' for ya?

On cue, the BABY gurgles. And they all chuckle.

Projected: A BEAR is eating some berries. Looks up, and out ... at a COYOTE, who is looking back at the BEAR. They see each other.

The lights fade ...

THE END.

▶ Go to Curtain Call / Post-Show, page 225

---

*   My grandchild.

SCENE 9

Abbey just returns the old Village Site to Frank's Band

The map of the land remains projected, showing the
*following, while **THE HOST** explains:*

THE HOST:

On Abbey's land:
    The eco-resort continues as planned.
    The access road moves so that it does NOT go through the Old
     Village site.
    A cell tower is put in.
    Abbey sells half of the land to a private developer.

On Frank's Band's section of land:
    They're permanently reoccupying their old Village Site but are still
     waiting for news of their Title claim to the entire area.
    They put in their own access road to their section of land.
    But their immediate housing needs on reserve are still not solved ...

*FRANK stands with a **BABY** in his arms, bouncing*
it gently.

On the projected map: A car drives along a road from
***FRANK**'s reserve to **FRANK**'s portion of land. The car*
eventually stops.

***FRANK**'s phone beeps. Projected on the screen, a text*
*from **NOAH** appears:*

***NOAH**'s text:* We've parked, don't see you.

***FRANK** texts back.*

***FRANK**'s text:* Walk over the ridge, west side of the
clearing, in the shade of some trees.

***NOAH**'s text:* Which way is west again?

***FRANK**'s text:* I'll drop you a pin.

A pin drops on the map.

***FRANK**'s text:* All hail the new cell tower.

***NOAH**'s text:* LOL. All hail.

NOAH and ABBEY walk on, following NOAH's
cellphone GPS.

FRANK: Morning.

ABBEY / NOAH: Hey, / good morning.

FRANK: Another beautiful day.

ABBEY / NOAH: Yeah, / yeah.

FRANK: Thanks to global warming.

    A beat.

NOAH: (*noticing the BABY*) Awww ...

FRANK: Abbey, Noah, I want you to meet my grandchild.

ABBEY: Beautiful ... oh my God, so beautiful.

NOAH: Grandpa.

FRANK: Don't even.

NOAH: Look at you ...! Hey there, cutie.

    NOAH touches the baby – it starts crying. NOAH is
    disappointed.

FRANK: Rain's getting some rest. Not a good night last night.
(*to the BABY, in baby talk*) Was it? Not a good night ...

ABBEY: So is this a permanent camp out here now?

FRANK: Is anything permanent? Some people like it, yeah. Still waiting
for money for houses with proper walls and ventilation, so yeah a few
folks have built kekulis.

NOAH: Coo-coo what?

FRANK: See the small bumps in the ground, there, there, and there?

    Projected: Small mounds in the earth.

FRANK: Houses built into a hole in the ground.

NOAH: Ohhh ... yeah, I've heard of those. Thought they were called "pit
houses"?

FRANK: Sure, yeah. Some people really feel the energy out here, it's
good for them.

A beat. FRANK has an edge to his voice:

So how's it all going? Still on schedule?

ABBEY: We're supposed to break ground next month, but we're behind.

Beat.

FRANK: You wanted to meet?

NOAH: Yeah ... a few bits of ... news and ...

ABBEY: Well ... first off: We wanted to ... invite you, and your family, to our wedding.

FRANK: Noooo! Really?

ABBEY: Yeah, June 9th. At our place.

FRANK: We'd be honoured. Thank you. June 9th?

NOAH: It's a Saturday.

FRANK: Ahh, I may have a Council meeting. But I can see if I can get out of it.

NOAH: Cool, cool. Let us know. There's seats for four.

Beat.

ABBEY: Also ... we heard you proved there's an old Village Site here. So that'll help your land claim.

FRANK: Where'd you hear that?

ABBEY: Around.

FRANK: Got your spies, do ya? Don't panic, it'll be a long process.

ABBEY: But if it's successful?

FRANK: Well, we'll see about that.

NOAH: A lot of people are really nervous. About what's gonna happen to their homes. Their lives. Should they sell their property now, before value goes ... y'know ... there's just a lot of uncertainty and you know how that affects the market.

FRANK: There's no need to be concerned, I don't think.

NOAH: But you have to realize there's a lot of questions.

FRANK: Hm-mn.

Beat.

ABBEY: I just wanted to see … if there was any way, you'd … leave our land out of the claim.

FRANK smiles.

NOAH: We know that, even though you're Chief now, you can't decide yourself, but … we were hoping you could put that forward, to your Council.

FRANK: I'll try.

ABBEY: Come on, Frank. You know how much we've sunk into this. You can already see how good it'll be – local business, jobs. We've even hired people from your reserve. We're a community now. Neighbours. We gotta work together.

FRANK: And good neighbours build good fences, do they?

ABBEY: We didn't put up that fence to keep anyone *out*, it's to keep our patrons from straying onto *your* land.

FRANK: Didn't talk to us about it first. Just put it up. Barbed wire.

ABBEY: Frank, I'm sorry, we should have consulted you first. But did you consult us about the road that passes right by my family's gravesites?

FRANK: I didn't know that. If I'd known –

NOAH: Soooo, lessons learned, we should all consult each other more.

FRANK: … That's a lot different than consent. Mutual consent.

NOAH: Well, we can't, we can't go there. We can't have to need your approval every time we – do you want to have to get our consent before you build pit houses? Come on.

ABBEY: Okay, consent would mean you'd need our permission to include our land in a claim.

FRANK: Oh no. That's different. That claim means we'd own your land, we wouldn't need your consent.

NOAH: It's only fair, Frank, she didn't *have* to give you this portion of land, for nothing. She didn't *have* to reorganize our plans, build the lodge further downriver, reroute the access road, costing even more money, but she did, in good faith. Out of fairness. It's only fair.

FRANK: Fair ...

Beat.

ABBEY: Look at us. We're people. We exist. We can't ... *not* exist. If we no longer have our land, our lives, everything we've – then it's worth nothing. We're nothing.

FRANK: Can you say that again? Cuz I just heard my Ancestors. Speaking through you. (*beat*) I'll bring the matter forward to the others. But I can't promise anything.

Beat.

ABBEY: Okay. Thank you.

Beat.

NOAH: Hey I've always wondered, actually. How do you ... you know ... how does your Band or Council like ... decide things? Is it by vote or –?

FRANK: Consensus. Some Bands do it other ways. But us? Always consensus. Your democracy always leaves some people out. Leaves some people unhappy.

NOAH: Totally ...

ABBEY doesn't say anything. A beat.

Projected: A BEAR is eating some berries.

Projected on another screen: A COYOTE stands on a ridge. Looking around.

The lights fade on the screens too ...

THE END.

▶ Go to Curtain Call / Post-Show, page 225

SCENE 10

Abbey has the land ...

The map of the land remains projected, showing the following, while **THE HOST** *explains:*

THE HOST
And on Abbey's land:
The eco-resort continues as planned.
Access roads are paved, right across the old Village Site.
A cell tower and septic system is put in place.
And Abbey has moved back into her childhood home ...
While across the river, day and night, Frank's people have taken up
    their drums in protest ...

The map focuses in on the edge of the property, out near the stream ... That's where **ABBEY** *is.*

ABBEY *is out on the land, down by the stream, dazed and defeated. The loud sound of constant drumming can be heard. Her cellphone rings.*

Projected: NOAH would like FaceTime ...

She answers. **NOAH** *is projected.*

NOAH: Hey.

ABBEY: Hi.

NOAH: Can you hear me?

ABBEY: Yeah.

NOAH: Sorry, Wi-Fi's spotty where I am right now.

ABBEY: It's finally good out here.

Beat.

NOAH: Christ, they're still drumming?

ABBEY: Yup. And there is nothing we can do to stop them. We just had a big meeting with the cops. Legally they can do whatever they want on their land. Who's gonna book into an eco-resort with that going on?

NOAH: Well ... you know ... they kind of have a right to be angry ... I mean, the cops really didn't investigate ...

ABBEY: Noah! He sent my dad to his grave and then he attacked us. It was self-defence. That's it. (*beat*) Are you enjoying your tropical experience?

NOAH: Um ... sure.

ABBEY: Good ... When are you coming back?

  Beat.

NOAH: I'm not totally sure, really.

ABBEY: What?

NOAH: Don't be mad, okay? I just haven't had enough time to, you know, process this.

ABBEY: You already processed it, you processed it a year ago. The construction is starting.

NOAH: I know, but ... listen, out here, with the waves and the ... I'm just beginning to finally ... hear myself again. I need to take my time with this. It's just all been so ...

ABBEY: I get that, I do, but I can't do this by myself anymore. The building, my mom – I'm exhausted. I need help. I need you.

NOAH: Yeah, well ... maybe you should sell it, cut your losses?

ABBEY: What?

NOAH: I mean, you're not tied to that place anymore. You could do anything – live anywhere.

ABBEY: I can't just move to Thailand, Noah. (*beat*) Are you bailing on me?

NOAH: ... I'm just looking at options. (*off camera*) Uh yeah, hold up. Give me a sec ... (*back to ABBEY*) Sorry. I'm just not sure how to continue on there. With everything I know.

ABBEY: Who is that?

NOAH: What?

ABBEY: Who are you talking to?

NOAH: What? Nobody. Just a, just a buddy. (*beat*) I mean, there's so much baggage over there, with the history, the land ...

ABBEY: Right. But you're totally fine colonizing another country.

A beat.

NOAH: I ... that's ... You know what, I'm not sure I'm gonna call again.

ABBEY abruptly ends the call. She breaks down ... then suddenly notices FRANK standing on the other side of the stream. Is it a ghost? Her mind playing tricks on her? Insanity setting in?

A beat. FRANK looks around, at the stream ...

FRANK: Some things never change, eh? Out here. I remember this stream like it was yesterday. Playing down here as kids.

A beat. The drumming is constant.

FRANK: You had enough yet?

ABBEY: They can't drum forever, Frank. Sooner or later they'll get tired.

FRANK: I don't know about that ... There are a lot of us over there. And we don't mind working together.

ABBEY: We?! You're not real. You're ... gone ...

FRANK: I'll never be gone, Abbey. I'm a part of this land. I'm a part of you now.

ABBEY: You killed my dad! And you were trying to destroy me too. I had no choice.

FRANK: Oh, you had choices.

ABBEY: And now your people wanna leave me no choice but to sell, is that it?

FRANK: We're not sharing the resources we need for our survival with a bunch of rich folk who want a back-to-the-earth experience. Period. And it's not what your dad wanted either.

ABBEY: According to you. I'll never know. I'll never really know ...

Beat. They stare at each other for a moment.

ABBEY: I've invested every bit of anything I have into this land. I am trying to do good with it. To do good by him. I'm staying, Frank. I was born here. My family is buried here. If your people win your land claim, then maybe I'll have to re-evaluate. But this is my home, and I am not about to leave, again, just because it's hard.

FRANK: Right, got it. You don't want to make a change, even though you can. Even though you have the power to do so, right here, right now. You'll only do it if the government tells you to, or you're forced into it.

>*A beat.*

FRANK: All right. Do what your heart tells you. I'll do the same.

ABBEY: YOU are not going to do anything! You're dead!

FRANK: Told you the battle would rage on.

>*FRANK turns to walk away.*

ABBEY: I was raised here, too. Don't forget that.

FRANK: Hope you don't meet up with a bear on your way back.

>*FRANKS leaves. ABBEY watches him go ...*

>*As the lights fade, the image of a BEAR, rummaging around in the distance.*

>*Then, on another screen: the image of a COYOTE, looking out.*

>*The light on the screens fades too.*

THE END.

▶ Go to Curtain Call / Post-Show, page 225

CURTAIN CALL / POST-SHOW

After the bows and once the audience has finished clapping ... the screen pops to life again. And the actors speak as themselves:

(**FRANK**): Wait. We thought you might want to see this. It's the story path you chose today.

A projection shows the story path the audience chose during this particular performance.

(**ABBEY**): And here are the paths you *could* have chosen.

Surrounding the path this audience chose, the projection now shows the map of all possible paths.

(**ABBEY**): (*invitingly*) Next time, maybe?

(**FRANK**): You're also now invited to stay in the theatre for a post-show discussion, and the introduction of a special Invited Guest. If you choose to stay, you can keep your clicker with you, and we'll begin after a five-minute break.

(**ABBEY**): But first, two final questions. Make sure your clicker is on.

(**NOAH**): Would you consent to your clicker responses at this performance being looked at by our team to help guide us with the potential future of this play? Your consent is optional, your responses are anonymous, and results from this question will not be displayed.

    A. I consent.

    B. I do not consent.

You have fifteen seconds.

The results are displayed.

(**FRANK**): And speaking of consent: here in this theatre, we are on Seymour Street, which was named after the second colonial governor of British Columbia. It was Governor Seymour's belief that colonizers did not need agreement or consent to occupy this land.

(**ABBEY**): Knowing that, if you were in Abbey's shoes, honestly, what would you do?

*The cast exits. THE **HOST** continues:*

THE HOST:

    A. Return all of the land

    B. Return half of the land

    C. Return a portion of the land

    D. Keep all of the land

And if you'd like to change how you responded, or try to change the way others responded ...

You have the rest of your life.

Appendix

The Host's Interactive Bits

ALTERNATE 1

In the event of a tie vote:

THE HOST: Ohhhh-ho-ho-hohhhh! Looks like we have a tie! So now, this is what's going to happen. I'm going to eliminate the choice that received the least votes. Let me go ahead and do that.

The choice with the least amount of votes slowly disappears from the projection screen.

Next I'll reopen the voting, and you will all have fifteen seconds to choose again from the options remaining.

But first, you might want to take a moment to talk to the people beside you and see if you can get them to vote how you're voting? Just a thought.

Okay, okay. Here we go. Make sure your clicker is on. Voting is now open. You have fifteen seconds.

The timer starts ...

Votes are in.

You've chosen ...

*The results are projected and **THE HOST** says the choice.*

ALTERNATE 2

If the vote is still tied:

Take Indigenous votes only.

THE HOST: OH-HO-HOOOOOOOHHHHHHHH! Still tied! All right, here's what we're going to do now. Instead of revoting, which could result in another tie, I'm going to consult the questions you answered before we started, and count only the votes of those who identify as Indigenous. Everyone else's votes will not count.

I know, I know, but think about it this way: Indigenous people in this country didn't have the right to vote until the 1960s without having to give up their Native status. So I think you non-Indigenous folk can tough this one out.

Okay. I've done my calculations, and this is what the Indigenous folks in the room want to see happen:

The results are projected and ***THE HOST*** *says the choice.*

ALTERNATE 3

If the vote is still tied and no one in the crowd identified as Indigenous:

Take "Over 55" votes only.

THE HOST: OH-HO-HOOOOOOOHHHHHHHH! Still tied! All right, here's what we're going to do now. Instead of revoting, which could result in another tie, I'm going to consult the questions you answered before we started, and count only votes from those who are aged fifty-six or older. Everyone else's votes will not count.

I know, I know, but you young folks still have a lot of voting years left. Let's see what would happen if the blue-hairs finally got their way.

Okay, I've done my calculations, and this is what the Over 55 folks want to see happen:

The results are projected and ***THE HOST*** *says the choice.*

Bibliography and Acknowledgments

Reproduction Credit

Sections from the book *Unsettling Canada: A National Wake-Up Call* by Arthur Manuel and Grand Chief Ronald M. Derrickson are included in *Inheritance* with permission from the publisher Between the Lines Books, the Manuel family, and Grand Chief Ronald M. Derrickson.

The playwrights wish to acknowledge the following resources:

Banks, Dennis, with Richard Erdoes. *Ojibwa Warrior, and the Rise of the American Indian Movement*. Norman, OK: University of Oklahoma Press, 2011.

Bellecourt, Clyde, and Jon Lurie. *The Thunder before the Storm: The Autobiography of Clyde Bellecourt*. Saint Paul, MN: Minnesota Historical Society Press, 2016.

Bouchard, Randy, and Dorothy I.D. Kennedy (eds). *Shuswap Stories: Collected 1971–1975*. Vancouver, BC: CommCept Publishing, 1979.

Budd, Robert. *Echoes of British Columbia: Voices from the Frontier*. Madeira Park, BC: Harbour Publishing, 2014.

Dennis, Darrell. *Peace Pipe Dreams: The Truth about Lies about Indians*. Toronto: Douglas & McIntyre, 2014.

Lambertus, Sandra. *Wartime Images, Peacetime Wounds: The Media and the Gustafsen Lake Standoff*. Toronto: University of Toronto Press, 2004.

Manuel, Arthur, and Grand Chief Ronald M. Derrickson. *The Reconciliation Manifesto: Recovering the Land, Rebuilding the Economy*. Toronto: James Lorimer & Company, 2017.

———. *Unsettling Canada: A National Wake-Up Call*. Toronto: Between the Lines, 2015.

Sellars, Chief Bev. *They Called Me Number One: Secrets and Survival at an Indian Residential School.* Vancouver, BC: Talonbooks, 2013.

Stangoe, Irene. *History and Happenings in the Cariboo-Chilcotin: Pioneer Memories.* Vancouver, BC: Heritage House Publishing, 2000.

Swanky, Tom. *The True Story of Canada's "War" of Extermination on the Pacific; Plus, The Tsilhqot'in and Other First Nations Resistance.* Burnaby, BC: Dragon Heart Enterprises, 2013.

Switlo, Janice. *Gustafsen Lake: Under Siege; Exposing the Truth behind the Gustafsen Lake Stand-Off.* Peachland, BC: TIAC Communications, 1997.

Vowel, Chelsea. *Indigenous Writes: A Guide to First Nations, Métis, and Inuit Issues in Canada.* Winnipeg: HighWater Press, 2016.

Younging, Gregory. *Elements of Indigenous Style: A Guide for Writing by and about Indigenous Peoples.* Edmonton: Brush Education, 2018.

The playwrights also thank the following for personal consultations:

Beverly Manuel, Secwépemc

Nicole Schabus, lawyer and Arthur Manuel's widow

Chief Judy Wilson, Neskonlith Indian Band (Secwépemc)

Grand Chief Ronald M. Derrickson, Westbank Kelowna

Nyla Carpentier, Tahltan/Kaska theatre creator

Hugh Fallis, retired rancher and president of the BC Interior Community Foundation

Henry Campbell, civil litigation and will/estate law

Corporal Scott Linklater, RCMP Chase Detachment

And the following for their participation during development:

Lorne Cardinal, Andrea Menard, Renae Morrisseau, Nyla Carpentier, Yvonne Wallace, Kim Sənklip Harvey, Quelemia Sparrow, Tai Amy Grauman, Veronique West, Emilie Leclerc, Krys Yuan, Sarah Garton Stanley, Daryl Cloran, Jaisen Vardal, Brenda Prince, Fonda Bullshields, Jessica McMann, Doreen Manuel, Ray Thunderchild, Kevin Kerr, Kathleen Flaherty, Matt Bedard, and Tania Carter.

Interview with the Creators

Clicking a Collaborative Path
Exploring What (Re)conciliation Can Look Like in *Inheritance: a pick-the-path experience*

by Annie Smith

The following interview by Annie Smith with the co-producers, director, and writers/actors of *Inheritance* took place on June 26, 2020, via Zoom. It is here excerpted from *Theatre Research in Canada* 42, no. 1 (May 2021), pp. 120–138, in an abridged form and reproduced with permission.* Warm thanks to Annie Smith and *Theatre Research in Canada* for their generous collaboration to this book.

Inheritance: a pick-the-path experience, by Daniel Arnold, Darrell Dennis, and Medina Hahn, was performed at the Annex Theatre in Vancouver, from March 3 to 15, 2020. The Annex Theatre was devised with alley seating, the audience sitting on both sides of an undulating stage that suggested both indoor and outdoor spaces. When the audience entered, we were handed a small "iClicker remote" with an instruction card in the program. Before the performance began we were given a clicker tutorial. When an impasse or decision point was reached for all the characters, the action would be halted and a voice over loudspeakers would inform us that we had choices, which were displayed on screens above the set. We were instructed to individually click our choice and there would be a few seconds while the iClicker app tallied the votes. The final choice would be announced and the play would resume following the direction chosen by majority of the audience.

---

* In addition, Geoff Scott of TriCities Community TV videotaped the interview and produced a video with excerpts from both the interview and the production, which can be viewed at: commediaportal.ca/en/media/interactive-play-inheritance-explores-issue-first-nations-land-rights and youtu.be/Z6sIOQuq338.

Annie Smith (interviewer): It is exciting to see you all. Please introduce yourselves and explain your role in or with *Inheritance*. My role in *Inheritance* is audience participant and chronicler.

Herbie Barnes (director): I am a teacher, a writer, a director, and an actor. I'm Anishinaabe from the Aundeck Omni Kaning First Nation on Manitoulin Island. I do all sorts of things. I call myself a "theatre cockroach" – any way I can survive in theatre, that's what I do. I was brought into *Inheritance* by [co-writer, actor, and dramaturge] Darrell Dennis, who introduced me to the whole gang. That was for a couple workshops about a year before we did the production.

Roy Surette (co-producer): I'm the artistic director at Touchstone Theatre. I've been an artistic director at The Belfry in Victoria, the Centaur Theatre in Montréal, Touchstone Theatre years ago, and have now been back at Touchstone for about three years. I grew up on the West Coast and went to Studio 58. I've worked in the industry mostly as a director and an artistic director. For *Inheritance* – [co-writer and actor] Daniel Arnold invited me to a reading of the first draft of this piece at the Friendship Centre. I was really intrigued by the ideas, the content, and the form. Touchstone is a forty-three-year-old company that has done a lot of new work and has an all-Canadian mandate. We like to do ambitious and relevant pieces and this fit the bill completely. I thought they were crazy ambitious in terms of the scope of the play and the many different paths it could take so we came on as a co-producing partner, pooling our resources to pay for it. I'm really happy to have Touchstone involved.

Marisa Smith (co-producer): I'm the artistic producer at Alley Theatre and I'm also a director and a performer. I've been in the project from the beginning, mainly writing a lot of grant applications and supporting Daniel when he was bouncing ideas and writing drafts, early research trips and outreach.

Daniel Arnold (co-writer and actor): My role with *Inheritance* is co-writer, performer, and co-producer with Alley Theatre and my wife, Marisa [Emma Smith]. I had this idea around 2011, so it's been a long time coming. I'm a third-generation settler with Scottish, Irish, and English ancestry.

Medina Hahn (co-writer and actor): I am a writer and actor and sometimes producer – on this project: writing and acting. About November 2018, Daniel called and I jumped on board. I've been singing, acting, dancing since I was a kid and I went to the University of Victoria and then the University of Alberta, where I met Daniel. I'm of Lebanese and Irish heritage.

Darrell Dennis (co-writer, actor, and dramaturge): I'm from the Secwépemc Nation in British Columbia. I started in theatre because I was a rambunctious child and I got bitten by the bug. I've been a professional actor, a playwright, and I've produced and directed too. I was brought into *Inheritance* by Daniel fairly early on in the process as a dramaturge and as the needs and process extended and became larger I came on as a co-writer and actor.

Annie: Where did the idea for the story come from and why is this story important?

Daniel: I wanted to address the idea of ownership and what has become known to me as stewardship. If someone has a cabin and they are not using it for a number of years, why couldn't someone else use it if they needed it? I actually told this idea to Medina and Darrell when we were doing a play together in Kamloops, which is in Secwepemcúl'ecw, the Territory Darrell is from. But it wasn't until 2014 that the idea actually cemented into something more tangible and meaningful for me, when I learned that Vancouver and the majority of what we now call BC is on unceded land. There are almost no treaties between the colonial governments and the First Nations. When I learned that, all of a sudden this seed of a premise became real. We can take an audience through a personal battle over, essentially, "Whose land is this? And whose land should it be? And how do we rectify the past?" It was at that point that I got Darrell involved as a dramaturge. And I've worked on it since then.

Herbie: Right now we're going through Black Lives Matter and this incredible change in our world. We've learned that oppressions are not only what we see but also how we live, and ownership is a big part of that. Certainly in Canada, First Nations people have been kept off of any kind of ownership. They're not allowed to own the land. It's Crown land that we're stewards of. When you talk about getting ahead to build a community, to get yourself into a place of wealth, those land ownerships have to be in place.

Annie: But it's such a colonial concept – to have land title.

Herbie: And we didn't have that. Possession wasn't such a big thing. If you were hungry, you took food. We talk a lot about the seventh generation in my community where we're looking now at the effects of what we do on the seven generations down the road. In the European mindset, they think about the seventh *decade*. "How am I going to exist when I'm seventy years old? How am I going to have enough money for myself when I'm seventy and beyond?" So with that mentality it's about hoarding, it's about making sure your pile is big enough that you can survive.

Medina: I'd also say that [it's important] to get information out to people. The ability to educate people about the history we were never taught in school. My generation wasn't. My son is being taught more. There is so much that we are ignorant about, as Canadians. When you start to crack that open for people to learn – and as they start to learn and realize – they will dive in more and hopefully it will touch the humanity in people to keep learning and rectify the history in whatever ways they can.

Annie: Can you explain the production's creation process? It's had a long gestation. Has the bulk of that span of time been scriptwriting? And when did you actually start workshopping it?

Daniel: I started writing it in 2014. The original idea was potentially a screen version and Darrell was story-editing on some of that. Then it morphed into a play the next year and we started doing readings of snippets of it publicly in 2016. And then in 2018, "Okay, this is going to become something." It was also around that point that I was starting to realize that, as the lead creator and writer, I could not do this alone, especially as a non-Indigenous person. There's only so much research I could do, so bringing Darrell from dramaturge to co-writer made sense. So both things converged and almost immediately Medina became involved. She and I had been co-writing plays and co-performing before. It made a lot of sense: there were three characters in this play and so, "Medina, bring us your gifts as both a performer and a writer, and let's take this from the idea that's been in my head for a while and is on the page, but let's actually get in the room all together and make this a thing."

Annie: When did the idea of audience participation come into the process?

Medina: Daniel has been talking about a "pick-the-path adventure" since I met him when he was, like, nineteen. So he's been talking about that kind of storytelling for a while.

Darrell: Even back in 2011 when [Daniel] first came up with the idea, he mentioned that this was audience participation, in whatever form it was going to take. We could easily have told this story on stage and that would have been fine, but what I really liked – going back to the question, "What did I think was important?" – was putting the onus on the audience, to have them not only reveal what their opinions and thoughts are on the subject but actually start discussions among themselves about why they chose the route they did or why they didn't choose that. That was a lot more important than just talking at an audience, three actors on stage telling them what to think.

Annie: In terms of co-producing, Roy, did you have any concept of what this would actually be like on the ground?

Roy: The concept was clearly present from the beginning – and the scale of it. It was such an ambitious adventure. Even for the audiences who only saw it once, by having the other propositions put before them, they would say afterwards how enriching it was to just imagine what if "B" had not won, if "C" had won, what would have happened? They were so intrigued not just putting a version of the story out there but looking at all of the choices that are being made through this intense drama that has a lot to say about a lot of current issues.

Annie: What did you see happening in the audience? I think that's what this is all about, in the end – what does the audience do? How do they respond?

Herbie: What I loved about it was how engaged they were. You would hear a vote happen and then you would hear an audible response from the audience that was like, "Ooooh, that upped it." So it became really interesting to see the excitement when their vote was chosen or when they lost a vote, too. All of that was fun to watch. Roy, what do you think?

Roy: It was always that question, because it was part of the process: Are people going to go for the high drama, the most dramatic choice, or the ethical choice? There was a point in the process where you were trying to guide them more towards an ethical choice and then you guys wisely, I think, said, "No, let them vote with whatever their instincts are." It was really fun to watch it go in different directions. I mean, there were some harsh choices that were seldom made but were rehearsed and teched that were really violent, and then there were some that were kind of a lovefest. It quite often landed in a similar place. I was there three or four times and there was a bit of a pattern that would often appear, but it did run the gamut, didn't it, during the run?

Marisa: The fact that it was staged in the round was beautiful. When you asked why is this piece important to you, the thing that comes to mind for me is, we're all in this together. And it's about something that only all of us together can change. And it really does put the onus on the audience to have the feeling of being empowered to change. And you look around the room – and sometimes I would be sitting across from incredibly honoured people – we would have these guests that would come in and they're Chiefs and they've been fighting this stuff for years and years and they're sitting across from me and they are voting on the same thing that I'm voting on and that, alone, was so incredible. I would see a twelve-year-old boy and then the sea of faces all reacting a little bit differently with the clicker in their hand, going "Ahhhh – what are we going to make happen?" It was really special.

Annie: Can you talk about the research? Where did you go? Who did you talk to? What were your sources?

Daniel: I started working with Darrell. I would ask questions. I also read his book, *Peace Pipe Dreams: The Truth about Lies about Indians.* It is a fantastic book. We actually sold it at the play. So I started there and then I read lots and lots of books. I read *Unsettling Canada: A National Wake-Up Call* by Arthur Manuel and Grand Chief Ron M. Derrickson, which we also ended up including in the play, with permission from the writers and publisher, and a number of other books.* But there's only so much you can get from reading. So I said, "Darrell, [Marisa and I are] going to take a trip to your Territory. We're going to go up there and we're going to meet some people. So can you hook us up?" So he reached out to some of his family members and we met with some of them.

Marisa: We met with quite a few people, but most importantly, Mayuk Manuel, Arthur Manuel's daughter. She's also one of the founders of the Tiny House Warriors. And we talked about our intentions for the project. We ended up going to a tattoo ceremony and helped them bring some food. And we talked to Kanahus, her sister, as well, and introduced ourselves. It was more about listening to what was going on for them and then asking for permission, in person, to include the book in the piece and to be doing this project, which is about their Territory. We also met, through Arthur's late wife Nicole Schabus, a man named Percy Casper. Daniel had talked to Nicole about the character Frank

---

* See a selected bibliography in this book, page 229.

INTERVIEW WITH THE CREATORS

and what he might have gone through with his own activism, and what his experience might have been. Percy came to mind for her. So we drove up to Bonaparte Reserve and talked to him in his home. That was quite an experience. He had a lot to say. He's just an incredible person. So Percy and Mayuk ended up becoming artistic advisors on the project. That whole trip was very informative. I can't really even speak to what we talked about. It was more at a heart level. I remember sitting in this truck stop outside of Cache Creek and I had this vision of the map of Canada covered over with the Canadian flag and there was this corner of the Canadian flag peeled up and behind was all this really bad shit. It's not like I'm completely naive in my life and knowledge at this point, but it was that next level of sitting with the damage this country has done to a lot of people. And also, just the beauty of this unceded land. We drove back down from Cache Creek to Hope and that drive is so striking and incredible – doing this play about land, it all just hit home.

Daniel: We also engaged an advocacy and advisory council,* and many of the members were Indigenous, specifically to create a bridge between the fictional world that we were creating in the play and the real world that exists. This advisory council was by and large non-theatre people. Some of them were Elders, [including] Elders from the Territories on which we live: xʷməθkʷəy̓əm, S̱ḵwx̱wú7mesh, and səlilwətaʔɬ. So that was research: they would read the play, talk about the play, and certain things morphed and changed because of that.

Darrell: When Daniel decided he wanted to set it in the Territory that I'm originally from, I was able to provide some context and we changed some things in the text because of my knowledge of the area. It's a very specific area that he's referring to. As far as research goes, I don't know anything about the immigrant experience which Medina's character spoke to, or even the non-Indigenous – I could only speak to my own experience. So I think that as far as the research goes, for me it was giving my opinion or what I saw growing up in that area or what that area's like and what I grew up experiencing as an Indigenous person. Earlier on, because of the work I'd done on *ReVision Quest* on CBC** and

---

* See the Production History, page 1.

** *ReVision Quest* is a radio documentary program that aired on CBC Radio One in the summers of 2008 through 2011.

through my book, I've done a lot of research on how the Department of Indigenous Affairs works, and how reserve land works. I think I was able to provide some context to Daniel as far as my understanding of all that goes – a lot of the general history of Indigenous people.

Annie: In production, in performances, did the tech team have to change things with each change of audience choice? Were they having to respond?

Darrell: On opening night, they were just as freaked out as we were. They also have to deal with whatever the audience picks. It was interesting. Our stage manager was freaking out, and we were freaking out, and I looked at the crew and they were freaking out ... There was a lot of electric energy as opposed to someone just pushing buttons.

Herbie: It wasn't only their first time doing it, it's the first time *anybody's* done that style – it has not been done like that before. Everybody was flying by the seats of their pants and learning.

Roy: We made up a form of theatre!

Annie: Renae Morriseau, the play's talkback facilitator, and I have spoken previously about "cultural work."* Renae identified cultural work as different from the theatre performance but included in the theatre event. Watching the witnesses giving feedback, to me that was cultural work. Would you frame it in that way?

Daniel: Yes.

Marisa: There were two components to this project: the play, and the audience engagement and outreach to the community. We applied to a couple of different granting bodies to do the audience engagement portion of the project. So we were able to compensate our outreach coordinator and all of the guest witnesses who came in with that funding. This had been part of the plan for a year and a half to two years before the show. But then, once we started talking to Eugene about bringing in guests, he brought up the word "witness." And we went, "Sure, whatever that is." We kind of glossed over it a little bit at first. When Renae came on board we started to talk about what that meant

---

* I interviewed Renae Morriseau with Savannah Walling, Rosemary Georgeson, and Kathleen Flaherty about Vancouver Moving Theatre's production *Weaving Reconciliation: Our Way*. The piece is published in *Canadian Theatre Review* 181 (Winter 2020).

in terms of the Coast Salish cultures. And so we came to the idea that the witnesses would come in before the audiences had come into the theatre and we would give them a blanket and tobacco and Eugene would usually talk about them and read their bio and introduce them to the cast and crew and company and we would honour them and thank them for witnessing the production. So when you talk about cultural work that definitely felt like a piece of that.

Darrell: One of the things about Indigenous cultures – and I find this not just in North America but every time I've gone to other countries with Indigenous people – there is so much ceremony attached to events, especially events where storytelling happens. And that was really an imperative part of what we did. So much of our culture is based on the Land and that is our ceremony; that is so much of the identity of our people. It was really interesting to bring that ceremonial part every single night, which is very much how our communities do Potlatches or any sort of ceremonies.

New paragraph — An important part of that too – having the witnesses and having the talkbacks afterwards and having these Native voices speaking – was that they were able to speak about what they saw on stage and either say, "I agree with that," or "I don't agree with that," or "That was not my experience." The important part about that was that my character in the play was not speaking on behalf of all Indigenous people. People can't go, "Oh, I saw that play – that's what Indigenous people want." So I think that was also a very important part and I appreciate that.

Annie: What are you hoping to do next with *Inheritance*?

Daniel: One of the things that came out of the reaction to the play is that people wanted not only for this to tour but to be seen by youth and also be adapted to other mediums. So Darrel and Medina and I have been developing an audio-drama version, a screen version, and are working to maybe make those things happen. And the play will be published by Talonbooks. And maybe there is a way to get this in front of high-school students – that's not particularly what Touchstone or Alley does, but Axis Theatre is interested in partnering on a remount. So we are definitely not done!

The *Inheritance* Study Guide

by Danielle Kraichy, Métis
B.Ed., First Nations and Indigenous Studies

This study guide is designed for youth aged thirteen and up in the education realm. It can also be useful for those outside of education: everyone can benefit from extending their world views. As with all educational resources and activities, educators should adjust the following activities so that they are suitable with their class or group and ensure they have the background knowledge needed to organize these activities effectively. If an educator wishes to have support with these activities, they may be able to consult their Indigenous Education Department or a local Indigenous organization for guidance.

Connection of Land
Activity 1 – Road Trip

Objective: Students will learn about the different legal terms for land ownership and build an awareness of real-world examples of where these lands are and how people interact with them.

Have students research the following legal terms. They should be able to provide real-world examples in Canada for each term. Then have students plan out a road trip (in pairs or individually) that must include staying on each type of land within one week. Let's imagine they have an electric car or van packed with camping essentials.

- Aboriginal Title
- Unceded
- Treaty (land)
- Land deed
- Land title
- Reserve
- Crown land
- Squatter

	Number of kilometres to location	Legal land type	Name of location	Resources needed: drinking water, waste management, grocery store, electricity ...)	Impact of your night's stay
Night 1					
Night 2					
Night 3					
Night 4					
Night 5					
Night 6					
Night 7					
Return trip					

Students will need to calculate how many kilometres they must travel to reach their destinations and return, what resources they will have access to once there (food, accommodation, etc.), and consider the implications of spending the night at each location: Will they be staying at a hotel or inn, camping, squatting? Who may be impacted by their occupying of the area? And so forth.

Have students share their road trips' itineraries with the class. The educator can follow up by asking the class the following questions:

- What difficulties did you encounter while planning your road trip?
- Who were you impacting and how so?
- What surprised you about the meaning and significance of the legal terms listed above?

Activity 2 – Interview on Land

Objective: Students will learn about the land they reside on and explore the different perspectives on land and inheritance.

Have students interview an adult family member or friend on the topic of land. Have them record their answers to the following questions or some of your own:

- What is your relationship to the land or area we live on?
- Do you or have you ever owned land or had family that did? What is or was that like?
- Were there any challenges?
- What were the benefits?
- Do you or did you share the land with anyone else?
- If not, who owns the building you live in and/or asserts ownership of the land you live on, and do you know how they received ownership?
- Did you inherit anything from your family? If so, what?
- What do you know about the history of the land you live on?
- The dominant world view in Canada is to view land as something you can own, as a possession. What do you consider a "possession"?
- What challenges could you see arise when a possession that was not freely given in the first place is passed down in a family?
- Have you ever considered putting anyone else but family members in your will?
- If someone inherited money or property from you, would you be offended if they chose to give all or some of it to the local First Nation(s)?

- Do you think we owe anything to the land?
- Is there anything else you would like to add about your relationship with land or territory?
- Are you okay with this information being shared with the rest of the class?

Ensure that students practice interview protocol and conduct culturally informed research. Below are examples of points to consider:

- Informing the interviewee on the nature of the interview project (class assignment, the topic of land, etc.)
- Sending a letter home about the project
- Thanking the interviewee for the interview
- Asking for consent to write down and share information

After the students have conducted their interviews, they can share their findings with the rest of the class or hand in written copies. The educator can lead a discussion on common themes that arose from the interviews: the importance of interview protocols, of culturally appropriate reciprocity in interviewing some Indigenous people, and so on.

Activity 3 – #LandBack Stories

Objective: Students will learn about the #LandBack movement and deepen their understanding of an Indigenous world view.

Though still a relatively new and rare act, there have been a few cases where non-Indigenous people have provided their land or the profits from their land to Indigenous people or Nations. Individually or in pairs, have students research news articles or stories that report examples of this. Provide them with the hashtag "#LandBack" and ask them to explore the movement, find a news article or story, and respond to the questions below. Students can use the following questions to guide their research.

- What is the #LandBack movement?
- What is the summary of your story or news article?
- What is the history of the land in question?
- Which Indigenous person or group(s) were involved? Which Nation(s)? Are there other people involved?
- What compelled the settler(s) to do this action?
- Did the settler(s) have something to gain from this action?
- How did the Indigenous group or person respond? Did any others respond?

- How long did the described process of sharing the territory or profits take, and what was it like?
- What did the settler(s) learn from this interaction? How did they benefit from this?
- Where on a map is the land in question located?
- What do you think about this story?
- Did any part of the story surprise you? Why?

Indigenous Identity and World Views

Activity 4 – An Indigenous World View through Quotations

Objective: Students will begin exploring the intersectionality between groups of people to better understand how discrimination towards Indigenous Peoples operates. In the process, students will also learn more about other minority groups.

In the play *Inheritance*, the treatment of Indigenous Peoples in Canada is compared to other oppressed groups throughout the world. The three points that follow will focus on specific sections of the play and will ask students to reflect on each section by answering the provided questions. Depending on the classroom culture, the educator can further open the discussion with their own answers to the questions or ask students to share their reflections with the class. This activity also works well for individual work.

1.

Reread pages 78–79. What acts of discrimination that led to historical atrocities does Frank mention? Do further research on acts of discrimination that led to atrocities unto Jewish people during the Holocaust, also known as the Shoah. What parallels can you find between the discrimination of Indigenous Peoples and Jewish people? How do they differ? What perceptions does society have of the Holocaust, and how do they respond to Survivors? As you reflect on the experiences of Indigenous Peoples, how does society respond to them today? Now having done your research, consider Frank's line below; why does he make this comparison?

> **FRANK:** So tell me. Is genocide simply a matter of "Might equals right"? Would you say to a Holocaust Survivor, "Well gee, survival of the fittest, why didn't your family fight back"?

2.

Read an excerpt from one of the paths you could have chosen: from Noah's line "Okay, but wait ..." on page 117 to Frank's "*You're* living off ours!" on page 118.

Research some current issues about racism against Black people in Canada and the United States. What did you find? Why do you think Frank makes the comparison with Black communities in the U.S.? How can the idea of "one representing the whole" be problematic? Where else have you seen this idea come up in your life? Was it accurate or problematic? How so?

3.

Reread page 81. Abbey mentions many details about herself; what are they? Research and define the term "intersectionality." What disadvantages or acts of discrimination does Abbey disclose as a woman of immigrant/settler descent? What acts of discrimination or disadvantages does Frank mention in the play? Noah mentions the issue of "making assumptions" (page 82); what assumptions do Abbey or Frank make?

Frank stresses the issue of comparing who is more oppressed in the following page. Read Frank's speech on page 82. What do you think Frank means when he states, "It must be nice to benefit from the 'systems' that we reserve Indians can't even participate in"? Why does Frank view the system his people face as a life-or-death situation? What point is Frank trying to make in this part of their conversation? What point is Abbey trying to make in this part of their conversation? Can both of their concerns be valid? Why or why not?

Activity 5 – Research Project on Acts of Discrimination

Objective: Students will learn about the many acts of discrimination and other forms of racism Indigenous Peoples face and become experts on one specific example.

In Scene 4, Frank discusses the legacy of colonization and its impacts, including the Indian Act and its policies of discrimination and oppression. Create a research project for students to learn about the acts of discrimination and racism towards Indigenous Peoples. Break the class into groups of three or four and have each group research one of the following topics brought up throughout the play:

- Indian Act
- Oka Crisis

- Gustafsen Lake standoff
- Residential schools
- Royal Proclamation of 1763
- Smallpox blankets
- Sterilization of Indigenous women
- Potlach ban
- Indigenous suffrage
- The Sixties Scoop
- Creation of the reserve system
- Racism and inequities in colonial public systems such as health care, law, and education

Have each group answer the following, along with any other questions you would like to add:

- Provide a summary of your topic.
- How did this affect Indigenous Peoples locally (if possible, give both personal and community examples)?
- How did this affect Indigenous Peoples nationally?
- What did Indigenous Peoples do in response to this discrimination?
- How did others respond to this (non-Indigenous/settler people, governments, other cultural groups, etc.)?
- What are the effects of this issue for Indigenous Peoples today?

Have each group present their research project to the class. Students can create visuals to accompany their presentations such as a slide deck, video, poster, or presentation board. Students can also take notes on other students' presentations to retain information on every topic.

The Three Protagonists – Character Analysis

Activity 6 – Land Use Proposal

Objective: Students will learn about the world view of each protagonist in *Inheritance* in a deeper manner by acting out a "land use proposal" scenario.

Have students break off into groups of three. Inform students that they will be working on a scenario as the three main protagonists from the play. Each student will be taking on the role of a different character so that Abbey, Noah, and Frank are represented in each group. Below is an example scenario you can present to your class once they are in groups and familiar with their character's values and personality.

Scenario: You have just been hired to create a proposal for how a section of land should be used. In your team of three, you must keep your values in mind during the decision process and come to an agreement for your proposal. The plot of land in question is the same plot of land from the play *Inheritance* and involves: an old village site, traditional fishing and hunting grounds occupied by one of Abbey's family members, and a proposed eco-resort – all located next to a First Nations reserve. The budget has not been finalized. Ensure you can justify your choices as boards from local governments will be asking questions!

Students can present their land use proposals through an oral presentation with accompanying visuals, such as slide decks, dioramas, or poster boards. Once students are ready to present their proposals, the educator and the rest of the class not presenting can act as "the board with representatives from local governments" and ask questions. Alternatively, students can independently answer these questions through written responses. The following are examples of questions:

- How did you all come to an agreement?
- Was anyone's voice left out during the decision process?
- Are you all satisfied with your proposal?
- Do any of you feel like you compromised? If so, on which values did [character's name] compromise?
- [Character's name], what was the biggest challenge for you in working with your team?
- Our budget has just been cut by one-third. What are you three wiling to cut from your proposal, or how would you make up for the budget shortfall?

Activity 7 – Character Analysis through Journal Entries

Objective: Students will analyze each character to better understand some of the different world views in Canada and deeply analyze a character of their choice through journal writing.

1.

Have students use a chart or create one like the one below to analyze the perceptions, values, and opinions of the three protagonists in the play, Abbey, Noah, and Frank. Students should include a column for their own perceptions, values, and opinions as well. Have students use evidence from the play to write the views of each character for each topic. Topics could include:

Indigenous Peoples, the environment, immigration, identity, the Canadian government, family, relationship to the land, and so on.

2.

After students have completed their charts, have them choose which protagonist they feel resemble themselves the most and write a response below their table explaining this resemblance. Have student do the same for the protagonist they find resemble themselves the least. Ensure students use the chart in their reasoning.

	Abbey	Noah	Frank	Me
Their own identity				
Indigenous Peoples				
The Environment				
The Canadian government				
Relationship with the land				
Family				
Immigration				
Music				
Non-Indigenous/ settler people				

3.

Students can then choose from which protagonist's perspective they would like to write a journal entry and base their writing on the above topics. A great challenge would be to have students write from the perspective of the protagonist they are most different from, in order to expand their understanding of different world views. Have students place themselves at the time of the beginning of the play, before all three protagonists have met. Students should use their chart as a reference and write in the style of their chosen character to explore what they might be thinking about at that moment. Have students write a journal entry, using some of the following sample starters:

- I feel so strongly about …
- The weather is pleasant today, perfect for …
- I am so excited to …
- I am worried about …
- This land could be something special. It could be …

Narrative Reflection

Activity 8 – Reflecting on the Pick-the-Path Narrative

Objective: Students will reflect on their choices in the pick-the-path narrative and ideas on decision-making.

Have students answer the following questions through written responses:

- Was there a time in reading the play when your group went against your vote and took a different path? If so, were you surprised by your class's decision? Why do you think you were in the minority in this case?
- Did those around you influence your vote? How so?
- Did you influence others' votes? How so?
- How often did your vote align with the majority's?
- If you were to read this play with members of your family, do you think the paths chosen would have been different? How so?
- In endings 1, 2, and 3 (scenes 7, 8, and 9), Frank mentions how his Band takes a longer time than other types of government to come to a decision because they value their cultural tradition of having a consensus. How do you think this type of decision-making would go in your class when picking a path in the play? Provide a hypothetical example.
- Reflect on the days during which your class read the play; how was someone's absence considered during your reading? How did their absence affect the path that was chosen and, therefore, the narrative? How was the decision-making style adopted on that occasion different from a consensus?

- What did you appreciate about the pick-the-path narrative and why?
- Now that you have gone through the play once, would you vote differently a second time around with the same class? Why?
- How would you attempt to influence others' votes reading the play a second time around?
- Would you suggest another "path" to vote for? What would it be? If not, why wouldn't you?

Extension 1:

As the educator, pick a Choice-Point in the play and have the class come to a consensus on how to proceed (by show of hands, for example). Discuss how it went and the benefits and challenges of this process.

Extension 2:

Have students go back and read the play independently. Then have students answer the following questions:

- What paths did you take and why?
- Read **all** paths. Which ones do you prefer and why?

Activity 9 – Indigenous Storytelling: Bear and Coyote

Objective: Students will learn about Indigenous storytelling and explore the significance of having it in the play.

Reread the story of the Grizzly Bear and the Coyote to your class (page 77). Lead a class discussion using circle protocol, or have students write a written response to the following questions. Alternatively, you can bring in a guest to hold a circle for the discussion and learn from them.

- What did you take away from the story of the Grizzly Bear and the Coyote?
- What is this story about?
- What lessons are in it?
- Is there anything in this story that doesn't make sense to you or that you are unsure of?
- How does this story connect to the play *Inheritance*?
- What do you know about Indigenous storytelling?
- What is the cultural significance of Indigenous storytelling?
- Why do you think the playwrights Daniel Arnold, Darrell Dennis, and Medina Hahn included this story?

- What is the significance of having Indigenous storytelling in this play?
- The Bear and Coyote are projected at the end of the play again; what do you think is the significance of this?
- How can this story and Indigenous restorative practices be applied in other areas of society?

Extension 1:

Have students research the term "Indigenous storytelling." Read the story to the students once more and ask them to share their own interpretation of the story using drawing or illustration. Have a gallery walk as a class, viewing each student's artwork. Ask students what similarities and differences they see in their pieces. Why might that be? What was important to the artist? How does the retelling of a story change one's understanding of the story?

Connection to Local Territory

Activity 10 – Putting Reconciliation into Action Locally

Objective: Students will learn about the history of the local territory and put their power into action by supporting a local Indigenous initiative.

1.

Lead a discussion with your class on Frank's quote from page 118: "We're Third – no *Fourth* World citizens in a First World country. So what can you *do*, you ask?"

Possible questions for discussion:

- What does this quote mean?
- How is it powerful?
- What is it asking readers to do?
- What does Frank mean by "Fourth World citizens"?

Conclude the discussion with the following points to lead into the next section:

Frank's feelings about reconciliation are clearly not idealized, but he does call on Abbey and Noah to put reconciliation into action multiple times in the play, such as sharing Abbey and Noah's condo, splitting the land, etc. Frank is not only asking Abbey and Noah what they can do but asking us readers what we can do.

2.

Have students individually or in small groups research whose Traditional Territory your school lies on. Possible questions could include:

- Whose Traditional Territory or Territories is our school on? Consulting the website native-land.ca is a good starting point.
- What type of Territory is it (unceded, Treaty, overlapping, etc.)?
- What is the history of this area? Ensure you have multiple perspectives: Indigenous, settler, immigrant, etc.
- What is the school's relationship with the local Indigenous Peoples? Refer to your school district's Indigenous Education Department website.

Have students share their information as a class and assemble one large document. The educator can collect information on flip-chart paper or in an electronic document projected for the class. Reiterate Frank's quote and the emphasis of "action."

3.

In their small groups or independently, have students research at least one local Indigenous-led initiative or one issue for local Indigenous Peoples, such as the lack of clean drinking water, mould in houses, etc. Have students report their findings back to the class and decide as a group which initiative would be best to support. If appropriate, support the cause by raising awareness, putting a new protocol in place at your school, or raising and donating money. Ensure you consult your Indigenous Education Department before you pursue an initiative to confirm that it is appropriate.

Below are some possible ideas to pursue:

- Ensure the school has an appropriate and accurate Land Acknowledgment (see page 5 of this book)
- Raise awareness of a local Indigenous-led initiative
- Connect with a local Indigenous-led initiative and see how your class can support their cause
- Raise funds for a local Indigenous-led foundation
- Build a positive relationship with the local Indigenous community

Connection to Frank's Nation, the Secwépemc

Activity 11 – Putting Reconciliation into Action: The Secwépemc

Objective: Students will learn about the Neskonlith Douglas Reserve and the Secwépemc people through research and discussion, and gain a deeper understanding of the Secwépemc people by researching Secwépemc-led initiatives to support, thereby putting reconciliation into action.

1.

Have a class discussion focusing on the quote from Frank on page 93: "You mean you don't recognize your power. Until someone walks up and asks you for some of it. (*beat*) I think we all have more power than we care to admit." Ask students to discuss with those around them what the quote means to them. After a few minutes ask students to share their interpretations of the quote with the class. Follow-up questions could include:

- Where does our power come from?
- Who has power?
- What makes us powerful?
- Is someone asking us to share our power the only way we can recognize it?
- What can limit our power?
- Why can we be hesitant to recognize or share our power, as Frank mentions?

End the discussion with the message that everybody has the power to make change, and to act.

2.

Inform students that they will be researching Frank's reserve and the Secwépemc people in hopes of putting reconciliation into action. Students will become "experts" on one portion of information of the Secwépemc people to inform the rest of the class through a presentation. Provide each pair with one of the topics below to research. Students can use visuals to accompany their presentations such as slide decks, poster boards, videos, etc. The following topics should be covered by at least one group each and could include:

- Location, history, and details of the Neskonlith Douglas Reserve
- The Secwépemc people's different Band names, along with their locations and populations
- Secwépemc government system, both modern and traditional
- Examples of Secwépemc/Indigenous-led initiatives
- Present-day issues for Secwépemc people
- History of the Secwépemc people and its Territory, Secwepemcúl'ecw (before and during early contact with settlers)
- Traditional regalia, art, food, and technologies
- Traditional housing and ceremonies
- Connection to land and environmental efforts
- The Secwépemc language, Secwepemctsín

3.

After students have made presentations on their topics, have students brainstorm what they think would be the best initiative to put into action or support by discussing the options with their classmates. Reiterate the quote that started this project, or have it written down for all to view as a reminder of how this project started. Have students consider time, Secwépemc needs and desires, and your class's resources. Then have a class discussion and come to a consensus for which initiative to support and how your class will go about it. This discussion may suit a circle protocol methodology if the educator is comfortable leading it. Ensure you consult your Indigenous Education Department before you pursue an initiative, confirming with them that it is appropriate.

Below are some possible ideas to pursue:

- Support the Tiny House Warriors
- Raise money for a Secwépemc initiative
- Write a letter of support
- Raise awareness of issues Secwépemc people are facing, highlighting how they affect and relate to all Canadians

Study Guide Glossary

Aboriginal Title – An inherent right, recognized in common law, that originates in Indigenous Peoples' occupation, use, and control of Ancestral Lands prior to colonization. Aboriginal Title is not a right granted by the government; rather, it is a property right that the Crown first recognized in the Royal Proclamation of 1763 (see that term). It has been subsequently recognized and defined by several decisions by the Supreme Court of Canada. Furthermore, subsection 35(1) of the Constitution Act, 1982 recognizes and affirms "existing aboriginal and treaty rights."

Band – Many First Nations communities are still governed by the Indian Act and are referred to as Bands. This means that their reserve lands, monies, other resources, and governance structure are managed by the provisions in the Indian Act.

Crown land – A territorial area to which the federal or provincial governments assert ownership.

decolonization – The process of deconstructing colonial ideologies and the effort to avoid the superiority and privilege of Western thought and approaches.

doctrine of discovery – A concept originally promoted by European monarchs in order to legitimize the colonization of lands outside of Europe. This colonial law gave imperialistic governments the power to claim land by travelling to and occupying territories that were not inhabited by subjects of a European Christian monarch; the land was said to have been "discovered," and therefore title ownership was claimed by the discoverer.

First Nations – A term used to describe Indigenous Peoples in Canada who are not Métis or Inuit. First Nations people are the original inhabitants of the land that is now called Canada. "First Nations" should be used exclusively as a general term, as community members are more likely to define themselves as members of specific Nations, or communities within those Nations.

Gustafsen Lake standoff – A month-long conflict (August 18 to September 17, 1995) between a small group of First Nations Sun Dancers and the Royal Canadian Mounted Police (RCMP). The standoff took place in central British Columbia, in Secwépemc Territory, near the town of 100 Mile House. Sparked by a dispute between a local rancher and a camp of Sun Dancers using "his" land for ceremonial purposes, the armed confrontation raised larger questions of Indigenous Land Rights in British Columbia. On September 11, 1995, in what was later called the largest paramilitary operation in the history of the province, RCMP surrounded the remote camp and a firefight erupted.

Hudson's Bay point blanket – A wool blanket with a series of stripes and points (markers on cloth) first made for the Hudson's Bay Company (HBC) in 1779. There is a history of Europeans intentionally giving blankets contaminated with smallpox and other infectious diseases to Indigenous Peoples.

Indian – A term that is now considered outdated and offensive to some, but has been used historically to identify Indigenous Peoples in South, Central, and North America. In Canada, "Indian" also has legal significance. It is used to refer to legally defined identities set out in the Indian Act, such as Indian status.

Indian Act – The principal statute through which the federal government administers Indian status, local First Nations governments, and the management of reserve land and communal monies. It was first introduced in 1876 as a consolidation of previous colonial ordinances that aimed to eradicate First Nations culture in favour of assimilation into Euro-Canadian society.

Indigenous – Ethnic groups who are the original or earliest known inhabitants of an area, in contrast to groups that have settled, occupied, or colonized the area more recently.

inheritance – A thing that is inherited. This could mean receiving property, titles, debts, rights, or obligations upon the death of an individual. It can also mean: being born with the same physical or mental characteristics as one of your parents or grandparents; or beginning to have responsibility for a problem or situation that previously existed or belonged to another person.

land deed – A land or property deed is a written and signed legal instrument that is used to transfer colonial legal ownership of real property from the old owner to the new owner.

land title – In British Columbia, colonial legal ownership of land is referred to as title to land (land title).

Neskonlith Douglas Reserve – A part of the Secwépemc Nation and caretakers of the Lakes area of Secwepemcúĺecw (Secwépemc Territory). In the nineteenth century, upon the request of First Nations, the Crown set aside lands and resources for the use and benefit of certain First Nations and their citizens; in some cases, reserves were established, including the Douglas Reserve. Subsequently, Crown officials took deliberate steps to implement a policy to unlawfully reduce and alienate lands which were reserved for the use and benefit of the First Nations, including portions of the Douglas Reserve. The Neskonlith

Douglas Reserve was arbitrarily reduced by two-thirds in 1864 in spite of protests made by the Band.

Oka Crisis – Also known as the Mohawk Resistance, was a seventy-eight-day standoff (July 11 to September 26, 1990) in Oka and Kanehsatà:ke, Québec, between Kanien'kehá:ka (Mohawk) protesters, police, and army. At the heart of the crisis was the proposed expansion of a golf course and development of condominiums on disputed land that included a Kanien'kehá:ka burial ground. Eventually, the army was called in and the protest ended. The golf course expansion was cancelled, and the land was purchased by the federal government; it has not yet been transferred to the Kanehsatà:ke community.

reconciliation – Reconciliation is about establishing and maintaining a mutually respectful relationship between Indigenous Peoples and non-Indigenous groups in this country. In order for that to happen, there has to be awareness of the past, an acknowledgment of the harm that has been and is still being inflicted, atonement for the causes, and action to change behaviour. (See the National Centre for Truth and Reconciliation, or NCTR, at nctr.ca.)

reserve – A tract of land, the colonial legal title to which is vested in Canada, that has been set apart by Canada for the use and benefit of a First Nations band.

residential schools – An extensive school system set up by the Canadian government and administered by churches that had the nominal objective of educating Indigenous children but also the more damaging and equally explicit objectives of indoctrinating them into Euro-Canadian and Christian ways of living, thereby assimilating them into mainstream Canadian society. The residential school system operated from the 1880s into the closing decades of the twentieth century.

Royal Proclamation of 1763 – Issued by George III on October 7, 1763, it established the basis for governing the North American territories surrendered by France to Britain in the Treaty of Paris (1763) following the Seven Years' War (1756–1763). With regards to Indigenous Rights, the proclamation stated explicitly that Indigenous people reserved all lands not ceded by or purchased from them.

smallpox – A highly contagious disease caused by the smallpox virus, *Variola major* or *minor*. It is spread by droplets from the nose and throat or by dried viral particles on blankets and clothing. Smallpox causes death in up to 30 percent of people infected.

squatter – One that settles on property without right or title or payment of rent; one that settles on public land under government regulation with the purpose of acquiring title.

terra nullius – A Latin phrase meaning "nobody's land." It was a principle sometimes used in international or colonial law to justify claims that a certain territory was unoccupied or uninhabited and therefore could be acquired by a state's occupation of it, even if the land was indeed occupied by Indigenous people.

treaty – Negotiated agreement that defines the rights, responsibilities, and relationships between Indigenous groups and federal or provincial governments.

unceded land – Land or lands to which Aboriginal Title has neither been surrendered nor acquired by the Crown through treaty, war, or otherwise.

Study Guide References

Assembly of First Nations, www.afn.ca/Home/

BC Open Textbooks, opentextbc.ca

The Canadian Encyclopedia, www.thecanadianencyclopedia.ca/en

Crown-Indigenous Relations and Northern Affairs Canada, www.canada.ca/en/crown-indigenous-relations-northern-affairs.html

The Indian Act (R.S.C., 1985, c. I-5), laws-lois.justice.gc.ca/eng/acts/i-5/

Indigenous Corporate Training Inc., www.ictinc.ca

Indigenous Foundations (University of British Columbia), indigenousfoundations.arts.ubc.ca/home/

Indigenous Services Canada, www.canada.ca/en/indigenous-services-canada.html

Investopedia, www.investopedia.com

Land Title and Survey Authority of British Columbia, ltsa.ca

Merck Manuals, www.merckmanuals.com/home

Merriam-Webster.com Dictionary, www.merriam-webster.com

National Centre for Truth and Reconciliation (NCTR), nctr.ca

Wikipedia: The Free Encyclopedia, en.wikipedia.org/wiki/Main_Page

A Short History of the Secwépemc People and Their Territory

This text is abridged and adapted from the following document: Adams Lake and the Neskonlith Secwépemc, "Human History and Landscape," pp. 25–59 in *Land Traditions of the Neskonlith and Adams Lake Shuswap* (Calgary [Mohkínstsis / Wincheesh-pah / otōskwanihk ᐅᒍᐣᗚᐢᐄ᙮ᣠᑊ / Guts'ists'i / Klincho-tinay-indihay], AB: Peter Douglas Elias / Perisor Research Services, 1999). It was generously approved for inclusion in this book by the Adams Lake Indian Band Chief and Council and the Shuswap Nation Tribal Council. Warm thanks to Celia Nord at the Adams Lake Indian Band for her revision and improvement of the text.

Origins

Secwepemcúl'ecw (the Secwépemc or Shuswap Territory) spans approximately 180,000 square kilometres and stretches across a vast area of the interior of what is now known as the Canadian province of British Columbia, from the Columbia River valley along the Rocky Mountains, west to the Fraser River, and south to the Canada–United States border. Humans have been living in Secwepemcúl'ecw for over ten thousand years, since the end of the Last Glacial Period. Initially people hunted mammoth, mastodon, and other large animals that flourished in the harsh post-glacial environment. Glacial ice disappeared fully around twelve thousand years ago, setting up the conditions for the kind of landscape found in the Territory today. Many settlement sites in the interior of British Columbia are found near salmon rivers, suggesting that by the time people were settling down into semi-sedentary lifeways, salmon were already an important part of the local economy.

By 6,000 BP (Before Present), the continental environment was no longer changing as rapidly as immediately after the end of the Last Glacial Period, and human populations stabilized. People began the tradition of settlement in villages of subterranean pit houses ("c7ístkteṅ" in Secwepemctsín*) located near salmon habitat, a tradition that persisted into historic times.

By four thousand years ago, evidence of plants reveals their importance in the economies of Secwepemcúl'ecw. Seeds, nuts, and roots were used for food, and plant fibres were used to make rope, twine, and netting. Cultures of the interior showed considerable variation as people adapted to the particular combination of habitats available in the vicinity of each village. Almost certainly, these cultures were ancestral to the Secwépemc and other Salish peoples.

Though previous eruptions had impacted Secwepemcúl'ecw over millennia, volcanoes erupting in Alaska and the Yukon about 1,300 years ago blanketed much of the north with ash and forced massive migrations towards safety, edging closer to Secwepemcúl'ecw. Hence, Northern Dene (Athabaskan) Peoples abandoned their old homes and moved south. Soon after, the Tsilhqot'in people arrived on the north of Secwepemcúl'ecw and quickly adopted a lifestyle similar to that of their Salish neighbours. These were the cultures of the region at the time of contact.

Secwépemc Culture at Contact

At the time of contact, the Secwépemc ("the spread-out people") occupied a large part of the southern Interior Plateau. By 6,000 BP, they had maintained semi-permanent villages where food and technology were stored, and a network of specialized base camps in the vicinity of particular resources which were extracted, processed, and transported to the villages. These resources included deer and other ungulates, fish (anadromous and freshwater species), plants including spring beauty (skwenkwínem), nodding onion (qwléwe), cow parsnip (xwtellp), and Indian celery (k̓utse), nuts of the white-bark pine (seléwll) and black lichen (wíle), and berries such as saskatoons (speqpeq7úwí) and huckleberries (wenéx).

Then, as now, salmon (sqlélten) were a staple in Secwépemc diet, economy, and culture. By midsummer, when the main salmon runs were underway, most people were camped at the riverside fishing stations. A frenzied time of fishing, processing, camp maintenance, and transportation

---

* "About Our Language," First Voices, accessed April 26, 2021, www.firstvoices
   .com/explore/FV/sections/Data/Secwepemc/Secwepemctsin/Secwepemc
   /learn.

to winter villages gradually ended as the fishery tapered off in late October.*
The fishing base camps were the centre of feasting, marriage, ceremony,
and dancing. Important fishing camps were also the point of trade between
neighbouring villages and nations. Major trade fairs in the region attracted
over one thousand participants.

Winter villages were almost exclusively on dry, well-drained sites on
river terraces. C7ístkteṅ (pit houses) were the preferred winter home, but
there were other styles of insulated houses as well. People delayed their move
into the village as long as good weather held, but usually they were settled
in by November. In deep winter, people stayed in the village and mostly
lived on their stored food. Games, contests, the manufacturing of much
needed tools and baskets, storytelling, and trade were important parts of
the winter season. During winter Secwépemc people did gather some foods,
such as by ice fishing for rainbow trout (písell) and sturgeon (xu7t'), and
also trapped smaller animals.

People left their winter houses as soon as weather allowed, usually in
February when melting snows and longer days made hunting easier, and even
a few early plants were sprouting. Spring was also the time to collect materials for making the basic tools of Secwépemc technology – bows (tskwínek),
arrows (stskwele7úẁi), containers (cpegpégt), tool handles (tḱmíple7), rope
(lop), and cordage – made from sap-filled willow (q̇welséllp), mock orange
(stth'ulhp), juniper (punllp), birch (qweqwllíllleṅllp), maple (ts'wéllten),
cottonwood (mulc), Saskatoon berries (speqpeq7úẁi), and bitter cherries
(pekllén).

Through March and April, families set up their summer base camps to
begin a new year of intensive and extensive harvesting. Most people returned
from the trout fishery and mountain or grassland hunting in early summer
to pick berries. The winter villages were visited throughout the summer
to store processed berries, meat, fish, and the many other products of a
summer's work. Elders and injured or disabled people stayed in the village
year-round. Most burials were on a prominent point near the winter village
on the river terrace.

---

* "Journal Thomson's River October 1841," in Royal BC Museum's online
  exhibition *BC's Living Landscapes*, "Records of the Hudson's Bay Company
  relative to the Thompson's River Post (Kamloops, BC), 1821–1865," accessed
  May 21, 2021, royalbcmuseum.bc.ca/exhibits/living-landscapes/thomp-ok
  /river-post/october1841.html.

Early Post-Contact History

The Secwépemc had contact with Europeans sometime late in the eighteenth century, after British traders established a flourishing fur trade with coastal peoples, who traded in turn with peoples living in the interior. European exploration of the interior began in 1793, when Alexander Mackenzie travelled west following the Peace and upper Fraser Rivers. His expedition, along with those of Simon Fraser in 1808 and David Thompson in 1811, encountered the Secwépemc and their Territory, and soon after other traders were in direct contact with the Secwépemc.

For the most part, relations between the interior nations and the traders were amicable. The traders were interested mainly in getting goods into the region and fur out, and they rarely drifted far from their stores. The stores were located at known village and base camp sites and were reached using the ancient system of trails connecting the entire region. The Secwépemc and the traders carried on together for forty years, from 1812 until gold was discovered in sand bars near Kamloops in 1857 and along the Lower Fraser River in 1858.

Later History

After the discovery of gold, intruders quickly crept up the rivers into the heart of Secwépemc Territory. During the early 1860s, the first road pierced the interior along the walls of the Fraser Canyon to serve growing European settlements. In 1886, the Canadian Pacific Railway penetrated the heart of Secwepemcúl'ecw. Once routes to the interior were "discovered" by Europeans, often using the system of ancient trails, the Secwépemc Territory was exposed to successive waves of encroachment from traders, miners, settlers, loggers, railroad builders, tourists, and government officials.

The traders did some hunting on their own, but most of their food was taken in trade from the Secwépemc. The traders demanded more food each year than was used by several average Secwépemc villages, and the Secwépemc hunted, fished, and gathered to supply the traders' needs. Almost as a sideline to food production, the Secwépemc also began trapping more than they did before contact.

Guns made killing game easier, and the Secwépemc and the traders had them. By the late 1820s, the use of metal traps had nearly exterminated beavers. In the 1840s, traders were demanding so much salmon that some families did not have enough for their own winter needs. By the 1850s, some Secwépemc were starving to death.

The Gold Rush

When gold was discovered along the Columbia, prospectors soon appeared on the South Thompson and the streams flowing into the Shuswap Lake. By some estimates there were over thirty thousand miners in the interior, and they all needed food, fuel, clothing, and construction materials. The miners attracted merchants who were importing food. Flour, rice, and beans purchased with wages replaced some of the more difficult and less rewarding plant foods in the Secwépemc diet. The miners' livestock needed pasturage and winter feed. By the early 1860s, elk were hunted to extirpation and caribou abandoned their southern range. Finally, the Secwépemc at Neskonlith and Adams Lake blocked miners from further entry in their Territory, but most of the damage had been done.

Once the easy pickings were gone and gold operations began using water diversions, sluices, deep digging, hydraulics, and shored pits and shafts, the demand for logs, timbers, and lumber rose. Soon the nearby mountain forests were under heavy attack. Gravel beds along and beneath streams, including the spawning beds of salmon and trout, were destroyed by dredging for gold.

The direct and indirect impacts of miners and mining were serious, but the core of Secwépemc culture remained intact, including patterns of land use.

Disease and Settlement

The small flood of miners who reached Secwepemcúl'ecw gained a new appreciation for the territory's potential; when the gold rush collapsed, some stayed and became settlers who in turn attracted other settlers. By the time settlers were carving out their homesteads on Secwépemc Lands, the region was under colonial administration with a policy of settling the interior as quickly as possible to create markets and a tax base, and to quell American influence. Before the law reached the Secwépemc Territory, however, the region was scourged by epidemics.

Not since contact had the Secwépemc experienced epidemics like those that followed the miners and settlers arriving from throughout the world. Early in the 1860s, smallpox reached the South Thompson. The colonial government tried to contain the outbreak near Victoria by removing non-whites from the town and vaccinating only white people. Hudson's Bay Company workers at Fort Kamloops and the outposts vaccinated as many people as they could.

In late summer of 1862, Chief Neskonlith reported four deaths and said he and his people were no longer going to Fort Kamloops. By the end of 1862, as much as two-third the Secwépemc population, from twenty-five thousand before contact to approximately seven thousand, had perished of smallpox. Later waves of measles, influenza, tuberculosis, and other infectious diseases battered the survivors. Only in the past generation has the Secwépemc population recovered to their numbers at the time of contact.

Indian Reserves

Officially, the colonial government said they created Indian reserves to protect the Indians from predatory miners, ranchers, and loggers, and coincidentally seized the best lands for purposes of settlement. A large block of land was set aside nearby to the junction of the North and South Thompson Rivers, the area now known as the Douglas Reserve. Before colonization, what are now known as the Little Shuswap Lake, Neskonlith, and Adams Lake Bands were part of one grouping. Chief Nesquaimlth was given a letter stating that "All persons are hereby cautioned not to cut timber, interfere, or meddle in any way with the rights of the Indians on this reserve." For a few years, the Shuswap Lakes Secwépmemc (now known as the Pespesellkwe) were able to keep settlers out by asserting and defending their claims to lands, but in time they were overwhelmed by the determination of government agents to free the land for settlers.

By 1865, settlers were taking up the lands best suited for frontier agriculture. That summer, Phillip Henry Nind, Gold Commissioner at Lytton, visited the reserve and saw the Secwépemc had "thousands of acres of good arable and pastureland, admirably adapted for settlement." The Secwépemc were clearly in possession of the lands; in fact, Chief Nesquaimlth was charging Canadian settlers a fee to graze on his people's lands.

Nind admitted the Secwépemc were "jealous of their possessory rights, and are not likely to permit settlers to challenge them with impunity." Nind added, "Such is [the Secwépemc's] spirit and unanimity, few settlers would think it worth their while to encounter their undisguised opposition." The Secwépemc, he said, would fight for their land. Nind suggested extinguishing the Secwépemc's claims, giving them "certain reservations for their sole use," and "paying them what is proper for doing so." Then all the prime land along the North and South Thompson and their tributaries could be settled. The Neskonlith, Adams Lake, and Little Shuswap people were left with reserves that were deemed too small to support even a single family of settlers – only twenty acres of land was allowed each family, whereas settlers struggled to manage on 320 acres per family.

The Secwépemc protested the loss of their lands and diminishing resources. In 1877, they met with the Joint Indian Reserve Commission, who agreed they did not have enough land. A new reserve (Neskainlith No. 2) was created on the south side of the river, opposite the much reduced first reserve (Neskainlith No. 1). Chief Nesquaimlth agreed the last of the best lands were already taken by Canadians and asked for a hay land at the head of Salmon Arm on Shuswap Lake. Instead, the Commission gave all three bands – Adams Lake, Neskonlith, and Little Shuswap – a small joint reserve and fishing place, keeping the best grassland for Canadians. The reserve lands, although somewhat larger, could not support their band communities. In 1892, the Salmon Arm reserves were divided among the three bands, resulting in a scatter of small reserves west and opposite the present-day city of Salmon Arm.

But the tiny reserves were not secure. The Neskonlith people applied for more land but, even though the government's officials agreed the Secwépemc needed more land, none was granted. Instead, parts of each reserve were trimmed off or occupied by intrusive rights of way and easements. Between the early part of the century and 1990, the small Neskonlith reserves were blanketed with railroad and road rights of way, electricity corridors, and water management easements.

Like the Neskonlith people, the Adams Lake people had to defend their interest in the reserve lands. Because the many small Adams Lake reserves are scattered throughout the main settlement corridor, they are the target of more than twenty-five rights of way and easements, including timber leases, highways, roads, electricity and telephone services, railroads, and several outright surrenders.

With reserves, the Secwépemc did have some protection from settlers, but only in the close confines of their villages. All the rest of the land from which they gained their livelihood was taken from them. In spite of it all, the Secwépemc may have done rather well with the lands they kept, as the three reserves gave the Neskonlith people control over the complete variety of ecosystems important in their traditional economic culture.

The Secwépemc never complained about the quality of their reserve lands. Rather, they complained about their extent. The kind and quality of reserve land they possessed enabled them to maintain a thriving domestic economy well into the twentieth century, but eventually population growth and economics eroded the environmental basis of the economy they could construct on their small reserves.

Missions and Schools

Preaching and teaching arrived when the Secwépemc were at their weakest, decimated by smallpox and dispossessed of their most important lands and resources. The spiritual dispossession of the First Peoples of Canada is well known. Missions and schools added incentive to confine Traditional Activities to special and often secret places where they could not be observed.

Ranching

Cattle were driven up the Okanagan trail starting in the 1830s, to supply the meat market and to stock settlers' foundation herds. Settlers quickly encroached on the best farming and grazing lands and woodlots. By 1865, settlers had taken over two thousand acres and took another three thousand between 1866 and 1871.

Ranchers were allowed to pre-empt lands for their homestead sites, and a few had leased pastureland, but many others simply allowed their cattle to roam at large without regard to whether the lands were used by the Secwépemc. These cattle quickly found the grasslands and parkland where the grazing is best and springs are numerous – the same places where the Secwépemc gathered plants for food and technology and set up their higher elevation summer base camps.

Before 1900, ranchers allowed their cattle to roam without the benefit of a lease. Soon the government land agents reported that the range was exhausted. Grazing lands in Secwépemc Territory are restricted to a few favourable places, but leases were also written for large areas where there is actually little grazing potential. To secure a lease, ranchers were obliged to fence their lease lands even though there were few cattle in some of the heavily forested leases. This fencing further disrupted access to land.

The livestock industry grew to fill all the available grazing lands, and by 1940 there were over one hundred thousand cattle and sheep in the Kamloops grazing district. Cattle were restricted to the low-elevation grasslands and parklands, but the alpine areas were extensively used as summer pasture for sheep. In time, government officials were complaining that domestic livestock was driving wildlife, especially ungulates, off the native ranges. By 1990, there were still over seventy thousand head of cattle in the district.

Roads and Trails

Until the 1860s, people occupying the interior used the system of trails established by the Secwépemc and their neighbours in ancient times. The most important trails ran north and south through the successive mountain ranges between the coast and the Rockies. The provincial government funded expeditions in the 1860s to find routes for roads between the Thompson River and the Columbia River and eventually across the Rocky Mountains. By 1865 the first rough cart trail was pushed through.

Immediately, the expanded trails were put to use by settlers and ranchers. By the early 1870s, most of the best agricultural land between Kamloops and upper Shuswap Lakes was settled. By 1914, even the most marginal arable lands at higher elevation and far up the smallest valleys were taken up. The government tried to limit settlement on the margins because few settlers could survive long enough to prove up their claims. Once they had exhausted their 160 acres of sparse land, the settlers moved away, leaving felled and burned clearings and fences that interfered with wildlife and destroyed the basis for traditional Secwépemc land use activities. Nevertheless, by the 1930s, the only low-elevation lands the Secwépemc could use and occupy were those within the boundaries of their tiny reserves.

Roads quickly penetrated most of the backcountry away from the rivers and lakes. By the 1990s, every place that could support a road was webbed with highways, secondary roads, logging access roads, private-access roads, and off-road vehicle trails. The rest was pierced by foot, horse, motorbike, and snowmobile trails.

Railroads

The colony of British Columbia agreed to join Confederation if Canada agreed to build a railroad to the Pacific Ocean. In British Columbia, these routes were largely based on original Indigenous trails found and mapped through direction from scouts hired from local First Nations. The colony gave the federal government almost eleven million acres of land in a strip from the Alberta border to tidewater at New Westminster. This land, to be sold and exploited to pay the cost of building the railroad, included much of the land used by the Neskonlith and Adams Lake people, and as the railroad was pushed through, settlers followed it. The real industrialization of the Secwépemc Traditional Territory began in earnest.

Logging

When the federal government took over the railway lands in 1884, large blocks were sold to loggers at very low prices and with minimal regulatory interference. Loggers stopped "trespassers" from entering their timber allowances whether they were in use or not. The Secwépemc were thus prohibited from using forested lands that were once integral to their economic culture.

Since roads and railroads were superimposed on the system of ancient trails connecting Secwépemc villages, the most heavily used Secwépemc lands disappeared under a blanket of timber leases. Dam raceways sent successive flash floods and logs scouring down the length of rivers and streams. For years, the famous Adams River run of sockeye salmon was all but destroyed.

Near the turn of the twentieth century, there were several large forest reserves in the railway belt under federal control. Although set aside to preserve the forest, the reserves were also leased for mining and as sites for schools, churches, cemeteries, summer resorts, and cottages. Each year domestic users cut many thousands of metres of wood for construction, heating, fences, corrals, and railroad ties.

By the mid-twentieth century, forestry was the key industry in the region and most accessible forests were either logged or scheduled for logging. Until the 1960s, small mills were scattered through much of the forested parts of the Secwépemc Territory, but then much larger mills were built and cutting in the forest increased.

Recreation

The Secwépemc Territory is a famous tourist destination with everything from alpine skiing to white-water rafting. Tourism began in earnest with the railroad, which delivered people to within a few kilometres of prime hunting, fishing, and boating. As the most accessible lakes became fished out, tourists used roads and trails to reach more remote lakes until they, too, needed restocking. By the 1970s, campgrounds in the vicinity of Shuswap Lake and Adams Lake boasted well over one hundred thousand camper-nights each year. Houseboats invaded Shuswap Lake, adding to the burden of sewage and garbage entering the lake's waters. In the mid-1990s, a multimillion-dollar ski resort opened for business on the summit slopes of Mount Tod (Skwelkwekwelt), the most recent intrusion in the Secwépemc's Lands.

Imposed Regulation

Regulations governing settlement, mining, ranching, farming, tourism, and rural and urban development had severe consequences for the Secwépemc people and the Secwépemc Territory. Secwépemc land and resource traditions were soon replaced by Canadian ones. For example, early in the settlement era, individual traders and settlers made their own arrangements for occupying Secwépemc Land in the form of a contract – goods or gold in exchange for use rights. Under colonial law, the Crown seized all Secwépemc Land without compensation and disposed of it as it wished and for its own profit.

By the late twentieth century, the entire Secwépemc Territory was blanketed with an imposed regime of timber, land, and mineral leases, fee-simple titles, pre-emptions, Crown interests, easements, and rights of way. Three levels of imposed legislation and regulation – federal, provincial, and municipal – manage forests, waters, and fish and wildlife in the Secwépemc Territory. There are few places where the Secwépemc can practise their land and resource traditions without running afoul of a Canadian law that could land them in jail.

Impacts of Contact and Settlement

By the 1860s, the mixed economy of the Secwépemc included activities such as hunting, fishing, trapping, and gathering, but also included such innovations as gardening and stock raising. Some people took on new forms of commodity production, especially production of fish, meat, firewood, and basketry for trade with miners and settlers. Chief Neskonlith and perhaps many others collected rents for grazing rights on their lands. The Secwépemc began to sell their labour for wages, at first as packers and guides for traders, explorers, and surveyors, and later for miners and settlers. A few established themselves in their own businesses.

By the early 1870s, the Secwépemc owned over four hundred head of cattle and thirteen hundred horses but, according to the Indian Agent, were already reaching the limit of their agricultural development. With agricultural opportunities diminishing each year as the best grazing and arable land went to settlers, the Secwépemc turned to more intensive forms of market gardening and horse breeding. The bands closest to Kamloops and other centres of settlement enjoyed good markets for vegetables and work horses, but the more distant bands up the South Thompson River relied more on trapping lands not yet reached by settlers. By the late 1870s, all the Secwépemc bands were as much involved in agriculture as their small land base would allow. Together, the Neskonlith and Adams Lake Bands owned about 350 horses and one hundred cattle, but their prospects for expansion were very limited. All the best available pastureland in the grasslands and lower elevations of the mountains were occupied by settlers' cattle, and the small terraces barely accommodated Secwépemc villages and gardens. The few streams that could be diverted for irrigation were the source of conflict between the Secwépemc and the settlers, with neither getting enough water to grow good crops.

Perhaps because the Secwépemc had selected wisely when their reserve boundaries were decided, the Adams Lake and Neskonlith people sustained a domestic economy from their reserve resources until well into the twentieth century. All reports from the 1870s until the 1910s said the Secwépemc were self-sufficient, hard-working people. Then, the population began to grow slightly, but even slightly was too much for the very limited reserve lands and resources.

In October of 1913, William Parrish addressed the McKenna–McBride Royal Commission on behalf of the Neskonlith people. He told the commissioners that all arable and pasture land was fully used, and that there was no room left on the reserves for expansion. In fact, several families had no place on the reserve they could call their own. Any land that was not cultivated or fenced for cattle was too far from water for either purpose.

By then, the Canadian Pacific Railroad had been completed, and the Secwépemc could no longer allow their cattle to graze at large. The few families living on the Salmon Arm reserve had grazed cattle earlier in the century, but all had been killed by passing trains. Through the first decades of the century, the band was barely able to survive through selling vegetables, cattle, horses, and chickens. Whenever possible, people worked for the settlers.

Through it all, the Adams Lake and Neskonlith Secwépemc continued to use the Secwépemc Territory according to Tradition, often in the face of threatening opposition from their competitors and all levels of Canadian government – a long history of systematic dispossession.

Contemporary Title and Rights Issues

Recently, the British Columbia government legislated their provincial version (the Declaration on the Rights of Indigenous Peoples Act, or DRIPA) of the United Nations Declaration on the Rights of Indigenous Peoples, or UNDRIP. Canada is also in the process of legislating a federal version. Over the last several decades, Specific Claims, Strength of Claims, and agreements between the Secwépemc people, settler governments, and other proponents have contributed to the improvement and development of these govern-ment-to-government relationships. The Secwépemc, now ten thousand people strong and growing, living in thirty-two Salish-speaking commun-ities divided by the Indian Act into seventeen bands, have never given up their fight to confirm their inherent Rights to Secwepemcúl'ecw and their roles as "Yucwminmen," stewards of Tmicw (the Land and everything on it).

Note: Secwépemc Knowledge Holders from the Lakes Division, who are part of the larger Secwépemc Nation, have rights and responsibilities to the cultural knowledges and symbols or the Secwépemc mentioned in this book. Any Intellectual Property Rights associated with these Secwépemc cultural knowledges and symbols inherently belong to the Secwépemc people and cannot be copied or adapted without permission.

Photo: Wendy D Photography

Daniel Arnold, of Ukrainian/Scottish ancestry, co-wrote and performed (with Medina Hahn) the award-winning plays *Tuesdays & Sundays* and *Any Night,* both of which garnered numerous awards and toured to places such as Ottawa, Edinburgh, Prague, New Mexico, and New York. He and Medina also adapted *Tuesdays & Sundays* into a radio play for CBC and the BBC (starring David Tennant), and adapted *Any Night* into a feature film script which won the Super Channel Screenplay Award. Daniel has also created work for the screen including the multi-award-winning feature film *Lawrence & Holloman,* and he is a co-producer with Alley Theatre.

Photo: Penny Moore

Darrell Dennis, a Secwépemc native, is the writer/performer of the Dora-nominated *Tales of an Urban Indian, The Trickster of 3rd Ave East, Home of the Running Brave,* and numerous other plays, television, film, radio, and the award-winning non-fiction novel *Peace Pipe Dreams: The Truth about Lies about Indians.* For four years he also produced and co-hosted the CBC Radio One doc series *ReVision Quest.* Darrell was the head writer, director, and performer of *Guilt Free Zone* on APTN and continues to write steadily for film and television projects in Canada and the United States. He currently lives in Los Angeles.

Photo: Kevin Clark

Medina Hahn, of Lebanese/Irish ancestry, is an award-winning writer and actress whose work has been seen on stages across Canada, the United States, Europe, and onscreen. She co-wrote and performed (with Daniel Arnold) the plays *Tuesdays & Sundays* and *Any Night* and also adapted them to radio and film. With performance degrees from the University of Alberta and the University of Victoria, she came to writing and creation from an acting background, having worked extensively on new plays. Thanks to mentor Daniel MacIvor, Medina and Daniel are the protégé recipients of Canada's largest theatre award, the Siminovitch Prize.